Welcome to Willowdale, North Carolina, a small town where the folks are friendly, the romances are as sweet as the tea, and the biddies at the diner gobble up gossip like it's peach cobbler. This may be their biggest scoop ever.

When sexy Hollywood bad-boy Teague "T-Rex" Reynolds comes to this quiet Southern town, he needs a fake girlfriend to hide the secret that brought him there. School nurse Kate Riley takes the job, but she won't fall for a movie star, no ma'am. That's fine with Teague. He hung a closed sign on his heart years ago.

Convincing the press they're in love is one thing. Fooling each other they're not is getting harder each day. Despite scandal, heartache, and misunderstandings galore, they might just find the sweet thrill of true love. Book one of The Willowdale Romances.

Coming in 2013

Book Two of The Willowdale Romances

Man of the Month

No Foolin'

A Willowdale Romance

by

Lisa Scott

Bell Bridge Books

This is a work of fiction. Names, characters, places and incidents are either the products of the author's imagination or are used fictitiously. Any resemblance to actual persons (living or dead), events or locations is entirely coincidental.

Bell Bridge Books
PO BOX 300921
Memphis, TN 38130
Print ISBN: 978-1-61194-214-9

Bell Bridge Books is an Imprint of BelleBooks, Inc.

We at BelleBooks enjoy hearing from readers.
Visit our websites – www.BelleBooks.com and
www.BellBridgeBooks.com.

10 9 8 7 6 5 4 3 2 1

Cover design: Debra Dixon
Interior design: Hank Smith
Photo credits:
Woman (manipulated) © Branislav Ostojic | Dreamstime.com

:Lfn:01:

Dedication

To my mother, who's always believed in me. If I told her I was going to colonize Mars, she'd say, "Call me when you get there!" Too bad she's not allowed to read this book because of certain scenes.

Lisa Scott

Chapter 1

KATE RILEY PULLED up in front of Scalia's Bistro, ready to go in and beg for a job she didn't want; her cut-off jeans and faded tank top made that clear. The tire of her Jeep bumped over the curb, and a hubcap clanged onto the sidewalk. She groaned. *One of these days, it's gotta get better, right?*

Main Street was usually quiet in the middle of the afternoon, but a horn blared as she backed up to fix her lousy parking job. She gave the driver a friendly wave instead of the not-so-friendly finger itching to pop up. Gotta be careful in a small town like this—it was probably someone she knew. Easing back into the spot, her gas gauge lit up.

"Perfect." She turned off the engine and slumped in her seat. Nope, this wasn't gonna be the day a sack of cash fell from the sky. Attached to Mr. Right. Although, she'd given up on meeting him after Mr. So Very, Very Wrong kicked a hole in her heart.

Not everyone's meant for love, sugar. That's what Mama always said about her own sorry marriage. Kate must've inherited *that* gene—along with hips that didn't quit.

"Thanks for the ride to work," her stepsister, Dina, said from the passenger seat. "Except for almost running down the pedestrians." She rolled her eyes, hopped out, and nearly tumbled over from the weight of her baby belly—not quite ready to pop, but getting there. "I'll find a lift home, really."

Kate leaned across the console and forced a smile. "Maybe the baby's daddy could give you a ride home? Ready to tell us who that is?"

Dina crossed her skinny arms and tipped up her chin. "I'm not talking *to* or *about* the baby's daddy."

Kate let out a sigh she knew was too long and exhausted for

3

someone her age. She sounded like Pansy Parker down at the Jelly Jar diner when they ran out of sweet potato pie. "Dina, if the cancer hadn't killed my mama, this would have."

Dina's eyes narrowed, framed by eyebrows plucked pencil-thin and highlighted with too much pink eye shadow. "Well, it did, and that doesn't suddenly make you my parent. I'm eighteen." She rubbed her belly. "Me and the baby will be fine."

Kate swallowed the angry knot in her throat along with the snotty comeback. "Someone's gotta be your parent now, Dina. George may be your father, but he sure doesn't act like it. He forgot to drive you to work today. You think he's going to help with a baby?" She shook her head. "Any idea where he is this time? Maybe out getting a job?"

Dina shrugged. "Doubt it." Then her lips quivered and her big blue eyes watered up. "He's not going to jail, is he?" The kid could go from surly to sad in two seconds flat. Amazing.

"No. They won't arrest him. They'd just take the house. But don't worry, I'll fix it." She wasn't going to let her stepfather lose her mama's house because he was too irresponsible to pay the property taxes. If only her job as a nurse at the junior high paid more. If only she had a brother or sister to help shoulder the burden. Or a husband. Scratch that. A husband seemed like a good idea until you got one. At least that's how it'd been for her mama. "I'll get the money for the taxes." Because that's what Kate did—she fixed things, whether it was a bandage on a boo-boo or finding a stack of cash to save her house. Kate always did what she had to do, and she was proud of that.

Dina put her hand on her hip. "Then you better get inside and ask about that waitress position, or it's gonna be filled." And her mood snapped back, just like that, the manipulative little . . . "Bye," she fluttered her fingers at Kate and lumbered into Scalia's Bistro, her dark ponytail swinging in time with her hips.

Working with her stepsister and a bunch of surly teens at Scalia's was going to make for a hellish summer. Plus, Kate had already worked there when she was a teenager. Not mortifying at all to come back at age twenty-six. Things definitely were not getting better, not this day, anyway.

She rested her head back on the seat and re-did the mental math. Again. She needed more than an extra ten-thousand dollars by summer's end to pay off the taxes and fines, or the folks at the town hall were putting a lien on the house. A waitressing job wouldn't pull that in. Double shifts, *maybe*—with a really tight uniform. What would that cost her pride? Plenty. Just one more reason for the chatterboxes in Willowdale, North Carolina, to talk about poor, poor Kate Riley. Being gossip fodder had never been on any bucket list of hers, yet here she was keeping the blue-hairs still chatting.

Kate looked up and down Main Street, empty of any other help-wanted signs. She'd had no luck at the hospital over in Whitesville or the residential-care facility in town. Wasn't much available in Willowdale besides this position, unless she learned how to change oil down at the Jiffy Lube or roll perms at Tonya's Curl E.Q. Salon. Her pal Jeanne had tried that once and had nearly run Tonya's business into the ground. Dot Klein's hair was just growing back after Jeanne forgot to wash out her perm.

So, Scalia's was it.

She got out of the car, grabbed the hubcap and tossed it in her backseat. Lingering in front of the town's fanciest restaurant, she was just putting off the inevitable. The garlicky smell of the early-bird special made her stomach curl. *The smell of defeat, sister.* She leaned against her car and wilted in the steamy afternoon, all sticky and warm like a long, hot yawn.

Pushing away from the car, ready to go inside—if only for the air conditioning—she spotted a man hurrying toward her: tall, drop-jaw handsome, and totally out of place with his new leather shoes, dark jeans and white linen shirt. He didn't belong here, yet he did look familiar. You'd remember a guy like him. Hell, you'd dream about a guy like him. Without thinking, she sucked in her cheeks and her stomach and took a deep breath. *Hot. Damn.*

The man glanced over his shoulder then approached her. He lifted his sunglasses, cocked an eyebrow and grinned. "Can you give me a ride?"

That brought her stampeding heart to a halt. *What about me screams taxi*, she wondered. "A ride?" Her shoulders slumped.

"Yes. Anywhere." His smile fell as he glanced around. "And fast."

Kate pointed at the restaurant. "I was just going in to ask about a job." She took a step back and looked him up and down. "And I don't even know you." *Not that I wouldn't like to . . .*

He held up two fingers. "Scout's honor, I'm a nice guy looking for a ride. And more importantly," he said, reaching into his pocket, "I will give you five hundred dollars to drive me out of this town right now." He plucked five one-hundred-dollar bills from his slim black wallet and spread them out like a hand of cards.

Kate wondered what kind of trouble this guy was in—and how long it would take to make five hundred dollars in tips without showing ample cleavage during happy hour. It wasn't a bag of money attached to Mr. Right, but it certainly was an interesting development. She nibbled on her lip. *What do they say about desperate times?* "Get in."

He ducked into the car and looked out the back window. "Go!"

Kate hopped in and screeched the car onto the street. "Where?"

"I'm not sure." He closed his eyes and rubbed his temples.

Kate stole another look at him. He had dark hair threaded with glints of copper, high cheekbones and a strong jaw that would undoubtedly hold up to some serious kissing. Major muscles lurked beneath that fancy shirt, and she glanced down at his thighs. Her car veered onto the shoulder. She snapped her focus—and her wheels—back on the road. She wasn't known as Willowdale's best driver, and this guy certainly wasn't helping improve her reputation.

He turned to her. "I'm sorry, I should've mentioned to drive *without killing me.*"

Kate slowed the car and jerked her thumb toward his door. "You want out?"

He held up his hands and faked a smile, showing off teeth

whiter than she'd ever seen. "No, no, we're fine. Is there somewhere we could hide out for a few hours?"

She drove faster, laughing nervously. "You're not running from the police, are you? Cause I guarantee Police Chief Tommy Larsen will find you." At least, he'd always had a knack for tracking her down. Kate glanced in her rearview mirror, making sure he wasn't on her tail again. "We're not going to get shot, are we?"

"The only thing we could get shot with today is a camera."

"Excuse me?" *I've picked up a narcissistic lunatic.*

He dropped his head in his hands. "I'm trying to dodge the *paparazzi.*"

"*Paparazzi?* In Willowdale?" She laughed. "I doubt Ned Shaw from the Weekly Saver's tracking anyone down, not even this week's high bowler. Who are you?"

He looked at her and made his voice all serious. "Teague Reynolds."

"Teague Reynolds." She twisted her lips, thinking. "Sounds familiar."

He let out a ragged, annoyed breath. "Teague Reynolds. I was on that TV series, *Big and Bad?*"

She blinked at him. *Sorry your hotness, no idea.*

He scrunched his eyebrows like a disappointed kid. "I got a Golden Globe Nomination this year for best supporting actor in *Desperate at Midnight?*"

Kate snapped her fingers. "You're the one who dates all the young actresses. What do they call you?" She tapped a finger on the steering wheel, trying to remember.

Teague dropped his head back and groaned. "They're not *all* young."

Kate's mind spun, searching for his nickname. "Some big, scary animal that stomps around . . . like all over women's hearts . . . Tiger . . . T-Bone . . ."

"T-Rex," he mumbled.

She smacked the steering wheel. "Yes! T-Rex. I know who you are." She squinted at him. "You look different in person." Then she frowned. "I can't believe you dated both Cameron twins."

His mouth opened and closed. "Not at the same time."

"Didn't Kimmie Cameron go for therapy after you dumped her?"

"Trust me, she needed it."

Kate slowed the car. "Are you running from a woman? I don't do catfights." Kate could be foolish, but she wasn't a *total* fool.

"No! No catfight." He crossed his arms and groaned. "Is there somewhere we can lie low, or not?"

"Quit pouting. I'm thinking." Kate sped up. "What in the world are you doing in Willowdale, North Carolina?"

"Nothing I want anyone to know about. But someone suspects I'm here and I don't want them to prove it and find out why." Again, he looked back. "Yep. Same black SUV that's been following me the last half hour. Do you have a hiding place? I'll give you an extra five hundred dollars. Sounds like you need the cash."

Anger snapped in her chest like a twig. It had become totally obvious to a complete stranger that she was broke, desperate, and willing to do anything for money. Well, just about anything. "A hiding place? Who do I look like, Batgirl or Buffy? I'm Kate, by the way, since you didn't ask." *Kate Riley, chauffeur to ungrateful passengers all across the Carolinas.*

He drummed his fingers on his thighs. "What about your place, Kate-by-the-way?" He pulled another stack of bills from his wallet—along with another sexy grin.

"It's Kate Riley. And you don't want to go to my place. My stepfather might be home, and then all bets are off." Willowdale was too small a town to hide in. She fluttered her fingers, thinking. Unless . . . ughh. Could she really take him there?

"Shoot. I've got one place we might try." She blushed just thinking of where she was proposing to take Hollywood's most badly behaved boy. She'd have to remember not to let her guard down around this guy.

Teague turned back around. "You should've let me drive. I could shake this guy in sixty seconds." He grinned, flashing his dimples. "I do my own stunts."

"How special," she said. "So do I." Gripping the steering wheel, she zoomed around a sharp curve and under the railroad bridge. She eased the car behind the trestle bridge where Chief Larsen liked to hide, looking for speeders—and ex-girlfriends—to harass. The man just refused to give up, even five years and several girlfriends later—her friend, Tonya, included. In fact, this was probably the very spot he was hiding when he pulled her over for speeding when Tonya first moved to town.

After the black SUV tore past them, down the hill and out of sight, Kate turned the car around and headed back toward town. "Before we go searching for a hideout, you're going to have to duck or blend in with the upholstery because I need to fill up."

"You look filled out fine to me." He gave her a big, cheesy smile.

She gave him her nastiest look. "I'm going to charge you extra if you keep coughing up lines like that." Kate pulled into the gas station right outside of town and reached behind her seat to grab her purse.

Teague crouched down, but his gaze followed her breasts as she hovered over him.

She sighed. "Lord, it's like I'm seventeen and babysitting the twelve-year-old McClacken twins again. Must've been a long time since you've seen a pair without silicone. All right, get a good look then keep your eyes to yourself."

He raised an eyebrow. "Good to know I haven't been picked up by a delicate flower."

"Watch out. I've got a lot of weed in me." She pulled her credit card out of her purse and hopped out to fill up. After plugging the nozzle into her gas tank, she looked up at the sky and rolled her eyes. What in the devil's name was she doing hauling an A-list movie star around town? She had half a mind to drag him around Willowdale and show him off to her friends. But her instincts told her the sooner she got him off her hands, the better.

When she finished up, she climbed back in the car. "Okay. I've got a good hiding place in mind but you keep your hands and your comments to yourself."

"Whoa, what kind of guy do you think I am?"

"T-Rex. Hollywood's hottest heartbreaker. Said so right on last week's tabloid I read at the beauty shop."

Still tucked down in his seat, he looked up and narrowed his eyes at her. "Right next to the article about my alien love child, I bet."

She stifled a laugh as they cruised through the heart of downtown and turned down an unmarked road that led into the woods.

"Where are we going?" Teague sat up.

She maneuvered the car along the bumpy road, hidden under the thick canopy of trees. "There's this out-of-the-way spot I thought we'd try." Her cheeks must've been red as an August sunset. "How long do we need to hide, anyway?"

"I've got a plane chartered to leave at eight over in Whitesville."

Kate blew out her breath. "That's over three hours to kill."

He grinned at her. "I've given you a thousand dollars. Not a bad rate per hour."

With a glare for him, she pulled into the clearing at the end of the road overlooking the valley. Gravel crunched under her tires as she parked the car, angled so she could focus on the beautiful, rolling scene below instead of the gorgeous view in the seat right next to her. "I guarantee no one'll find us here."

The place was deserted, with huge pine trees flanking either side of the overlook, providing plenty of privacy. A few crushed beer cans littered the ground and old tire tracks from generations of long, steamy nights left grooves in the dirt. Not that she'd know. But it must've looked much different beneath a moonlit sky instead of the big blazing sun. She swiped the back of her hand across her forehead even though the air conditioning was cranked on high.

A grin split his face. "This looks like a place where kids come to make out."

Her cheeks burned and she looked away. "It is. But I figure we're safe here on a Tuesday afternoon." Unconsciously, she checked to see that her seatbelt was fastened. It was. Of course it was.

He set one hand against the back of her seat and leaned toward her. "Or maybe you're just trying to take advantage of me, find out if my reputation is true." He put his hand over his heart. "I'm hurt, really." Then he pressed the latch on her seatbelt and smiled. "But I'll get over it." His breath was hot and inviting on her skin like a warm breeze at the beach. *A nudie beach,* she thought, probably turning five kinds of red.

She slapped away his hand and clenched her teeth. "I could always drop you off back in town."

Both his hands shot up. "No, no. I'm kidding. We can sit here and play twenty questions. Rock, paper, scissors. Truth or dare. Whatever you want."

She refastened her seatbelt and flicked on the radio. "Or we could sit here and ignore each other." Which was the best thing to do with a guy like Teague Reynolds—the triple fudge brownie sundae of men: hot, irresistible, and gone before you know it. Totally bad for a girl's heart. She was smart enough to recognize his kind.

He turned the radio off. "So, what kind of job are you looking for?"

She turned the radio back on. Her heart quickened as she glanced at the patch of silky brown hair peeking above the neckline of his shirt. Most actors waxed their chests. She hated that; real men had chest hair. Every inch of Teague Reynolds looked like a real man. And every inch of her wanted to find out for sure.

His lids lowered, watching her eyes take him in. "Well?" One eyebrow perked up, ever so slightly.

She felt her face turn red. "What?"

He smirked. "I asked what kind of job you were looking for."

She looked past him, out the window. Now that she knew who he was, she was *not* interested. At least that's what her brain was telling her; other parts were disagreeing. But no. No, no, no. He might have ten million women drooling over him, but she wouldn't give him the satisfaction of being number ten-million-and-one. She'd managed to salvage a little bit of self-respect through all the heartbreak she'd suffered. "I have a job."

"I thought you said you were going to see about a job back on Main Street?"

Kate drew in a deep breath and got a whiff of warm, sexy male. How could someone so appealing be so annoying? No wonder Kimmie Cameron needed counseling. "Yes. I'm a school nurse, which pays squat, and I need something for the summer this year."

He rubbed his stubbly chin. "This year? But not usually?"

"I never agreed to twenty questions." She pointed a finger at him. "You've played a few too many cop roles."

He turned the radio down. "I've only asked you three questions."

She pinched the bridge of her nose and prayed for a dose of patience. She did not want to get to know this man; he might turn out to be even more enticing. "No, you asked me four."

"Fine. Ask *me* four questions." He shifted in his seat to face her, his arms crossed, mouth smirking, and hair curling around his shirt collar.

Kate exhaled, wishing the tight quarters in her Jeep weren't forcing her to be so darn close to this guy. "Fine. Question one. What are you doing here in Willowdale?"

He shook his head. "No comment."

"Hey, that's not an answer," Kate protested.

Teague shrugged. "I didn't say I'd answer, I only said you could ask. Next?"

"Cheater!"

He dropped his smile. "I am not a cheater. Those rumors aren't true."

Trying to suppress a dramatic eye roll, she drummed the steering wheel. "Where are you going after here?"

"L.A., then the Sunshine Film Festival." He held up two

fingers. "Two more."

"Did you really tattoo Simone Peters' name on your butt?" She held her breath.

He leaned toward her. "I'll let you check to find out for yourself."

Kate closed her eyes, trying to convince herself she wouldn't enjoy that assignment. "Who are you going out with now?"

"No one," he said, hesitating. "But I should check *People* magazine first to be sure. You never know."

His intense gaze unsettled her. She gripped the gearshift in the center console, hoping it would steady her wild, girly, hormones, which were screaming like she was in the second row at a Toby Keith concert.

He looked at her hand. "Time for rock, paper, scissors?" He hovered one palm over her fist. "Paper beats rock every time." His hand covered hers, swallowing it with big strong fingers. "That was easy."

She stared into his icy blue eyes, noting the amused and satisfied expression. She'd seen that look before; it made acid swoosh in her stomach. "I am not easy."

He arched one eyebrow. "No doubt about that."

TEAGUE HELD ONTO her as she tried to pull away. He liked the feel of her small hand in his. He imagined tracing his fingers across her palm, up her smooth, white arm. Or maybe he'd use his tongue. She looked down at her sandals and blushed like she knew his wicked thoughts. What was behind her resistance? Hell, women lined up for that kind of thing with him.

He tried to remember the last time he was with someone who hadn't been featured on the cover of *Cosmo*. He couldn't recall, but it didn't matter. Kate had an easy beauty that intrigued him. He'd twine her long, dirty-blond hair around his finger to see if it was as silky as it looked. No fancy highlights, either—it was her natural color. Kate seemed as simple and pretty as this little town. He frowned. A town that had just seriously complicated his life.

He pulled his hand away. "How often did you come here as a teenager?"

"Sounds like we're moving on to truth or dare." When she stared at him, he noticed the flecks of green and amber in her blue eyes, like someone had painted them in as a final, perfect detail.

And that surprised him; he wasn't used to noticing women's eyes. Other parts were usually much more interesting. He leaned closer. "What color are your eyes? I thought they were blue, but now they look green."

She shrugged. "Blue-green, I guess."

What color are your eyes? Holy Pickup 101. *Don't flirt with her!* He tugged a hand down his face and tried to shake off the feeling. Despite what the tabloids liked to say, Teague was more talk than action. Okay. There was action. But he always made it clear that he wasn't looking for a serious relationship and never would. That didn't deter anyone from trying, though. So Kate's resistance was a surprising turn-on. Teague usually got what—and who—he wanted. But Kate didn't seem to want him. *Huh?*

They stared at each other, as if in a standoff. And they both jumped when someone tapped on the window.

"I guarantee no one will find us here." He did a bad imitation of Kate.

She sneered at him, glanced out the window, and slumped back. "It's Chief Tommy Larsen. The very last person I need to see right now." She turned and gave Teague a look that probably scared the hell out of students faking sick in her nurse's office. "Thought he wasn't looking for you."

Damn, she's even cuter when she's mad. "Didn't think he was."

She rolled down her window. "Hello, Chief, what brings you out here today?"

A tall, thick man peered in the window and lowered his shades. "I should ask you two the same thing. Who you got with you there, Katie? It's awful early to be out here at Lookout Point. Remember?"

She gave him a great big smile. "No, I sure don't. You must be remembering all your other girls. Confusing me with Ellen, maybe?"

Chief Larsen ran his fingers through his short, dark-blond hair. "We were taking a break, remember? Ellen happened during our break."

She crossed her arms, showing off her cleavage nicely. "That would've been something to mention when I asked if you'd dated anyone during our break. Lie by omission, isn't that what they call it?"

The chief sighed. "Stupid young men deserve a second chance."

"You want another go-round with an ex? Call Tonya. She's still single."

The chief swatted away a fly and let out a long sigh. "Now you know that didn't work. Only made me realize how much I missed you."

Kate shrugged and said, "How about Jeanne? The three of us gals all went out with LeRoy Jenkins. Although that was at the same time . . ."

Teague sucked in a breath and she turned to swat at him. "Not like that. The three of us went out on separate occasions."

Teague nodded quickly like he understood, but he was mostly trying to shake the image from his brain.

The chief continued. "Now you know how Jeanne feels about my brother. Besides, I'm just teasing. I know where you stand."

Don't blame him for trying, Teague thought. *I'd want a second shot with her.* The idea startled Teague, but he shook it away. He had bigger problems than curiosity about kissing Kate; he had to figure out what to do about the baby.

And didn't that thought quiet the fire down below.

"Aren't there any missing cows to find? What are you doing out here?"

The chief took off his sunglasses and polished them with a handkerchief. "Just making the rounds. Got a few reports of some suspicious vehicles in town." He planted his hands on his thighs and peered in the window. "Now let's get back to business, 'cause you didn't answer my question. Who's this here with you? He's not giving you any trouble, is he?"

Teague leaned past her and waved. "I'm an old friend in town for a visit."

The chief folded his arms. "An old friend from where? As I recall, most of Kate's friends are from right here in town."

She glared at Teague. "Why don't you explain? You tell such a good story."

He opened his mouth and let out his deep, rumbling laugh. "Well, you see—"

The chief stepped back. "Teague Reynolds?" The chief pointed at him. "T-Rex! What are you doing here?"

He'd been meaning to kill the *ET* reporter who came up with his nickname. He bumbled his words and fiddled with the empty soda can in the cup holder. "Well, like I said, I'm visiting Kate."

The chief laughed. "I must say I'm surprised. I knew T-Rex got around, but our own sweet Katie?" He rocked back on his heels and shook his head. "Can't compete with a movie star. Maybe it really is time to give up the chase."

Teague was surprised to feel his hands fold up into fists.

"No, it's not what you're thinking. Heck, you should know I'm done with men." She frowned. "Guys like you and T-Rex, anyway. Now keep quiet about this. I don't need people talking."

The chief pretended to zip his lip. "Don't you worry. I don't want to hurt you anymore than I already have. I might be jealous, but mum's the word on your little afternoon delight." He turned to leave.

She tried to protest, but Tommy spun around. "Hey, T-Rex, did you really get arrested for skinny-dipping in a fountain with that supermodel out in Vegas?"

Kate glared at Teague. "Hadn't heard that one."

"Don't believe everything you read." *She wasn't a supermodel. Just a regular model, right? And a citation isn't an arrest.* He held up both hands, protesting his innocence. "You can check my record, Sheriff. No arrests. Clean as a whistle."

Chief Larsen clucked his tongue. "Too bad, I would've enjoyed that story. Well, looks like you're getting lucky today." He winked.

Kate's cheeks turned an adorable shade of red, which definitely made those blue-green eyes stand out. "I told you, we're just sitting here talking. We're about to leave."

"We are?" Teague asked. He'd been enjoying himself, forgetting all about the problem he was so desperate to hide.

"We are now," she growled.

"In that case, I'll escort you," the Chief called back, climbing in the cruiser. He waited for Kate to pull out.

She backed out of her spot and eased down the dirt road, a swirl of dust clouding their wake.

Teague tried to fight back his smile. "So, you two were an item—"

Her grip tightened on the steering wheel. "We're just friends now."

"But you were?"

"Twenty questions is over," Kate snapped.

"Where to now?"

"I don't know, but I should think about leaving town with you. That man has a big mouth."

Leaving town with *him*.

The idea didn't seem so bad.

Chapter 2

KATE CHECKED THE rearview mirror to make sure the Chief wasn't tailing them. "How were you planning on getting back to the airport?"

"Same way I got in—a cab." He scratched his head. "But that's out of the question now. The photographer will be looking for it."

"We've got three hours to kill." She sighed. "I guess we'll take the scenic route down Antique Alley. Let me know if you'd like to stop in any of the stores." *Sure Kate, he wants a tour of the local scenery.*

He stared out the window for a few minutes. "Did you grow up here?" he asked.

Kate turned down the country road that led to the tiny airport in Whitesville. "Sure did. Lived here all my life." Ramshackle shops and tiny diners dotted this road, along with the occasional farm. The mountains beyond made a beautiful backdrop. Most folks who lived along this stretch set out stuff for sale on their front lawns: fresh tomatoes and peaches, old bikes and kids' wagons they'd fixed up, or yard sales that lasted all summer long. In between the homes were acres of farm fields. A far cry from Hollywood.

Tourists often spent the weekend poking along the road to Whitesville, searching for treasures. Her heart stung as she thought of her mother and their own Saturday antiquing expeditions. Kate figured it had been Mama's way of coping; like Depression glass could fix a depressing marriage. She pretended to study the big scrub trees, dripping with moss and vines, set back from the road. She didn't want Teague to see the tears pricking her eyes.

"Sure is a tiny place," Teague said, as they stopped to let a line of cows pass.

She smiled and waved to Farmer Peterson. "If it's so small, what are you doing here, Mr. Big Time?" Not that she expected an answer.

He ignored her. "Your family still live here?"

What's left of it. She nodded and drove on once the cows had passed.

Her mom had married George Riley when Kate was twelve. Kate and Mama took his last name, even though he wasn't really her daddy. She never knew any other father than him, but she had never felt the love for him she imagined a girl would feel for a real dad. The kind of man who loved his wife and daughter enough to keep from chasing any pretty blonde who crossed his path. Redheads, too. One thing she could say about George, he didn't discriminate.

"I really appreciate this." Teague smiled at her with one side of his mouth. Now that she knew who he was, she recognized that grin from many a magazine cover. She'd been known to toss a few of those rags on top of her grocery order when her lousy love life left her eager to gobble up some celebrity break-ups.

A bug splattered on the windshield and she flicked on her wipers. "Like you said, you're paying me well." She wasn't going to let someone like Teague work his charms on her. She could thank Chief Larsen for that lesson. A pretty guy with pretty words was bad news. And Teague was pretty in every way. She needed a nice, simple guy who laid out his cards and didn't play games. Hadn't found a man like that so far. They probably didn't exist.

Teague pointed to a restaurant a little ways up the road. "Let's stop and get a drink. I haven't seen that SUV since we drove away from your make-out point." One eyebrow arched.

"*Lookout* Point. Some people just go there to *look*." She pulled up to the Kissin' Cousins diner and antique shop. It was far enough outside town that she thought it was safe. It's not like she could take him in to the Jelly Jar in town. Half of Willowdale would show up to pose for pictures with him. Dolly Jackson would probably sneak off with him and hold him captive in her closet. "Want me to get something so you don't have to go in?" She didn't want anyone else to spot them together.

Teague glanced out the window at the empty gravel parking lot. "Looks pretty quiet. I'll take a chance. Can I borrow your ball cap?" He reached to the backseat for the baseball hat she'd tossed back there. "Or maybe the hubcap?" With a quizzical look, he held up the shiny silver disk.

"It's been a bad day."

"I know the feeling." He tucked his hair behind his ears and put on the hat.

She tilted her head and studied him. "You still look like Teague Reynolds."

"So call me by a different name."

"How about Eugene?" Unfortunately, even the nerdiest name she could think of didn't make him any less attractive.

He screwed up his face. "Eugene's the kid in school who eats his boogers."

"Fine. We'll go with T-Rex, then. It suits you."

He narrowed one eye. "Eugene works."

They went into the diner, and she relaxed as she scanned the big, empty room. Clatter echoed from the kitchen and the ceiling fans hummed full blast, but other than that the place was quiet enough to hear crickets. Teague grabbed a booth in back and slid onto the red leather seat.

"I thought you only wanted a drink, Eugene?" How long were they going to be here? The longer they spent together, the more nervous she got. She didn't like the way this man made her heart beat so fast. "You're hungry, too?"

He rubbed his hands together. "We've got time to kill and the smell of hot grease gets a man's stomach working overtime."

An older woman walked over and set two menus in front of them. "How are y'all today? Can I get you a drink?"

She looked back and forth between them and Kate tensed, waiting to see if the woman recognized Teague. He seemed unfazed and smiled at her. This time, it was his wide-eyed, broad smile. She'd seen five or six of his smiles in the few hours they'd been together. Had any of them been sincere?

He craned his neck to see the waitress's big, yellow nametag, made up to look like a road sign. "How are you today, Delores?"

"Oh, we're doing okay. Business is slow. You're my first customers in three hours. What can I get you kids?" Her pen hovered over her order pad.

"I'd love a nice tall diet soda, Delores. How about you, Kate?"

"Same thing, Eugene."

Delores left to get the drinks, and Teague flashed Kate a thumbs-up. "I think we're in the clear."

"Wow." She scanned the menu, not seeing anything she wanted. "We found the one woman in America not in love with you."

"Don't forget I met you today. So that would make two of you." He waggled two fingers at her and his eyes danced.

Stupid twinkly blue eyes. Kate raised her chin and said nothing.

The waitress came back with drinks and set her order pad on the table. "Don't I know you?"

Kate's heart sped up. Sure, they were a few towns over, but word might make its way back to Willowdale that she'd been shuttling around a superstar. Is there any way to keep a secret in this state? She blew out a breath to stay calm.

"No, I don't think so," Teague said, slowly unwrapping his silverware from the napkin.

Delores waved him off. "Not you, your girl. You're Margaret Riley's daughter, aren't you?"

Kate winced at Mama's name, her memory stinging like a thatch of nettles. "Yes, I'm Kate."

Delores set a freckled hand on her shoulder. "It's such a shame about your mama. She was a regular at our antique shop. Sure liked her Depression glass."

Kate nodded, her heart slowing down a bit. She'd been to lots of shops with Mama, but not this one. She must have come on her own. "You should see all of it at home." She'd been meaning to thin out the collection, but couldn't bear to sort through it just yet.

"She had that lovely Victorian just outside of town, right?"

"Yes." Kate forced a smile. "I moved back in when she got sick. And now I'm there helping out my stepfather and stepsister."

Delores patted her hand. "She was real proud of you. I saw you at the funeral but we weren't introduced. It's been, what, eight months now, hasn't it?"

Kate nodded. Delores certainly knew a lot about Kate and her mama. She must be plugged in to gossip central. If she found out who Teague was, they were in trouble. She was probably as bad as the gals at the Jelly Jar. Didn't even need cell phone service the way news spread there.

Delores looked at him. "And who's this here with you today?"

She swallowed hard. "Just a friend from out of town. Eugene."

Teague gave her a wave. "Hello."

"Hello, Eugene." Delores smoothed her apron. "Enough of my chitchatting, what can I get y'all to eat?"

Kate relaxed once she realized his cover wasn't blown. She ordered a salad and tried to push away her bad feelings. But the ache of her mother's death was there again, like a low-level infection she couldn't shake. And there's no pill or potion to make that go away.

"I'll have the burger, thanks," he said.

Delores shuffled off and Kate let out her breath. "I don't think she recognized you."

Teague waved his hand in dismissal. "I'm sorry to hear about your mother. Were you close?"

Kate nodded. If she told him anything more about her mother and how her real father had died when she was just a baby, she'd probably start sobbing like a toddler on vaccination day. She certainly wasn't going to let that happen. "What about you and your folks?"

He laughed. "Close is not how I would describe my relationship with my parents. We'll just leave it at that." He stared off at the old road signs hanging on the walls.

The two of them sat there, lost in private sorrows, but Delores soon bustled over with their plates of food. "You kids enjoy."

"Looks absolutely delicious, thank you," Teague said with one of his big, fake smiles.

Kate stabbed a tomato with her fork. This day couldn't end soon enough. She should go right back to Scalia's and apply for her own waitress job. One thousand dollars from Teague would certainly help pay the property taxes, but it wouldn't dig her out of this hole. And she didn't know what she'd do for work if she couldn't get that job, as humiliating as it would be. If only Teague hadn't sidetracked her, she'd probably be getting ready for the dinner crowd in that dumb Italian peasant dress the waitresses still wore. Her sadness was morphing into a hot little ball of anger: at Teague, at George, at Tommy. She glared at him.

"What?" he asked.

"You."

He pointed a French fry at her. "Listen, just because the Sheriff of Mayberry broke your heart doesn't mean you should take it out on all men."

Kate dropped her fork. "He didn't . . ." She was too flustered for words because he was right. She had loved Tommy. Oh, the lure of the varsity jacket. They had dated in high school, then through college. Tommy was a state basketball champion and they were the most popular couple in town. Everyone loved Tommy. Especially the girl he got pregnant when he and Kate decided to take a break after college graduation. Kate snapped out of her sad stroll down memory lane and was surprised to see Teague staring at her.

"I don't know what he did to you, but I'm sorry."

Well, that was like an unexpected nibble of sugar in your lemonade. Then she stabbed another tomato because Teague had two things going against him: he was an actor and he was a man. And she would never believe anything either of them said. Lies and heartbreak, that's all men were good for, which was why Kate was done with them. "Tommy taught me some hard lessons."

"Like what?"

She pushed her salad away. "That not everyone's meant for love. And it's a fact, not an opinion." Oh, she always tried to play it off like she was over it all, doing her best to be friendly with Tommy. Heck, she'd even set him up with Tonya. But when she let herself sit and think about everything that had happened, it hurt like a dozen bee stings to the heart that never went away.

Teague stared at her for a moment and Delores dropped off their check in a little black tray with a couple of peppermint candies. "You two should take a peek in our antique shop. We've got a sale going on. There are some nice pieces of jewelry for your girl, Eugene. I can tell you got real special feelings for her," she said, nodding at Kate.

Teague reached for Kate's hand. "She's special, alright. Thank you. We'll take a look."

Kate's eyes widened and she snatched her hand away when Delores walked back to the kitchen.

He shrugged and unwrapped a peppermint. "What? She thinks I'm Eugene, your boyfriend." He popped the candy in his mouth. "I'm just playing the part."

"Trust me. That would never happen. Not with someone like you." *The devil would get into the snow cone business before that ever went down.*

TEAGUE LIFTED AN eyebrow. She talked a tough game, but there was a lot of hurt behind those pretty eyes. He wanted to tuck her hair behind her ears so he could kiss away that frown. He bounced his leg under the table, surprised by his reaction. He hadn't been around anyone so real in a long time. It felt good. Scratch that—it felt scary as hell. Good thing he was leaving town soon. Kate Riley could be very bad news for someone like Teague.

He got coffee to go for the two of them, paid the bill—gave Delores a fifty percent tip so at least *someone* would be having a good day—and walked into the antique store. He went right to a display cabinet filled with old jewelry. He felt bad for Delores and this struggling shop. He had a soft spot for anyone or anything unwanted. When you're an unwanted kid, you watched out for rejected people, discarded things. Didn't take a trip to the psychologist to figure that one out. That's why he'd always paired himself with confident, brash, women; the women *everyone* desired. His heart was certainly safe with them. They'd never need him for anything other than a good time. And that's all he ever expected in return. So far, it had been working quite nicely.

He scanned the necklaces in the display case, imagining them looped around Kate's long neck. He felt an odd desire to soothe her, make the ache go away. Just like he'd always wished someone would do for him when he was a kid.

He tapped the glass. "Can I see that ring in the back? The silver one with the big pearl."

Delores handed it to him and folded her spotty hands. "It certainly is gorgeous. Just like Kate."

Kate walked up to him, letting out a big sigh at Delores' words.

"Can you try this on?" he asked.

She slid it on her finger and splayed her hand. "It's lovely. I think any woman would be tickled to have this." She took it off and set the ring on the counter.

"I'll take it," he said.

Maybe he'd give it to Kate, or . . . oh, hell. Just say her name: Jennifer, who'd toppled his world today. Maybe he'd give it to her the next time he was in town. Would he stop and see Kate, too? Maybe then they could get down to business and have a good time. He closed his eyes and tried to ignore the feeling. Why was he thinking about that at a time like this? He had "the problem" to deal with. Jennifer's big problem.

No, *his* big problem, now.

They walked out to the Jeep and he settled in the seat. He closed his eyes, wishing he were back in L.A., lying by his pool, maybe getting a massage from that lovely Swiss masseuse. A few more appointments with her and those massages would be much more interesting, he just knew it. He wanted to leave this town and never come back.

But that was impossible now. He'd probably have to make more trips back here after his visit today. But at least he'd gotten the call in time. The baby was due in two months and he'd have to make appropriate arrangements. But what would those arrangements be? He scratched his head. Was there any way to handle this without the entire free world finding out? Jennifer didn't stand a chance if they did.

Kate climbed into the car and slumped back in her seat. "So you heard my history with Tommy, and you know my mama died. Do you trust me enough now to tell me what you're doing in town?"

He shook his head and took a long gulp of not-so-horrible coffee. He couldn't trust anyone with this secret. He'd rather die than let the news out.

"It's crazy and it's complicated and I don't want to talk about it," he said.

She held up her hands. "Trust me, I'm not going to say anything to anyone. I fuel the gossip mill plenty around here, so I know what it's like. Might help to talk it out."

He turned and looked her in the eyes. "I've learned one thing in Hollywood. Trust no one." Actually, he had learned that a long time ago, when he found out his own mother didn't want him and gave him up for adoption—and not when he was a baby, either. No, when he was two years old, like he'd been a mistake. Like he wasn't good enough. Well, he'd proven to the world he was good enough by now, hadn't he? So why did he still feel so alone?

And why did this woman next to him make him feel so damn antsy?

Chapter 3

THEY DROVE ALONG Antique Alley until the airport was visible just up the road. Knowing Teague would be leaving in a few minutes, Kate was surprised by the mixture of regret and relief storming her heart like twin tornadoes.

But this is good news. She needed to hightail it back to town to apply for that lousy job. She needed to get her butt to the Jelly Jar to meet up with Tonya and Jeanne and tell them all about this crazy day.

Her phone beeped and she pulled it out. It was a text from Dina. *My dad's back home. He'll pick me up tonight. And the job's filled. Told ya.*

"Of course it is," she mumbled, putting away her phone.

"What's wrong?"

"The job I needed is filled now."

"You missed it because you were helping me." Teague puffed up his cheeks then blew out his breath. "I'm so sorry. I really am. But you have no idea how important it is the press doesn't discover why I'm in town. Thank you." He handed her the bag with the antique ring. "I want you to have this."

Kate's stomach did a little flip-flop. Again, her stupid emotions were bucking her common sense. But then she remembered all those trinkets George used to bring home for her mother, like they were get out of jail free cards from a Monopoly set. He always found a way to weasel out of any situation. It seemed Teague had learned the same trick.

Kate's mouth tightened. "Keep it. No doubt you'll have some new girlfriend to give it to next week. You paid me a thousand bucks, which was more than generous." She wondered which starlet would be wearing it at the next award ceremony.

Teague set the bag on his lap as they pulled into the tiny

airport. She saw his eyes sweep across the parking lot, packed with cars and vans. A light on top of a camera flicked on. Then another and another and another. He dropped his head back. "Damn it. They're here."

Kate pulled into a parking spot, and the cameramen and photographers ran over to the car, jostling for position, snapping photos and shouting questions. It was like a pack of dogs chomping and yipping outside a meat wagon.

"*T-Rex, what are you doing here?*"

"*Teague! Is this your new girlfriend?*"

"*How did you meet a small-town country girl?*"

Kate felt the blood drain from her face. "That photographer told everyone you were here."

Teague shook his head. "Any photographer would've loved an exclusive piece. No, that guy didn't unleash these hounds."

Kate looked to the heavens. *What were the penalties for killing a cop?* "Tommy. He's got TV reporter friends in Asheville."

"Looks like Chief Larsen made a few phone calls. So much for keeping mum."

Kate turned around, trying to count them all. "How did they get here so fast?" She imagined the whispers that would follow her around town when this news broke.

He frowned. "All the tabloids and magazines have stringers across the country."

Kate twisted her hands in her lap. "What do we do?"

Teague smiled. "I can think of one way to handle this." He took a deep breath. "Pretend you're my girlfriend." His grin widened.

Kate tried to swallow her laugh. "Oh, I don't think so, sugar."

He raised a hand of reason. "Strictly business. I'll hire you for the summer to pose as my girlfriend. Today is June fifth, let's say we break up . . . August first."

"No way." He was the absolute last person she needed to spend more time with. "I've got responsibilities here. I can't just fly around the world to bail out your behind." Kate looked out at the throng of reporters. She looked back at Teague. "What's with the grin?"

He turned up his hands and shrugged. "They already think you're my girlfriend," he said. "So does your cop friend. Oh, and Delores, too. No one's going to believe you're not. Plus, that job you were going after is filled."

Teague looked way too smug. Kate tried to slow her breathing and find her composure, though it was usually nowhere to be found. She let out a sigh for the ages. "What does being your girlfriend entail?"

"Like I said, strictly business. But we need to spend some time together and you need to come to the Sunshine Film Fest this week."

"Pose as your girlfriend." She reached for the coffee cup in the console and took a deep gulp. *Why couldn't it have been Scotch?* She looked over at Teague. How could she ever go back home when it was over? And how could she agree to be part of such a preposterous lie? It'd be the juiciest gossip to ever hit Willowdale. Folks talked for weeks when Tonya and Tommy had started dating—and then for weeks after they broke up. What would they say about this?

But then she thought of all that money she needed to keep her mother's house off the auction block. Kate gently bounced her head against the back of the car seat, trying to lodge some great idea in her brain. But the only solution that seemed possible was Teague's ridiculous . . . impossible . . . fool suggestion.

People were going to be talking about her anyway, once they saw these pictures. Somehow, Teague's proposal seemed like the sensible thing to do. And Kate was all about sensible these days. It was exhausting, really.

"Fine," she said through her teeth. "I'll pretend to be your girlfriend. But I want ten-thousand dollars." She raised an eyebrow.

"Let's make it twenty."

She sucked in a breath. "But only for one month." She poked his chest with her finger. "And *do not* think I'm going to fall for you. I have zero interest in someone like you. Let's make that clear from the get-go."

Teague grabbed the finger pressed up against his chest and pulled her knuckles to his mouth. "Sorry, don't want the press to think the lovebirds are bickering." He kissed her hand and looked up into her eyes. "And an extra twenty thousand says you *will* fall for me."

She snatched her hand away. "Fall for you? Pigs will not only fly, they'll open their own airline before that happens. And by the way, I get to break up with you." She would not suffer another round of sympathy after a humiliating public breakup. This one was going to be on her terms.

He shrugged. "Go ahead, break my heart, baby. You'll be the first one to do it." Teague smiled. "Ready, milady? Follow my lead." He opened the door a crack, but the photographers moved in closer, shouting more questions. He finally got out and they backed up. Camera lights flashed like one of the big Fourth of July displays in Whitesville. Teague walked around the car to open her door.

Kate suddenly regretted slapping on that *I think, therefore I'm single* bumper sticker Tonya had given her last Valentine's Day. Teague took her hand as she stood up on wobbly knees. She felt the same stab to her gut she had experienced back at Lookout Point when he'd curled his fingers over hers.

Cameras flashed; more questions came. Bugs danced around the lights in the dusky sky. When Teague raised a hand, the reporters shut up. "I'm surprised to see you all here. We wanted to keep things quiet. But yes, this is my new girlfriend, Kate Riley."

Kate tried not to roll her eyes.

Reporters hurled more questions at them—so many, she couldn't even gather what they were saying.

"What are you—"

"Where did you—"

"How did you meet?"

Teague turned to Kate and smiled. "It's such an interesting story. And you tell it so well, honey."

That weasel . . . Kate dug her fingernails into his palm. *He asked for it.*

She dropped his hand, clasped her hands in front of her and shrugged, doing her best *aw, shucks* country-girl impression. "Well, ya'll, we met on the Internet. One of those dating service thingies? I did it as a joke, but dang, he was serious about it, and here we are." She shrugged. "You should've seen his funny profile picture. I felt bad for him, actually, figured he wasn't getting many responses, so I emailed him." She batted her lashes at him, determined not to make this arrangement easy on him.

"T-Rex, why did you join an Internet dating service when you could have any woman in the world?" The reporters scribbling in tiny notebooks paused and looked up.

"You're certainly not hurting to meet women," another shouted. Plenty of chuckles followed that one. "Why come all the way to Willowdale for a date?"

Teague laughed and paused, and she wondered how he'd handle that one.

"I joined anonymously under a different name, with a bogus picture." He rolled his eyes and shrugged. "Haven't had great luck with the ladies in Hollywood, in case you haven't noticed."

The crowd laughed.

More confident, he straightened. "So, I thought I'd meet a nice, old-fashioned girl." He looked at her and smiled. "And that's how I met Kate."

She felt herself sucked into those eyes, wondering what it would be like to believe those words. It was like lapping up sugar. But then another light flashed and broke her gaze.

"Kate, were you surprised to learn the guy you met on the Internet was Teague Reynolds?"

She glanced at him, aware of his body heat, the firm stance, his very being, and shook her head. "Surprised wouldn't begin to describe how I felt."

"What were you two doing in town today?"

Good one. The pavement was hot under her flip-flops and she shuffled around a bit. She sucked in a breath, figuring this was the question that would stump them. But Teague kept up.

"It was our first official date. I even bought her this ring." He took the ring out of the bag and slipped it on her finger. "Now if you'll excuse us, we've got a plane to catch."

We?

The crowd of journalists followed them to the tiny plane sitting in the middle of the tarmac. The sun had slipped in the sky, setting the night aglow in purple and orange. The heat and stress of the day hung on her like a cloak.

She hugged her arms around herself. "I'm going with you right now? I didn't even pack." She looked up at him, panicked, aware of the delicate ring circling her finger like a tiny shackle.

"We'll go shopping tomorrow. I'll buy whatever you want."

"How about a goodbye kiss for the cameras?" a reporter called out.

Oh, this isn't good.

Teague flashed a look at the throng of cameras and slipped his hand across Kate's lower back. It was a nice, big hand. Fit, like it belonged there. He pulled her to him and his lips parted. Those easy blue eyes of his closed, and his mouth was on hers. Well good lord, she was in a movie scene.

Right, we're pretending. We're acting, she reminded herself. *I can do this.* She wrapped her arms around his neck and kissed him back, surprised at how hungrily she returned his kiss. This was more divine than taking her time with a box of truffles. Their lips moved like they'd been together many times before. He pulled away and her mouth ached for more, her lips still tingling and her stomach rolling. Damn. Why did that have to be so good? She could not, would not, fall for this guy. No way, no how.

But as they stared at each other, she wondered how a fake kiss could have felt so darn real. "Are we going to be able to pull this off?" she whispered.

One corner of his mouth curled up. "Trust me." He grabbed her hand and she followed him up the stairs onto the small plane, not trusting him at all. No ma'am, not one tiny bit.

Chapter 4

"WHEN CAN I go back?" Kate asked as the plane lifted her away from the only place she'd ever called home. She snapped the window shade shut.

"We've only been gone five minutes. Homesick already?"

Suddenly chilly, she rubbed her bare arms. "I hadn't planned on flying away from my life today. It's not like my calendar for the summer is entirely open." Even though it was. She pulled out her phone and texted Dina. "I had to go out of town on an emergency. Will call tomorrow to explain."

Teague scratched his head. "I'm not sure when you can go home. We'll be at the Sunshine Film Festival for a week. Maybe after that you can come back for a few days to visit. We're going to play it by ear. Don't forget, you agreed to work for a month. And I have to say, you were pretty good back there, especially with that kiss. Have you ever done any acting?"

She tried to think of something funny to say, like she always did when emotions got too close. But the joke didn't find its way out soon enough. Her eyes felt heavy with tears, so she looked away from him.

She hadn't ever been an actress—more like a liar, to protect her mother. Kate had caught George in compromising positions more than once. "Let's just keep this between you and me," he'd say, slipping her a twenty-dollar bill. "You don't want to hurt your mother, do you?"

She'd always wanted to say *Of course not, so why do you keep hurting her?* So Kate would take the money, keep her mouth shut, and use the cash to buy her a mother a trinket on one of their antique excursions.

Tears flooded her eyes, as she remembered the feel of the dirty bill in her hand and the way she'd crumple it up and shove it in her pocket. *And here I am doing the same thing again, taking money to keep a secret, embroiled in one big lie.* She promptly reached for the airsick bag and threw up.

Teague called for the flight attendant, then unfastened his seatbelt. He rushed next to her and set his hand on her shoulder. "You alright?"

"I'm fine," she snapped. She held up a hand to prevent him getting closer. "Stay away from me. Nothing is going to happen between us unless it's absolutely necessary, like for the cameras back there." She jerked her thumb over her shoulder.

He nodded. "Of course. That's the agreement."

The flight attendant emerged from the back of the plane and took the bag from Kate. "I'll be right back with a drink for you both." She gave Teague an appreciative look then bustled away.

Teague reached into his pocket and pulled out a small bottle. "Sleeping pill? Knocks you right out. Looks like you could use some rest, Kate."

She shook her head. "It's been an overwhelming day."

He looked at her, and for the first time, she thought she saw a flash of sincerity on his face. "Tomorrow's going to be even worse."

With a groan, she sat up. "Why?"

"Your face is going to be on tabloid magazines and newspapers across the country."

The flight attendant arrived just in time to hand her another flight bag. Kate threw up again and then held out her hand to Teague. "I'll take that pill."

TEAGUE WATCHED KATE'S fingers twitch, then her eyelids flutter closed. "Dating" her gave him the perfect excuse to go back to Willowdale so he could deal with the baby situation over the next few weeks. It really was a fantastic solution. Heck, maybe there'd even be a few more of those staged kisses. Just so long as she didn't try to get to know him. Not the real Teague. He'd worked too hard to keep the truth from everyone. He was relieved, really, that she was so adamant about nothing happening between them.

He covered her up with a blanket. "Team Teague" was going to have a cow when they found out about this. His publicist, June, thought she should have final approval on his potential girlfriends. She'd chosen a group of A and B list actresses he was allowed to date. His agent insisted his private life greatly impacted his public life and had to be strategized. His manager thought he should ditch women for a while and concentrate solely on his career.

Never mind his personal assistant, stylist, driver, chef and housekeeper. They all had opinions and liked to share them. How many people did he require to take care of him, anyway? Either way, he was in for an earful tomorrow. It was part of the Hollywood scene he hadn't planned on when he'd gone there looking for a new life.

Settling back in the comfortable leather chair, he pulled out a book, a thriller that a producer friend had optioned for a movie. He was considering casting Teague as the lead. That was his life—chasing the next big gig. And the ultimate gig would be landing the lead in an action adventure film: the number one goal for Team Teague these days.

He tried not to jostle Kate, who was slumped against him in a deep sleep. She'd sat in the small row of seats across from him when they'd first boarded, but he was reluctant to leave her now. He closed his book and set it on his lap. He couldn't concentrate. He felt like a voyeur, watching her sleep. She curled up on her side and settled her head on his shoulder. He set his hands on his thighs, determined not to touch her.

What he was going to do with this woman for an entire month?

Chapter 5

"WHY COULDN'T YOU get Kate to drive you home?" Dina's father asked as she climbed into his pickup. "I had a business meeting this evening." He slammed the rickety door shut.

Right, Dina thought. More like cards over at Roy's house. Even without Kate constantly reminding her, she knew her father's shortcomings. "She wasn't around." She decided not to mention Kate had left town. She was too tired to deal with one of her father's moods.

He tapped a cigarette out of the pack and tucked it between his lips.

She fanned her hand through the air. "Excuse me? Pregnant woman in the car. You can't smoke that in front of me."

He sighed and set it down on the console. "You mean pregnant *girl* in the car."

Dina swallowed hard. She hated disappointing everyone like this. She chewed on her bottom lip and looked up at the stars in the sky. What would she wish for if she saw a shooting star? That she wasn't pregnant? That Mama Margaret hadn't died?

She blew her bangs off her forehead. Kate was wrong. Dina could raise this baby by herself. She had to. Bitty-Bump's daddy wouldn't be around, that was for sure. Bitty-Bump's daddy had a new girlfriend. She rubbed her tummy.

George pulled into the driveway, but didn't turn off the engine.

"Aren't you coming in? It's eleven o'clock."

He ran his hand down his face. "Nah, I'm headed back to Roy's for a bit. Oh, I picked up a playpen for the baby at a yard sale. It's the in the back of the pickup. I'll get it out tomorrow."

Dad surprised her sometimes, acting thoughtful and kind

like he had when she was a little girl. What the heck had
happened to him over the years? "Thanks. That was real nice."

She hopped out of the car and let herself in to the dark
house. A year ago, a night alone would have been a dream come
true. But now it just felt lonely and sad. Mama Margaret would
have brought her a glass of sweet tea and asked her all about her
day. Mama Margaret probably would have been in her rocker,
knitting a blanket for the baby.

Dina slumped on the couch. She probably wouldn't be
pregnant if Mama Margaret hadn't died. Mama never would
have left her home alone with a boy. But that's what happened
soon after she died.

Dina kicked off her black flats and lowered herself onto the
couch, settling her feet on top of a throw pillow. The baby's
daddy had asked if the kid was his. Said he'd be there for her.
Dina laughed to herself. *Right.* She wasn't about to be with
someone who didn't really love her. Look at how things had
turned out for Dad and Mama Margaret. She loved them both,
but they shouldn't have gotten married. All they did was fight.
She didn't want a marriage like that. Plus, Dina had only been
out with the guy a few times before this happened. It was her
mess to clean up. And that's why she had lied and told him no.
No worries. The kid wasn't his.

But now as the due date was getting closer, her stomach did
giant flip-flops at the thought of raising a child all by herself. She
rubbed her hand across her big tummy. Should she give it away?

The very idea brought tears to her eyes. Giving the baby
away almost seemed like having it die or something. She ran the
back of her hand under her nose and pressed her eyes shut.
Where are you Kate? I need to talk to you. That was easy to say when
she was all by herself in a dark room. Admitting it to Kate was
another thing. She'd have to listen to a long lecture on
responsibility and consequences. Dina sighed, but she knew it
was true. Without Kate, she couldn't take care of this baby. And
she really, really wanted to keep it.

She pulled out her phone and typed in a text message to
Kate. *Can u come home? I need u.*

Then she erased it and turned off the phone. She wasn't quite ready to admit she couldn't do this. And she still had some time to figure things out.

KATE WOKE TO VOICES shouting. She sat up and rubbed her eyes and looked around the big, airy room. Light streamed through gauzy curtains, the sunbeams stretching across beautiful hardwood floors. Pulling the silky lavender comforter around her, she remembered what she had done. She was pretending to be Teague Reynold's girlfriend. Last thing she remembered, she was on the plane. How had she gotten in here? She groaned and rolled out of bed.

"You're going to ruin your career!"

Following the angry voice coming from below, Kate ran her hands through her hair and stepped out of her room. She stood on the second-floor balcony overlooking a huge living room with a big fish tank, giant paintings—probably originals, not that she would know—leather sofas and chairs, and an immense stucco fireplace. Now that's a room she could spend some time in. But no one was in there. A set of curved, iron stairs beckoned her downstairs. She took two steps and froze as the fighting resumed.

"Calm down, June," she heard Teague say. "She's a nice girl. She's not going to hurt my career."

"A nice girl *will* hurt your career." The woman's shrill voice got louder. "Remember Marcy Winters?"

"She got arrested for punching a chick who grabbed my ass," he retorted. "Not nice at all."

"Exactly. Tons and tons of press. That was the juiciest gossip of the week."

Kate thought she remembered that particular scoop. She sat down on the stairs, interested to hear more.

The ranting woman continued. "You date the divas, the wild girls, and you should be shooting for A-list. Or B-list, but only if she's up-and-coming or totally wild. What did you do with that chart I gave you?" The woman's voice felt like shards of glass in Kate's ears. "*Like* people date *like* people, you know? But T-Rex jetting off to pick up his little hick-town girlfriend? Please! You've just unraveled a year's worth of my work."

Kate held on to the cold metal railing and tried to think of ways to disappear.

"It got me in the papers," Teague said below. "And you said that's what's important."

"Sure it did, but this isn't the kind of press you want. Feature film stars don't date nobodies." Her voice hit a high note. "If you want to land your first leading action-film role, you've just sent yourself five steps back."

Kate's heart tumbled out of place. She'd been thinking how this would affect her, never realizing she could be bad news for him.

Teague was quiet for a moment. "June, it's complicated. And she's nice. I think she's just as pretty as any of the women I've seen here in Hollywood."

Pretty? He thinks I'm as pretty as anyone in Hollywood? Kate wrapped her arms around her knees. *Then he's an actor and a farmer, because he's a hauling a load of you know what.*

"Then you better get her cleaned up. Because the pictures in the paper today ain't pretty."

"She looks great."

"She looks small-town."

"She is. She looks real."

Ugh, real *what?* Kate thought about going back in the room and scouting for a second-story leap.

"Think about ending this, Teague."

"You handle my public relations, not my private ones."

"Your private relations are public. I told you, you can't keep a secret in Hollywood. Internet dating? What were you thinking?"

Kate's heart pounded like she'd just sprinted down the hall after one of her students who bolted from the oh-so-pleasant *You and Your Body* presentation. She stood on the stairs, trying to calm her heart, and watched a tiny woman with dark, cropped hair march out the front door.

Teague closed the door and pressed his back against it.

Kate turned to go back upstairs, but the stair creaked and Teague looked up. "You're awake." He rubbed the back of his neck. "I'm sorry. How much of that did you hear?"

Enough to know I'm social suicide for you. "I just heard shouting and came down to see what was going on. Who was that?"

"My publicist, June Meehan. She wasn't entirely thrilled I sprung this on her."

Kate hugged her arms around her torso. "So, how bad are the articles?"

He shrugged. "I've had worse."

She climbed down the stairs and went to the kitchen to see for herself. The tile floor was cold on her bare feet. She slid onto a stool and noticed the stack of papers on Teague's kitchen table. She picked up the one on top. "Kissing Kate: T-Rex's Online Love," she read out loud. *Not bad.* "T-Rex Goes Country." *True enough, she* was *country.* "Is Mighty T-Rex a Gentle Giant?" *No, ma'am, he is not.* "Me T-Rex, You Plain Jane," she said, incredulously. *Well, now that's just not fair.* She slapped the paper down on the table. "God, I do look like a country hick."

"Kate . . ." Teague didn't argue.

She studied the two of them kissing, and it certainly was a juxtaposition. Teague in his designer clothes, tanned and toned, kissing Kate in her frayed and faded jean shorts and flowered tank top. Her hair flew in a hundred directions. Tonya was going to get an earful about that new volumizer when she made it back to the salon.

But Kate couldn't take her gaze off the picture of his lips locked on hers. A sharp pain of longing shot through her, remembering the spark she'd felt in that fake kiss, which she quickly shooed away. He must be a good actor to put that kind of emotion into a pose for the press.

Kate looked down at her clothes, the same ones she'd been wearing the day before. "I really need something else to wear. I've got nothing with me, no shampoo, none of that stuff." She felt dizzy just realizing the scope of this whole set-up.

Teague stood and ran his hand through his hair. He was

already dressed in another pair of jeans and a form-fitting t-shirt, somehow looking even hotter than the day before. "Photographers are camped out at the end of the driveway, and if we go out they'll follow us on our shopping spree. That might raise some suspicions. So, I'm going to have some things delivered to us." He pulled out his wireless. "What size are you?"

Kate gritted her teeth. She was a fine size back home, but about seven sizes too big for Hollywood. "I'm a six," she lied. She bit her lip. "Or maybe an eight."

WHY DO THEY ALWAYS care so much about the damn number on the tag? He saw the uncomfortable look on Kate's face. She was not happy with all this. Hell, who would be? He thought she looked great like she was, all curves and softness. Skeletal was not his type, and that's what most of the women out here looked like. There's nothing sexy about a pointy hipbone jabbing your thigh when you're getting busy, that's for sure. He dialed his stylist and asked her to bring a wardrobe over for Kate. "And we'll need some red-carpet stuff, too."

"This for your new gal I saw in the papers today?"

"Yes. Bring a few things for her to try. I want her to be comfortable. She wears a six."

"Maybe get some eights too," Kate called from across the kitchen. "Just in case small town sizes aren't . . . so small." Her face was turning red and Teague thought she looked darling. *Darling?* What the hell kind of word was that? Damn, he was infected with a little bit of Willowdale. He sat at the big, long island in the middle of the kitchen and drummed his pen on the counter.

"Eights?" Justine asked over the phone. "The designers don't have sizes that big hanging in their sample racks."

Teague looked out at his pool and imagined that beautiful size-eight body in a bikini, lounging by the water. Maybe one strap sliding down her shoulder and him tugging the bottom off in the deep end . . . He shook himself from his daze. He needed to keep this strictly business like he'd promised—for both their sakes.

He cleared his throat. "Tell the designers she'll probably be the most photographed woman at the festival. They might want to come up with something in her size."

Kate sat on a stool with crossed arms, jiggling her foot. He wouldn't have been surprised if she stuck out her tongue at him. She did not look happy.

Justine let out a long, slow sigh over the phone. "And you want me to bring in someone to do hair and makeup. I'm not asking, I'm demanding."

"Sure. But here's the thing . . . we have to sneak you guys in here. The press is camped out at the end of my driveway. They'll be all over anyone coming in or out."

"Then explain to me how we're going to get in."

Teague smiled as the perfect solution hit him, one that just might make Miss Panties-In-A-Snarl over in the corner drop the glower. "I'll send someone to get you."

THE PHOTOGRAPHERS swarmed the Fantasy Florist delivery truck as it pulled through Teague's gate three hours later. The deliveryman carried in two big vases filled with deep, red roses. Kate gasped, trying so *very* hard not to be impressed that she almost missed the small army following the florist, weighed down with shopping bags, makeup kits and styling tools. She plucked a card from one of the vases—probably Waterford. She knew this was just a ruse, but still, four dozen roses in crystal vases from the baddest bachelor in the world would send a shiver through any woman's nether regions.

She opened the tiny envelope. *Kate, I'm so glad you came into my life. Teague.*

Perfectly coy. She tucked the card into her pocket. When she was serving the clam linguine special a month from now, she'd need some proof to convince herself this had all really happened. She braced herself against the dark granite countertop and wondered *what next?*

"Do you like them?"

She looked up at Teague, who was all smiles and hotness. *Damn him.* "Perfect diversion for the press." She motioned toward all the strangers in the kitchen, with its terra cotta tile floor and gleaming stainless steel appliances that looked like they'd never been used. The kitchen, dining room, and living room in Mama's house would probably all fit in this one room. What did one person do with so much space? But the space was filling up with strangers.

"Who are all these people?" she asked. Apparently it was going to take a small village to make small-town Kate Riley Hollywood ready.

Teague set his hands on her shoulders. "I think you'll be a lot happier the next time the press catches us together."

Trying to ignore the heat of his hands on her skin, she glared at him. But that only made him smile more, and that smile only made him look more gorgeous. She let out a little "hmph."

A woman came at her with scissors and a smock. "Take a seat, this won't hurt a bit. I'm Monica."

Kate flopped down in a chair.

Monica rubbed Kate's hair between her fingers. "What do you think about some highlights?"

"No," Teague said. "I like her hair. It's a beautiful color."

"Well, we need to cut in a few layers, give it some movement," said Justine, the slim stylist, coming up behind them. Kate wanted to offer her a snack so she wouldn't disappear into thin air before this whole makeover thing was done.

"But not too short," Teague said.

Why was he so concerned about her hair?

Justine and Teague circled around her like she was on display.

Kate blushed, angry at his presumption that he had any say in how her hair looked, and way too pleased he thought it was a beautiful color. "Do I get a say in this?" Tonya would kill her when she found out someone else had messed with her 'do.

"Of course," Teague said.

Justine wedged herself between them, being so skinny and

all. She pushed her cropped red hair behind her ears, releasing a whiff of something that smelled stupidly expensive. "Kate."

She knew that look; she used it on students complaining of a stomachache before finals. *Nice try, sister.*

"Kate, I don't know how this unorthodox relationship blossomed, but if you care about Teague and his career, then you need to understand that the press expects his girlfriends to have a certain . . . look. A certain style. I hope you can cooperate with us." She smiled again, like it hurt to move her lips. Which it probably did. They were way too puffy to belong to that little body.

Kate plucked a piece of fruit from the counter and handed it to her. "Would you like an apple, darlin'?" she asked, sweet as pie.

Justine winced. "Are you going to cooperate with us?"

Kate sat back, closed her eyes, and bit into the fruit. Wave the white flag already, she was surrounded, outnumbered, defeated—done. "Fine. Like Teague said. Cut it a little, but don't change it too much."

By the time she was trimmed, plucked, powdered and polished, she thought she looked like her long-lost, sophisticated twin sister. Teague had watched the whole thing, just to make it extra super-duper fun. Kate saw him behind her in the huge wrought iron mirror in the living room, looking at her. She wondered what he saw.

"Quite an improvement," Justine said, walking over with an armful of gowns. "Now, we need to get you properly dressed." She motioned for her to take off her clothes.

"Right here?" Kate looked at Teague, who sprouted a big smile.

Justine snorted. "What? It's not like you're showing him anything he hasn't seen."

Oh no, girlfriend, the horse has not been taking that trail.

TEAGUE GAZED AT KATE, the way the hair grazed her cheeks, the way her eyes sparkled, the way her lips were plump and moist and ready for him. He wondered if he'd have the chance to feel them against his again.

He shook his head. *No.* This was business. She wasn't interested in a relationship and neither was he, no matter how damn irresistible she looked. No matter how close they were to his bedroom. No matter how . . .

"Teague . . ." Kate was calling him.

He shook himself out of his daze. "What?"

"Seems your girlfriend's shy about you watching us dress her," Justine said.

"Oh, of course. I'll go check on our travel arrangements." He went to his office and smoothed his sweaty hands on his thighs. Why was he feeling so nervous? Kate was playing along nicely. The ruse was working. The press had only dug far enough to learn she worked as the school nurse, that she loved the fried catfish at the Jelly Jar diner—sometimes asking for seconds—and that folks in town had no idea the two of them were dating. Oh, yeah, they dug up a pregnant teenage stepsister. Was it something in the water in Willowdale?

But smokin' Kate popped back in his mind, doing things he shouldn't be imagining. He smiled, picturing how sexy she'd look in her new clothes. She'd been overwhelmed by the dozens of new outfits Justine had unwrapped: gowns, sundresses, shirts and pants, shoes, sunglasses. Kate's eyes had gone wide as she'd unpacked the bags and boxes. His throat tightened, wondering how she'd look in them.

Out of them, too.

"You can come in now, Teague," Justine called.

He was more excited than he wanted to be. He walked over to her and planted his hands on his hips, taking it all in. A sparkly blue dress the color of the summer sky clung to a body that was even curvier than he'd dreamed. It pooled around her toes, which peeked out of silver high heels. He could imagine the whole ensemble heaped on the ground.

He cleared his throat. Her hair was piled on top of her head, exposing pale shoulders and a long neck. He wanted to run his thumb along her bare skin, skate his tongue along her jaw, up to her ear. Drop that hair down to her shoulders . . . *Damn.* He was in trouble. He hadn't expected this. He didn't want to deal with this. Not now.

"Well?" Kate asked, her smile faltering as he stood there.

"Very nice," he managed to say. He went into the kitchen, because he wasn't certain he could keep himself from taking her in his arms and hauling her off to bed. Which wouldn't be a problem, he'd carried her up the stairs the night before when the sleeping pill had knocked her out, and she was his "girlfriend"—they did have an audience he could claim he was trying to impress.

But Teague didn't need a girl like her anywhere near his arms, and certainly not his heart. A girl like her would find her way in. And she wouldn't want what she found. She wouldn't want him—the real Teague. The Teague no one had ever wanted.

Chapter 6

KATE LOOKED AT herself in the big mirror that hung over a couch and she didn't recognize the woman staring back at her. *Miss Least Likely To Raise A Ruckus Or An Eyebrow* didn't look half bad. Even so, apparently she didn't look Hollywood enough for Teague. He'd barely squeezed out a compliment before stalking out of the room. How would she pull this off? What had she been thinking, agreeing to pose as his girlfriend? Despite plenty of cajoling from Tonya and Jeanne, she never even dressed up for Halloween, and here she was in the ultimate costume party: girlfriend to a Hollywood hunk. Insanity.

"I think that will do, Kate," Justine said. "I'll make arrangements for you to have a hairdresser and stylist for the premiere. We'll have these clothes packed up and shipped with you." She smiled primly. "I do hope you enjoy your adventure. Must be very exciting for a small-town girl to scoop up a guy like Teague." She raised a red eyebrow. "I hope you're aware of his track record."

Kate gave her a great big smile. "I'm not worried about the women he's dated."

Justine widened her eyes. "You should be. Most of them are going to be at the Sunshine Film Festival. Better have Monica sharpen your claws before you go. Simone Peters will be thrilled to see you."

Simone Peters. Voted *People's* Most Beautiful Person last year. The beauty who'd reportedly prompted Teague to get that tattoo on his butt. Dread coiled through her belly as Monica, Justine and the crew filed out to the delivery van.

The black leather couch in the living room beckoned, and she flopped onto it to check in with Dina. Fifty-six voice mails and text messages waited for her. She read one. *You've got some major 'splaining to do,* Tonya had texted her. Exactly. She tapped out a quick message for her friends. *Surprise! We'll have lots to talk about when I get home. Until then, XOXO.* If Tonya or Jeanne got her on the phone, they'd have the truth out of her in two seconds flat.

She called Dina, but got her voice mail, so she left a message. "Hope you're okay. I have one crazy story to tell you when I get back, probably in a week or so. Call if you need anything and if you can't reach me, try Tonya and Jeanne." She hung up. And what would she do if Dina did need something? She was a world away. But Dina had never come to her before for anything more than a ride. She'd have to pin George down for a lift to work now. Unable to deal with the other messages, she turned off the phone and wandered toward the kitchen.

She heard Teague talking on the phone. "Morty, I've been over this with June. This is my life. I date who I want, no matter what you think. And it's not a long term thing. You know me."

The words stung, and Kate chastised herself for being silly. It wasn't a long term thing—she had insisted on it. And it wasn't even a "thing." It was part of their deal, for crying out loud.

Teague slammed the table with his fist. "Enough. This is not going to blow my chances with Stan Remington. He wants me in his next flick. Trust me. Doesn't anyone trust me?" He ended the call and tossed his wireless on the table.

Kate stepped into the room and cleared her throat. "Never trust anyone, wasn't that your advice yesterday?"

He jumped when he realized she was in the room.

She wore one of the casual outfits the crew had brought her: the dark, skinny jeans Oprah had named one of her favorite things, and a silky pink t-shirt she loved enough to wear forever. The outfit was probably slumming it by Hollywood standards, but she still felt like she was showboating. It would fetch hundreds of dollars on eBay. Maybe she could take the clothes with her to sell later after she left this fantasyland. "So what am I screwing up for you now?"

"Nothing." He walked toward her. "That was my agent. He freaks out whenever I show up with someone new. Just like my publicist and my stylist did. And you're not only new, you're different. Unlike anyone I've ever gone out with before. They don't know how to handle you."

Kate wondered if he regretted their agreement. She walked toward the window overlooking his pool. Several chaise lounges sat underneath a white pergola alongside the long, narrow swath of turquoise water. A fountain in the middle sprayed arcs of water into the air. Potted palm trees dotted the concrete patio. "When do we leave?" She'd be happy spending her month right here, hiding. "And where is the Sunshine Festival, anyway?"

He followed her to the window and laughed. "It's in Maui, and we leave at six in the morning."

She sank into a chair at the table. She couldn't remember when she'd last eaten anything besides that apple. "Do you have any food?" The walls were lined with dozens of huge mahogany cabinets in the kitchen. Surely one of them held some goodies—the sweeter, the better.

Teague frowned. "I gave my chef the week off since I wasn't going to be around. I could scrounge around in the cupboards, or we could order out."

She perked up. "I'd love to see some of L.A. Do you think we could dodge the cameras and sneak out, Eugene? You seem to be pretty clever."

He pulled her up by the hand. "I just might be able to arrange that."

Teague slipped out his back door, still holding her hand. They dashed across the lush lawn, past the pool and the pool house, leaped over a low row of boxwoods, and squeezed through a hedge to the neighbor's gate. Teague unlocked it, and pulled her over to a huge building, which turned out to be the garage.

Breathless and still holding her hand, he smiled at her. "Ready for some fun?"

She stood facing him, just like she had in front of the plane. It was too easy to imagine another kiss, so she tried to imagine a big wart on the end of his nose. Didn't help. "I'm ready."

She thought Teague might move in for another kiss, and

she was trying to round up her defenses, when he stepped back and said, "Come on. You're gonna love this." He unlocked the door and flicked on a light. The place looked like a car showroom. He weaved through the dozen or so shiny sports cars, dropped her hand, and hopped on a Harley.

"You're stealing your neighbor's bike?" Kate asked. "Wow. You are a bad boy."

He laughed in that way that made the pit of her stomach hum, and patted the side of the big black machine. "No, it's my bike. My neighbor's an architect, works all around the world. He's never home. Said I could store my bike here for just such an occasion." He swung his leg over the bike and sat down. "This is the first time I've ever taken him up on the deal. Usually I come through the front door like a normal person."

She froze, staring at his legs wrapped around the machine.

"You haven't done this before, have you?" He crossed his bulging arms.

Oh, there were so many things she hadn't done. She shook her head and found her voice. "I'm a motorcycle virgin."

He laughed and handed her a helmet before patting the seat behind him. "I promise, it won't hurt a bit. Climb on."

She stopped breathing for a moment.

"Straddle me," he said.

She stared at him. *The bike, Kate, the bike.* Right. Nothing wrong with an innocent bike ride. She swung her leg over the bike and set her arms on his shoulders. She could feel the muscles through his t-shirt and knew her knees would buckle if she hadn't already been sitting down.

"Hold on tighter or you'll fall off. Wrap your arms around me."

She gulped. "You're the boss." Sliding her hands across his abdomen, she wondered if the moan in her head had slipped through her lips. Luckily, Teague started the engine, the roar deafening her thoughts and any unintended gasps.

They zoomed down the driveway, and she glanced back at the photographers still bunched up in front of his house. They didn't even turn to look.

Darting through the streets with a speed that sucked her breath away, Kate clung to him as they flew along the road. Her body moved with his—a whole lot closer than felt right—until they finally stopped in front of a small outdoor café. It was mid-afternoon and a waiter swept up around the empty tables. A woman in spiky gold heels walked past with three giant dogs on leashes, palm trees rustled overhead, and the sun hung in the sky like a juicy orange waiting to be picked.

I'm really in L.A., thought Kate.

She hopped off the bike, almost embarrassed to look at Teague after their intimate ride. Kind of felt like the morning after—without the fun.

He slid on a pair of sunglasses and traded his helmet for a ball cap. "Just call me Eugene."

"You know I will."

They settled at a table outside and Kate relaxed a bit. Until she remembered their trip lined up for the next day. "Do you have a movie in the Sunshine Film Festival? Is that why we have to go?"

Teague leaned back in his chair. "Yep. Supporting role in a small film that's been getting a lot of buzz. But for me, it's more about the networking. Stan Remington is going to be there, and if I want to break into the big time, I need to be in one of his films. It's the action-adventure actors who make the big bucks." He grinned his hundred-watt Hollywood smile. It was hard not to stare at him and marvel that they really made men like him. And that she was sitting right across from him.

She set her glass down and ran her finger across the condensation. "Am I really hurting your image?" Why did she care what his team of managers thought? She wasn't his girlfriend and didn't want to be his girlfriend—but still, it hurt hearing how inappropriate she was for him.

"So, you heard that." He sighed. "I'm not worried about it. I've defied them before. It kills them that I won't let a bodyguard tail me, but what kind of action-hero wannabe goes around with a bodyguard?" His eyes locked on hers, and Kate's heart caught in her throat. "I know this must be weird. We probably all seem crazy to someone like you. I really appreciate you going along with this." He sat up, snatched her hand and leaned over the condiments for a kiss.

"Teague . . ." She breathed his name. What was he doing? She leaned toward him and he took her face in his hands. He dragged his lips across hers and she answered back, knocking over the ketchup in the process. Her fingers curled around his forearms, tightening, as the kiss intensified. Finally, he pulled away with a smile.

Same spark as before. She was speechless.

But he wasn't. "Don't look now, but there's a photographer hiding between those potted ferns across the street." He shrugged. "Sorry to take you by surprise."

Kate licked her burning lips. "Oh, of course. I thought it was probably something like that." Damn. She'd gotten carried away again. Round and round she twisted the ring he'd given her. She'd have to keep up her guard—no matter what happened, no matter how often his lips came near hers or he grabbed her hand, this was all a show. They were acting.

He reached over and took her hand again. "Just in case they're still watching."

She nodded. "Right. Of course." She picked up the ketchup bottle and started rearranging the table with her other hand, like this was her nurse's station. It's a curse being organized, really. "How many of your ex-girlfriends will be there? That'll be a nightmare." Her hand was still in his, and she was aware of every wiggle of a finger, every change in pressure between them. His skin was moist against hers.

"Hey, I had to face the wrath of Chief Larsen back in Willowdale. He called in an army of *paparazzi* to get back at me just for sitting in the car with you. I doubt any of my exes could do worse."

She straightened the packs of sugar in their little black holder and then swiped away a few grains. "No, he was trying to hurt me, not you."

He squeezed her hand, and she sucked in a surprised breath. "Why? You're the nicest woman I've ever met, saving a stranger's backside like you did."

I'm 'nice.' Perfect. Every man's dream. "Because I won't marry him."

"Why not?"

She paused, wondering how much of the story to share. It had changed everything in her world. She sighed and let the words tumble out. "You heard me say we took a break after college, right? Well, a few months later when we got back together, he proposed."

Teague's blue eyes looked confused. "And that was a problem?"

"No, it wasn't. I said yes." She took a deep breath and closed her eyes. "Then the girl he slept with during our break showed up pregnant."

"Ouch." Another squeeze on her hand.

Kate nodded, not opening her eyes. "Yeah. He left that part out when he proposed, said he hadn't been serious with anyone. I can't stand a liar. Once it all came out in the wash, I gave him back the ring. He turned around and gave it to Ellen. Said it was the right thing to do, taking responsibility for his actions. I had to admire him for that, at least. He's a good person." The pain still tugged at Kate's heart, all these years later. That's why she was never going to let herself get hurt again. That feeling just didn't ever go away. She pulled her hand from Teague's and tucked it under her chin.

"He's a fool who broke your heart. And now he's married and chasing you again?"

"They divorced after two years."

Teague frowned and leaned toward her. "He still loves you."

She looked down. "I doubt it's love. I think it's just knowing that I won't take him back. Kills him that I won't give him a second chance. A couple times a year—if he's single—he comes back, trying that proposal on me again. Usually when he's had a few too many at The Hideaway."

"Not with the same ring, I hope."

She laughed softly. "No. He's doesn't actually offer up a

ring. I keep trying to tell him it's not going to happen." She shrugged. "I doubt he's serious, anyway."

Teague's jaw tightened. "You deserve better than that."

Kate swallowed hard and forced a smile. "It's not ever going to happen for me. And that's fine, really." Lordy, she talked too much when she was tired.

He sat back in his chair and cocked his head. "Just because of one disappointing guy?"

Kate shrugged. "Heartbreak kind of runs in my family. Must be some mutant gene." She looked away and twisted her straw wrapper until it snapped.

He was quiet for a moment, but she knew he was studying her. Finally, he said, "I doubt that."

The waitress arrived with their food, and Kate realized how hungry she was. She took a big bite of her mango salad.

Teague grinned, watching her eat. "I guess that's good."

She nodded, her mouth full. He probably wasn't used to watching women scarf down their food. But she was too famished to be dainty. She certainly wasn't going to fake a wimpy appetite for him.

He cut into his steak. "That's one thing I never do."

She paused with her fork in the air. "Eat salad?"

He laughed. "No, cheat. Don't believe everything you read in those rags. I may make the rounds, but I'm very loyal. Even to fake girlfriends." He set down his silverware and settled his hand next to hers.

Kate looked at their fingers, just a whisper apart. She wanted to correct Teague that Tommy hadn't cheated on her, but it didn't really matter. After seeing Mama's horrible relationship with George, then experiencing it firsthand, she knew Mama was right about love—not everyone was meant for it.

"Loyal is good." She looked up from their hands, into his eyes. This certainly wasn't the mean, heartless T-Rex she'd read about. He was kind and attentive—even thoughtful.

Then she remembered Tommy had been that way once, too. Of, course. This was probably how Teague did it. He lured in a girl by pretending to be a nice, sensitive, caring guy. Once the unsuspecting sap fell into his trap, he moved on. Kind of like how he wrapped up when he was done with a movie. On to the next project.

He was more like a calculating spider than a ferocious, dating demon. And he probably thought Kate was the easiest of them all. Just a few sweet words tossed her way would get a country girl like Kate to fall at his feet. Plus, there was that wager they'd made. He was just trying to win.

But no way would she let that happen. She pulled her hand away from his.

TEAGUE FELT A JAB to the gut. He swallowed his disappointment. She was probably smart, doing that. He needed to stop this foolishness and remember this was just an act. He'd experienced phantom feelings before with his co-stars. Those feelings had always faded, and Kate was just another co-star. This would pass, too. He stole another glance at her and winced. Was it just knowing he couldn't have her that made him want her? Was he no better than Chief Larsen?

"Let's go." He flipped a few twenties on the table and told himself he wasn't getting back on the bike just so he could feel her arms around him again. She hopped on behind him, looping her arms around his waist. He liked the feeling. Two cars pulled out onto the street, with photographers hanging out the windows.

"Hold on!" He sped down the street and blew through a light just as it turned red. Dodging down a few side streets, he lost them. He was aware of every move her body made against his. Man, she fit against him nicely. The way she clung to him made him feel needed. *Needed.* That's something he didn't experience very often.

They cruised along the coast until the sun started to set in a puddle of orange, dribbling into the sea. He pulled into his neighbor's driveway, stashed his bike, and they snuck back into his house. "At least I can show you to your room tonight. You were pretty out of it yesterday." He smirked, remembering it.

Her smile fell. "That's right. How did I get in?"

One eyebrow raised. "I carried you."

"Oh," she said in a tiny voice. "Up the stairs?" She pointed to the second floor.

He shrugged. "My pleasure." And it had been. There'd been something wildly provocative about sliding his hands underneath her thighs and neck, carrying her off the plane and then out of the car, settling her on her bed, like a treasure he couldn't touch.

Her cheeks were pink. "And you didn't have any problem getting me up there?"

Teague flexed his bicep. "Did it with one hand." He winked at her.

She looked up at him shyly and smiled. "Right. You do your own stunts."

"And so do you, as I recall." He could think of a few stunts he'd like to try out with her right now.

They stood at the base of the stairs like a pair of preteens at the front door after a first date. He scratched his head. "We should probably turn in. We've got an early start tomorrow."

"I almost forgot." She rolled her eyes.

"Come on." Laughing, he led her up the stairs to her room. "Do you need anything?" He leaned against her doorframe, just inches from her. It would be so easy to pull her to his chest and take a taste of those perky little lips that somehow always seemed to be formed in a smile. Kate was exceptionally cute when she was trying to be mad; it was a hard look to pull off with those lips.

She rubbed her arms and stifled a yawn. "No, I don't need anything. I have enough supplies to stay here for a year." She paused, and pressed her hand against his chest. "Don't worry. Not like I want to or anything." Again, with the lips and the dimples. Then she yanked her hand back and a blush crept across her cheeks, as if she hadn't realized she'd touched him.

He smiled. A year with this woman? He'd never last. He needed to kiss her again, to see if that spark was real. The one he'd felt when he first laid his lips on hers, and then later at the café. He'd like to carry her to bed now that she was awake. He'd peel her clothes off and find out if this magical attraction was really there or just the result of this charade. Maybe then he'd be able to shake this longing he couldn't ignore any longer.

He blew out a breath and took a step back from the door before jabbing his thumb over his shoulder. "I'm down the hall if you need anything." But he knew she wouldn't come to him.

He spent much of the night staring at the ceiling, wishing he'd been wrong.

Chapter 7

DINA ALMOST DROPPED the phone. Good thing she didn't; it was getting hard to bend over these days. "Kate? And T-Rex? It's gotta be a different Kate." When she said she was out of town she should have mentioned the part about the hot guy.

"It's in all the papers. Just go online and check it out," her friend, Chelsea, told her. "Didn't you know? She lives with you. She never talked about her movie-star boyfriend?"

"I'll call you back." Dina hung up the phone and did a quick Internet search. And sure enough, there was Kate kissing Teague Reynolds in front of an airplane. Her chest tightened. Did this mean she wasn't coming back? How could she do this to Dina? She swallowed the giant lump in her throat and realized she shouldn't have claimed she didn't need help with the baby. And she should have agreed that Kate was right, that George wouldn't stick around.

Dina paced around the room, nibbling on a cookie. There was a stash of them in her nightstand. She couldn't let Kate know how desperate she felt. She'd probably come back in a minute and blow everything with gorgeous T-Rex. Someone should live happily ever after. So, she texted Kate: *OMG. T-Rex? U R So Lucky!*

Dina dropped the phone when someone knocked on her open bedroom door. She looked up. "Oh, it's you." Flopping back on her canopy bed, she studied the boy-band posters that still lined her walls. Probably should take those down now that she was going to be a mama.

"That's a fine way to greet your father."

She shrugged. "Did you hear about Kate? She flew out of town yesterday with Teague Reynolds, the movie star."

Dad's eyes widened.

Just one more thing perfect Kate did right. I get knocked up and she hooks up with a celebrity.

"Movie star?" Dad knitted his brows. "She left town and didn't tell me?"

Dina rolled her eyes. "She's twenty-six, Dad."

"Who did you say it was?"

"Teague Reynolds."

He widened his stance and crossed his arms. "I don't like this," he said. "Not one bit."

She picked at a hangnail on her thumb. "What's not to like? If she's lucky, she'll get knocked up, too."

He frowned at her and left the room.

So that was it. Dina really was all alone; all alone with a baby on the way and no one to help. Her throat clogged, and she blinked back tears. She hated crying. Oh, she faked it when she needed to, but real tears were another thing.

She stared at her closet, which was taunting her with cute clothes that no longer fit. Favorite childhood stuffed animals sat on top of her dresser. Old issues of *Cosmo* peeked out from under her bed. Not too many parenting articles in those. It was like she didn't even belong in this room anymore. But where did she belong? She just wasn't ready for this.

Pressing her fingers against her eyes, she sucked in her breath. There was only one thing to do; there was only one person who could help her. She had to talk to the baby's daddy, tell him he was right. But would he want her now? The baby kicked, and she rubbed her belly and stared out the window.

GAZING OUT THE WINDOW, Kate felt like she was in a different world when the plane ducked under the clouds and she saw Maui rising from the sea. Of course, she'd been in a different world since she met Teague. But Hawaii was paradise. Pale pink clouds steamed over mountain tops, and white foamy waves rimmed the shore of the jewel-green island. This tiny land mass had appeared out of nowhere in the vast gray-blue sea. It was as if she'd entered a tropical dream when the flight landed. Fitting, she thought. This whole thing seemed like a dream.

They climbed into the fanciest limo she'd ever seen, but still, she was distracted by the sights and sounds. She fingered her orchid lei as the limo shuttled them to their hotel. Spiky green fronds danced in the breeze on top of tall, skinny palm trees. Sunlight glinted off the ocean while gulls bobbed and swooped down to the water. She lowered her window to get a better look. The weeds growing along the highway looked like her houseplants back home. She inhaled deeply and decided it even smelled exotic.

Teague was watching her. Dang, she felt stupid. Like a dog out for a ride, sniffing the breeze. She put up her window and shrugged. "I never thought I'd get a chance to come to Hawaii. It's probably no big deal to you, but I think it's incredible."

He stretched out his legs and draped his arm across the seat. "You're right. It is incredible. Sometimes I forget."

She shifted in her seat and looked back out the window again, her chin in her hand.

He reached across her and put the window back down.

A THRONG OF photographers clustered outside the hotel, snapping photos as they checked in. *Don't these people ever take a break?* she wondered. Teague just smiled and laid his arm across her shoulder. Then his grin dimmed. Kate followed his gaze to the most beautiful woman she'd ever seen holding court in the lobby.

The woman perked up when she saw him. "If it isn't T-Rex." A beautiful, petite blonde, she stood with a hand on her hip, tapping a high-heeled toe. "I'm still wiping your big track marks off my heart." Her wild, curly hair spilled over her shoulders like ringlets of spun gold. Her huge, round eyes were the oddest shade of amber, and she had breasts that were big, firm and on display for the world to see, but she was pointing them at Teague.

Kate cursed the anger bubbling inside her. How could a

normal person be jealous of someone so unreal?

Teague's arm slipped off Kate. "Hey, Simone. How have you been?"

She walked toward him. "Not as busy as you." Her eyes flicked over to Kate. "Always looking for a way to keep your name in the rags."

Kate looked for the nearest floral arrangement to hide behind, but Teague snagged her hand before she could flee. "I'd like you to meet my girlfriend, Kate Riley."

Simone stared for another moment, like Kate was an informational safety display. "I read in the papers." Simone did not offer her hand.

"Nice to meet you," Kate said checking out Simone from head to toe hoping to find some tiny flaw. No such luck.

"We've got to check in, Simone." Teague wouldn't look Kate in the eyes.

Kate had to sneak a peek at Simone again to make sure she was real. The woman looked like she'd been airbrushed.

Simone shook her hair off her shoulders. "I'm sure I'll be seeing you, Teague," she said, ignoring Kate. "I'm in the suite on the 27th floor." She winked at him and sauntered away.

Kate blew out the breath she'd been holding. "I deserve hazard pay for that."

Teague frowned. "My relationships don't end well, I can tell you that."

She glared at Simone and her perfect backside—perfect everything. Kissing Kate must have been like locking lips with his sister in comparison.

Teague grabbed her hand. "Come on." They walked up to the desk to check in.

Kate couldn't wait to hunker down in her room and hide. Maybe they wouldn't have to spend much time together at all. She glanced around the lobby, wondering who would make a move on Teague next.

A slender Hawaiian woman with long, black hair, and a grass skirt approached them with another lei. "Aloha."

"Aloha," Kate said, letting the woman place the flowers

around Kate's neck.

"And for your husband?" the woman asked, gesturing to Teague.

"No, not my husband," Kate said nervously.

"Boyfriend," Teague added helpfully, kissing Kate's cheek.

"Now, now, honey. Plenty of time for that later," she said with a tight grin.

"As you wish." He smirked.

The clerk at the desk tapped on his computer. "Ah yes, Mr. Reynolds and guest." He stared at the screen and his mouth formed a thin line. "I'm afraid we could not accommodate your last-minute request for a suite. But we've upgraded you to our beach bungalow. There's a nice big king bed, and you're right down by the water on your own private beach."

"There's *one* king bed?" Kate gripped the counter for support.

He looked up from the computer. "Yes. Don't worry. It's very private. I assure you, these are our finest accommodations." He nodded with a smile.

Teague's lips curled into a grin like the Grinch's after he plundered Whoville. "Sounds perfect." He snatched the key card and grabbed Kate's hand.

She could barely take in the glorious setting: the crisp, white, poolside cabanas, the manmade rivers and koi ponds, the gigantic tropical floral arrangements. Good golly, she didn't know places like this were real. But her mind was swirling around something even more unreal: she and Teague would be sharing a room. A room with one bed.

"I couldn't exactly say no," he said, as if reading her thoughts.

When they arrived at the bungalow, the bellhop opened the door and several attendants carried in their luggage. Once they left, they closed the door behind them, leaving Kate and Teague alone in the little love nest.

"This is nice," Kate said, trying to sound casual when she really wanted to squeal. She walked around the big airy space, running her fingers over the finery. Gauzy netting draped the big bed tucked in the corner. A marble table held a basket of tropical fruit and a bottle of champagne. A couch and giant TV flanked the opposite wall. She peeked out the window. The cabana was tucked in a small cove surrounded by tall palm trees, providing plenty of privacy, just as promised. A hammock hung between two of the trees, and a hot tub bubbled on a small patio off the living room. It was breathtaking. But there was just the one big room and a bathroom. There would be no hiding from Teague.

"I'm sorry you don't have your own accommodations," he said, sitting on the couch, stretching back. "I can sleep on this tonight."

She hugged her arms around her. "I'll take it. I'm smaller, you wouldn't get any sleep." So much for spending very little time together. "Can I just stay in here today?"

The bungalow seemed like a dream, with no photographers or superstar girlfriends kicking around. "If you want to go out by yourself, that's fine," she said. "Say I have jet lag." That was probably her best plan: spend as little time with Teague as possible. A gorgeous man in a gorgeous setting was too hard to resist. There was probably some mathematical equation to prove it.

He grinned. "I'll say we both have jet lag. Let's stay here together. We can order room service later. But first, I'm dying to lie in the sun." He got up and rummaged through his suitcase. "Be right back." While he ducked into the bathroom to change, she fished out her swimsuit and groaned. The damn makeover team sent her a bikini. A bikini! She was definitely a one-piece girl.

Teague walked out of the room and she sank to the bed. There wasn't an ounce of fat on the man. His biceps bulged as he reached for a towel, and his abs would certainly inspire some naughty dreams. She gulped down the squeal that might slip through her lips and looked up at him. *Wow.* Lord, she didn't say that out loud, did she?

He stood with his legs apart and put his hands on his hips. "Your turn."

For what? She nodded and scuttled into the bathroom like a crab trying to outrun a seagull that could swallow her whole. She undid her ponytail and shook out her hair. It fell in waves past her shoulders, but the circles-under-the-eyes jet-lag look wasn't working for her. She slipped off her clothes and stepped into the shimmery gold bikini. *Bada-Bling.* She might blind Teague. She slid on sunglasses that covered half her face and walked out.

"Whoa."

She rolled her eyes. "I know. Talk to your stylist. She picked this flashy thing out for me." She grabbed a book and a tube of sunscreen and left the room.

He followed her and plopped into the chair next to her chaise lounge, then looked out over the sea at the misty mountains beyond. "That's Molokai over there," he told her. "Isn't this gorgeous?"

A light breeze warmed her skin. She squeezed a dollop of white cream into her hand and smoothed it on her legs. "I don't even have the words to tell you how amazing this is." She rubbed the cream into her skin, fretting about the size of her thighs which had never bothered her before. Wondering if Simone had any arm jiggle at all, she tried imagining what a set of fake D's would look like in this suit, all the while one hundred percent aware that Teague was watching her every stroke.

Was he amazed how much sunscreen it took to cover a regular-sized woman? She reached for her back and realized *that* wasn't going to happen. Guess she was gonna burn, baby, burn.

"Let me help you with that." Teague got up to squat next to her chair.

Her mouth turned into a tiny circle as she considered his proposition. "Sure." She handed him the sunscreen and rolled onto her belly, relieved Teague couldn't see her face. Or her stomach. She heard him squeeze the tube and held her breath as she waited for his touch. He started at the base of her neck and his strong fingers slid down her back. She gasped.

"I'm sorry. Is it cold?" His sultry voice might be enough to warm her up.

"Cold. Yes," she lied. But no worries. Her medical training had prepared her for situations like this: situations of intense shock and trauma. Keep the victim talking, that's what she had been told. Only this was the first time Kate had been the victim. Pick a boring topic. Something mundane, not at all related to bodies or sex or . . . *Aw, hell!* "It's hot out, huh?"

Teague laughed. "You want to talk about the weather? Those are the kind of generic thoughts I generate, huh? Right, I forgot. You'd never be interested in someone like me." His fingers moved across her shoulder blades with a nice, firm stroke.

"No. Yes. I mean, I just was wondering, is it always this hot here? I've never been to Hawaii. Or is this because of global warming or something?" *Shut up, Kate.* "What do you think about global warming? I mean, do you think it's all real or just a load of bunk? You're concerned about the environment, right?" *What's this nonsense?* Blathering idiot, that's what she was. She could address an auditorium full of twittering pre-teens but couldn't carry on a simple conversation with a gorgeous man?

Teague was silent for a moment, probably stifling a laugh. She could hear him squeezing out more lotion, rubbing the cream between his hands to take the chill off, bless him, and then smoothing it along her spine.

"You mean, do I think things are getting hotter?" He snickered.

She was experiencing her own personal global warming. A sudden surge of embarrassment and desire can do that to a girl. "Well, yes. It is hotter, actually. Scientists say glaciers are melting . . . and temperatures are rising . . . New York could be underwater one day . . ." She caught her breath as his hands slid farther down her back and he ran two fingers under the string of her bikini top. Good golly.

Now his hands were flat, spread wide across her back. He massaged the lotion into her skin. This was much, much more than a sunscreen application. He grunted. "Is that such a bad thing? I like it hot."

So much for her neutral, distracting topic.

The tropical smell of the lotion made her dizzy. "I just think it's an important concern, is all." Her tense muscles relaxed under his strong strokes. She tried not to think about what she looked like from Teague's point of view and just enjoyed the feel of his hands on her warm skin, working down to her lower back.

Teague Reynolds was rubbing her where very few men had rubbed before.

"I agree, global warming is important," he said. "And I want to be kept up to date on any temperature fluctuations around here. So let me know when things are getting too hot for you." And with that he swiped two fingers under her bikini bottom, right over her buns. He leaned over her and dipped his mouth to her ear. "Or if they're not hot enough." His breath was fire on her skin.

She rolled over to face him and found herself between his arms. She was a silly rabbit caught between the paws of a tiger that was still deciding what to do with its prey. She let go of her breath. "Thank you." He was inches away from a kiss.

His lips twitched into a devious smile. He'd promised this was going to be strictly business, but this didn't feel like business at all. Risky business, if anything.

He traced his finger along her shoulder. "You have gorgeous skin. I'm happy to help you take care of it." He brushed a strand of hair off her cheek. "No tattoos hiding anywhere?" His eyes danced as he hovered over her, teasing her.

And with that, a big wet blanket blotted out the flames licking her belly. "You mean like someone's name on my butt?" Her chest tightened as she remembered the way he and Simone had ogled each other in the lobby. "Simone is definitely still interested in you." Her stomach felt like an empty pit.

He sat back at the end of the lounge. "Hey, cool it, hot stuff. I told you, I'm not a cheater. It doesn't matter what she wants."

The magic moment had been swept off to sea. Kate crossed her arms. "We're not actually dating, so it's not cheating." How easily she could channel her bratty twelve-year-old self. Probably because she spent her days surrounded by just such children.

Teague looked out to the ocean. "I wouldn't want it to look that way." He grabbed a handful of sand and let it slip through his fingers. His mood had definitely cooled.

So had hers. She wanted him to protest, that no, he was over Simone, that she was a nasty, beastly woman hiding in a perfect body for which she must have bargained with the devil. But he hadn't.

Kate pushed up off the lounge and walked out into the water. She dove under without looking to see if he was following her. She realized she was being completely, embarrassingly, ridiculous, but she couldn't help it. There was no fooling herself anymore—she wanted him, no matter how much she tried to deny it, no matter how hard her sensible side took her by the shoulders and shook no, no, no.

Luckily Miss Sensible would never let her give in. And that twenty-thousand-dollar bet would help back her up. Wanting something and going after it were two different things. She would not be going after Teague. Luckily, she had excellent willpower when it came to denying herself pleasure.

Chapter 8

TEAGUE WATCHED HER walk away. Saunter was a better word for it, with that sexy sway to her hips. Was she doing that on purpose? She looked amazing. Soft and rounded, like an old-fashioned Hollywood starlet, with her long wavy hair and big sunglasses. And that bikini might kill him, the way it molded to her curves. He could picture her as a pin up on some teenage boy's room. In his room.

And putting on sunscreen? Pure torture. He wet his lips. If he didn't know better, he'd think it was a trap she'd set for him, with that not-so-subtle discussion of global warming. But he must've been wrong. The way she skittered off into the ocean made it perfectly clear what she thought of him.

Teague got up from the beach chair and sloshed into the water. How did he manage to repel the one woman he found utterly intriguing? He didn't have to do a damn thing to attract the attention of most women—they just showed up. But Kate couldn't stand to be near him. What the hell? He was used to being the one pushing people away. He'd done it his whole life.

He dove in the water and swam after her. The water felt good on his skin; she would feel good on his skin. "We can blow off the festivities tonight, if you want. Let's stay here. This is nice." He could imagine pulling her against him right there, slipping off her bikini, finding each other in the warm, salty sea.

She stepped back, swaying her hands through the water, not looking at him. "I can stay here alone. Go do your thing. I'm fine here, really." She fell back into the water, floated on her back for a moment—which really seemed like torturous teasing, the way her breasts peeked above the waves as if they were saying, *Hey there, come join me big fella*—and then swam away from him, like an indecisive siren.

Well, damn. Why couldn't he find the words to get through to her? Was he so used to a script that he couldn't come up with his own lines to ask a beautiful woman, *Hey, you thinking what I'm thinking?*

Kate surfaced several feet away from him, peering off across the ocean. Her hair was sleek against her head, and drops of water clung to her skin like jewels. She saw him staring at her and snapped her head away. She looked so damned appealing, but she didn't want him. She just wasn't interested. Deal with it, dude. *She really wants to win that bet.* He shook his head in disbelief and walked back to shore. He lay on the chaise and his phone rang.

It was his publicist, June. That was one way to bring his boil down to a simmer. "Yes?"

"How much do you know about this woman? I just got a call from a reporter asking about her stepfather's outstanding taxes. She's bad news, Teague. Dump the hick and hook up with an old girlfriend. That'd get the press riled up. Restore your bad-boy persona. Right now, they're painting you as a hopeless romantic. Not good."

"Drop it, June. I'm not dumping Kate."

He thought he could hear her teeth grinding. She sighed dramatically. "Then I'm going to recommend you don't bring her when you meet with Stan Remington this week. He doesn't give second chances, and you've got one shot with him."

Another call beeped on his phone but he ignored it.

"Listen, I need you to head to the hotel bar right now," June said. "One of the producers from *Late Night* wants to meet you. I want you on the show when you're back in L.A. Just say hi, have a drink with her."

He looked at Kate floating on her back, fanning her hands through the water. She looked like a treasure washed up from the depths of the ocean. He groaned. "Right now?"

"Yep. She's going to be there in fifteen minutes."

"Fine." He hung up and noticed that the missed call was from Simone, though she didn't leave a message. What did she want? He could only imagine. She had taken it badly when he broke up with her. They'd had fun for six months. Good sex and all that. But then she got too close, wanting to stay over every night, wanting to come along everywhere he went, wanting more, more, more—more than he could give. She thought she was the one who could tame him, that's what she'd told him. She even wanted to spend the entire Sunshine Film Festival together last year.

He laughed. That's exactly what he was doing with Kate, and it didn't bother him a bit. He looked out at her, still floating on the water. "I'm going up to the hotel for a bit," he shouted.

Kate held up a hand to indicate she'd heard him. She was probably glad. It had taken his mother two years to decide she'd had enough of Teague. It had only taken Kate three days.

KATE WATCHED TEAGUE walk up to the hotel. He'd dressed in linen pants and a Hawaiian shirt. He wasn't just dashing up there for food, he was going to see someone. She dug her toes into the sand and swished the water around her.

What would her mother think about what she was doing, lying like this for cash? Posing as a girlfriend, allowing him to kiss her just for show? Kate's mother had been old-fashioned. Despite the hell George had put her through, she had looked out for him even from her deathbed.

"A marriage isn't always an easy thing. You don't leave it when you hit a few bumps. You don't leave when the love's gone. George has his faults, but he's a decent man. He took us in when we had nobody." She'd squeezed Kate's hand with as much force as she could muster. "Watch out for him and Dina. Promise me."

Kate shook the bad thoughts away, walked up to the shore and settled on the lounge chair. She didn't care where Teague had gone. Who knew what these Hollywood types had to do at festivals? He'd left his phone on the table next to the chair. She looked at it a few times like it was a snake that might bite her, then finally picked it up and checked his last call. *One missed call from Simone Peters.* She thought about tossing the phone in the ocean.

She buried her nose in her book but stayed on the same page for fifteen minutes. She dropped it to the sand and grabbed her own phone, checking in on Dina. She really should call her friends, but she didn't know what to say. *Surprise! I forgot to mention I was dating a Hollywood hunk?* She'd call them once the festival was over and the media attention died down. She texted Dina, asking if George was home and if she and her bitty bump were okay.

Dad's here. We're good. Photographers all over the place. Dina texted back. *When R U going 2 tell me what's going on?*

When U tell me who the baby's father is.

Nice try, she texted back.

Well, it was worth a shot, Kate thought, and she texted back. *It's complicated. We'll talk later.*

Kate wandered along the beach, picking up tiny white shells as she went. The money Teague promised would more than pay the property tax bill and penalties. But George also had a second mortgage on the house, and he'd hinted that it was overdue, too. An extra twenty thousand from winning her bet with Teague could help there. But how long would Kate have to bail him out? Her mother had only been dead eight months, and keeping an eye on George and Dina had already cost Kate plenty. She frowned and tossed the shells back into the sea. She'd probably be cleaning up his messes until she died. She'd have to, if she wanted to keep that house. And since Mama and her daddy had bought that house and fixed it up before she was born, she really wanted to keep it.

TEAGUE SMILED AND nodded throughout the meeting with the producer, catching none of what she said, ignoring the way she and her cleavage leaned closer and closer to him. A month ago he'd have had her in his hotel room by now. That's what she wanted. But damned if he wasn't busy wondering what Kate was doing. Maybe he should leave her back at the bungalow during the festival and pretend she was ill for her sake—and for his. The press might speculate she couldn't handle the heat of the spotlight.

He frowned. He didn't want her hurt or smeared in the tabloids. He'd already changed her life forever just by bumping into her on the street in Willowdale. That town had changed everything for him. First Jennifer and the baby on the way, now Kate. His life had been turned upside down and inside out—then twisted and hung out to dry. What was he going to do with this baby? How was he going to protect *Jennifer?* He didn't even know he had a sister until he'd gotten that phone call. And he wasn't prepared for what he'd found.

If only he hadn't been too proud to examine his past, he would have tracked down Jennifer earlier and none of this would've happened. He was still wondering how to deal with her, but he had a more pressing issue waiting for him at the beach.

He wrapped up his visit with the disappointed producer who'd been practically panting by the end of their meeting. He stopped by the *maître d'* and ordered a dinner of champagne, chocolate-dipped strawberries, mahi-mahi, steak and other delectables. Maybe it would work, prove to Kate he wasn't really T-Rex, that he was more like good old Eugene. If not, at least there was a record of him wining and dining his girlfriend. And that was the most important thing, he reminded himself: keeping up appearances with Kate, even if he couldn't make any progress in private. No matter how attracted he was to her, he had to keep the baby and Jennifer out of the news.

He walked back toward their room, a canopy of palms whispering above him. Was adoption the best option for the baby? He was disgusted with himself for even thinking it. Knowing his mother gave him away had haunted him his entire life. Would he do that to this child? Or could he keep the child and cover it all up to protect Jennifer? Ugh. It was impossible. Just like the situation waiting for him in the bungalow.

"KATE? Are you hungry?"

She looked up from her book and rubbed her eyes. "Yeah, I

am." Or at least she thought the burning in her belly was hunger. "What time is it?"

"It's six here, but it's midnight back on the east coast." His bronzed cheeks and tousled hair gave him a sexy look that sent her reeling. He walked toward the bed and planted his hands on his hips.

"I'll get dressed." She yawned.

"No. You look . . . perfect." His voice was low and husky. "I ordered dinner for us. Here. Room service."

She tipped her head to the side. "I figured you'd be out with Simone."

"What?" He looked genuinely confused.

"Isn't that why you went back to the hotel?"

"No, we broke up a year ago. It's over. Really. I went to the hotel to meet with a producer." He took a deep breath. "But I couldn't wait to get back here."

Kate looked around at the lovely room that had become her refuge. "I know what you mean. It's so private and comfortable." Her heart had betrayed her, pinging her chest since he walked in the room. She dropped her feet to the floor and stood up, stretching and inhaling the warm, fragrant air.

Teague shoved his hands in his pockets. "I wanted to get back here to you."

Kate froze mid-stretch and then dropped her hands to her side.

Teague took a step toward her, and then another.

She backed up, but the bed was in her way. Swallowing hard, her hand fluttered over her throat. A few grains of sand were stuck to her skin, which was still warm from the sun.

They faced each other, and Kate waited for him to crack a joke, to tell her it was a test to see how well she could stand up to the press's questions. But he didn't laugh. He just stared at her, then his lips parted ever so slightly. Big fingers brushed over hers, still resting on her throat. Her lips tingled just imagining another kiss, a private kiss meant for her, not the cameras. She could fall into a kiss like that and never be found.

No, no, no, her sensible self chanted. *This is dangerous, this is bad.* Kate made a mental note to toss Miss Sensible into the sea with a rock tied to her practical pumps.

Teague brushed her hair off her face and ran his thumb across her cheekbone. Tilting her head back to look up at him, she suddenly stopped. Why *was* he doing this? There were no cameras, and certainly no attraction on his part. Just part of his nature, probably. *Have woman in hotel room, must kiss her.*

Kate looked down; perhaps she could break the trance.

His other hand wrapped around the back of her head and pulled her face up to his, knocking the breath out of her lungs. He nudged her nose with his and brushed his lips across hers, testing them. Testing her.

She shivered, and he tightened his grip.

Who wouldn't want to kiss Teague Reynolds? It was pure female nature to want more. He was a luscious chocolate pie taunting her with a taste. It was useless to resist any longer. Kissing him didn't mean she'd fallen for him. Not at all. *Oh, hell.* "I suppose we should practice making this look good." Kate's voice came out in a breathy whisper. "We want people to believe we're attracted to each other, right?"

His mouth spread into a delicious smile. "Right." He ran his tongue along her upper lip, while she snaked her hands up his arms. Her knees dipped as he slowly licked her lips. Then he stopped when someone knocked on the door.

"Room service."

Kate's mouth hung open and she snapped it shut.

Teague's shoulders slumped, and he set his forehead against hers. "We'll try that again later." He smiled and offered his hand. "Come on. You've got to see this."

She felt like a kite that had fallen straight out of the sky. She even lost her appetite—and that hadn't happened since the stomach flu knocked her on her butt a few years back. But after stepping outside, her hunger found its way back. A table, set with china and crystal and probably five different forks, sat beneath a small white tent. The white linen tablecloth rippled in the breeze. A waiter stood to the side, ready to serve them.

Teague pulled out a gleaming teak chair for her and she sat

down, hoping he couldn't tell this was the fanciest damn thing she'd ever seen.

Scalia's could take a few notes here.

Two candles flickered on the table in the blue-black evening. "Wait, what time is it? It's dark out." How had he managed all this?

"It's after six. The sun sets early here." His face glowed in the candlelight, and she wanted to return to that kiss.

But she yawned instead, being the temptress that she was. "Sorry," she stifled a giggle. She was still tired from the time difference. She looked up at Teague across the table and smiled.

"You like it?" He looked like a hopeful kid showing off his class project.

She could only manage to nod. No one had ever done anything like this for her. She fingered the napkin in her lap. Her heart lodged in her throat, and she had to look away.

The waiter poured their champagne, and she closed her eyes. The scent of the lingering coconut suntan lotion and the salty brine of the ocean left her swooning. She sipped her drink and let the bubbles tickle her tongue. The waves slapped against the shore and the night was so quiet it was easy to imagine they were alone on a desolate island. *What would it be like to make love in the surf,* she wondered.

The waiter lifted the silver lid off her plate and the savory steak set her mouth watering. Yet she barely tasted the food. She was too busy replaying the scene in the bungalow. Had he been serious? He'd come back to be with her? He was going to kiss her because he wanted to and not because someone was going to take a picture of it?

Kate's insides hummed just thinking about it. So loudly, she could hear it inside her head. It was getting louder—a lot louder. What was wrong with her? She put her fork down and looked up. It was the thrumming of a helicopter flying toward them. A photographer leaned out the open door, pointing a camera at them, practically close enough to reach down and snag one of the shrimp cocktails.

Teague threw his napkin on the table. He kicked at the sand, swearing, then grabbed the plate of strawberries. "Can you get our drinks?" he shouted.

Kate snatched the champagne flutes and followed him inside, her hair swirling and her insides plummeting. Miss Sensible had kicked off her cement-filled shoes and clawed her way back to shore to add up all the facts. Teague must have known the photographers would find out about their private beach bungalow. That's probably what he'd been doing up at the hotel, calling in a tip for them to come document this intimate moment with his new "love."

Lordy, she was a fool. He hadn't set up a romantic dinner for them at all. He'd set up a photo op.

He closed the door behind them, and she shoved the champagne bottle at him. "You can finish this. I'm going to bed." She would not be played a fool like her mother had and give her heart to a hound. She was smarter than that. Clenching her teeth, she seethed.

He reached for her but she jerked her arm away. She shivered in the chilly, air-conditioned room. Wrapping her arms around herself, she scanned the room as if there might be a secret hidey-hole back to her world. She couldn't go outside; the photographer was probably still there. She was stuck in paradise with a man totally messing with her heart.

Defeated, she flopped onto the couch and tucked herself into the corner. Was she more angry or sad? She couldn't decide. She stole a glance at Teague, standing across the room, staring at the floor, rubbing the back of his neck. He looked ticked as all heck, but who knew if it was just an act?

Still, her heart flip-flopped, watching him, despite the curse words rattling round in her head.

This man should have come with a warning label.

TEAGUE RAN HIS HAND through his hair. This was too much to take. The *paparazzi* weren't just eating Kate alive; they were turning her into a five-course meal, much like the one he'd arranged outside. Curled up on the couch, she looked so vulnerable. He wanted to scoop her up in his arms and continue where they'd left off before dinner. Only, he wasn't sure if he'd get a kiss or a slap in return.

He drew the curtain closed over the French doors leading to the patio. "Kate, I'm sorry. The press is more interested in you than I thought."

Her eyes narrowed. "What's that supposed to mean?"

He set the champagne on the coffee table in front of her and knelt beside her. "You're different from the typical actress or model I'm seen with. Not many Hollywood types do the Internet dating thing." He softened his voice. "I didn't anticipate all this. I'm sorry." Of course she didn't want anything to do with him. He was ruining her life. "Maybe things will die down tomorrow with the first premieres. They'll have other people to stalk, other stories to follow."

"I just want to sleep," she said in a thick voice. She wouldn't look at him. He couldn't blame her.

Although he was desperate to feel her lips against his again, he knew the best thing now was to leave her alone. "Take the bed."

She didn't move off the couch, but he pulled back the bedcovers and fluffed the pillow, hoping she'd make herself comfortable. He went outside to give her some privacy. The bungalow was just one big room. There was no hiding from each other.

He closed the door quietly, sat down in the lounge chair, and stared at the foamy waves lapping the shore, the swooshing sound of the sea taking his mind far away. His plan to become a star and keep anyone from getting close had worked. It was working perfectly tonight, he thought. *Never thought it would backfire like this.*

When he had left home after high school, it was with zero regrets and one wish: to make sure he never loved someone more than they loved him. Somehow, the idea of being a star, of having so many people seeing him on TV or the big screen seemed like it might fill up his empty self-esteem.

It hadn't, he'd learned, after hitting it big three years earlier with a supporting role on *Big and Bad*. The fans loved him, and the producers gave him a bigger role on the show. That led to his first movie deal, then another, until he realized films were the way to go. It turned out his habit of hopping from girl to girl left an impression in the tabloids. That was okay with him, too. He couldn't pretend he hadn't enjoyed it.

His agent and publicist encouraged it. "Once you settle down, fans can't imagine themselves with you as easily. The last thing you want is to get serious with someone for too long."

"Won't be a problem," he'd assured them. And it had been good fun. But never much more than that.

So what was happening to him now? He glanced back at the bungalow and frowned. Why couldn't he stop thinking about the woman who was here for 'strictly business'? He jumped up from his chair and eased the door open, just wanting to talk to her, to hear her laugh. But she was asleep on the couch, long blue shadows and moonlight stretched out across her.

After watching her sleep for a few moments, he slid his hands under her neck and thighs and lifted her, just like when he had carried her off the plane. The back of her legs were moist on his skin and he could only imagine how the rest of her would feel against him. She murmured in her sleep and wrapped her arms around his shoulders. Her fingers teased the nape of his neck as if they were searching for something to take hold of.

When he set her on the bed, her hair spread across the pillow, and her lips curled in the slightest smile. He breathed in her sweet scent, tinged with that coconut sunscreen from earlier. Remembering how nervous she'd been as he smoothed the lotion across her skin made him smile. Now he hovered over her again, wanting to kiss her, longing to hold her, hoping she'd wake and invite him to join her. "Kate?"

Her dark lashes brushed her high cheekbones and she sighed in her sleep. He'd be happy just to wrap his arms around her and pull her to him. He'd burrow his nose in her neck, smelling the sweetness of her. That would be good. That would be enough. He didn't even need to make love to her, though he wanted to fiercely. If she woke, she'd see the evidence for herself.

He cursed under his breath. He ached for her, literally. It hurt to be near her. But he resisted even the urge to kiss her forehead. He needed to get out of this room. He had to get away from her. She didn't want him, and he'd have to find a way to stop wanting her so badly.

He slipped out the door into the night, his breaths coming fast and heavy. What was wrong with him? It was probably just the stupid bet, right? He had something to prove. Was that it?

He trudged to the Tiki bar outside the hotel, next to the pool. He needed a drink to help settle his emotions and certain body parts. These feelings frightened him. This wasn't part of his plan.

He sat down and ordered a beer, turning the bottle round and round, thinking about Kate. How could he be concentrating on her full lips and that little freckle right next to her left ear when he had to figure out what to do about the baby? She'd been a good distraction from *that* at least. He asked the bartender for another drink and tipped back his second beer.

"Don't you look lonely?"

Teague looked up as Simone settled on the barstool next to him in a very tight, very short, green sundress. He knew that was her favorite color, the one she thought played up her eyes. She crossed her legs and bobbed her foot so that the tip of her shoe grazed his leg.

He rubbed his eyes. "Kate's tired. Jet lag and the time difference knocked her out. It's tough when you come out here from the east coast."

"Right, some little hick town in Nowhere, North Carolina?" She squinted her eyes at him seductively, just like she did whenever a camera came her way. "This can't be real, right? Is this some publicity stunt? Why do it now, right during the festival?" She flipped her long blond hair over one shoulder and lifted an eyebrow. "You can tell me. What's the real deal?"

Polynesian music played in the background and the beer was leaving its buzz. Teague shrugged, trying to keep his voice even. "It is the real deal, Simone. I met a beautiful girl on the

Internet and fell for her."

She poked him in the chest with a pearly pink fingernail. "You don't fall for anyone. You let me fall for you, then you walked out the door." She popped open her sparkly silver clutch and fished out a cigarette.

Teague wrinkled his nose. "You started smoking again?"

Simone rolled her eyes. "I only stopped for you. I'll stop again if you want."

He grabbed a handful of macadamia nuts from the bar. "That's why I like Kate. She doesn't pretend to be who she's not." He tossed them in his mouth, enjoying the satisfying crunch.

Simone lit the cigarette, inhaled, and laughed out a plume of smoke. "Oh, please. She's pretending to be whatever you want her to be. What do you think she wants from you? You think this could lead to love? How?" She shook her head and laughed. "You're not fooling anyone. The photographers have a pool going to see when you two break up." Those big, pouty lips of hers that had once begged to be bitten and nibbled like a plum looked like thick ridges of old rubber puckered around her cigarette.

Teague waved the smoke away, wishing he could do the same with her. "You know I don't care what the press thinks."

"You should. Stay with her too long and you're going to ruin your street cred. Right now it's amusing and different, shocking even. I'll give you that. It's gotten you a ton of press, but they'll be over it soon enough." She set her hand on his shoulder and leaned toward him until her nose was touching his cheek. Her breath smelled like menthol and olives.

He leaned back but she moved closer.

"Now, if you and I were to get back together, that would be something to talk about. We're reunited at the festival, where our movie debuts. Cool, right? That's what people expect." She shrugged, a move that pushed her breasts together. Smiling, she paused, probably so he could take a good long look.

He turned from her and shook his head.

Her finger grazed his cheek, guiding him back to face her.

"It would get tons of press for the film. Total career boost for us both." She stubbed out her cigarette and set her hand on his knee. "And it would be fun. It was always fun with you." A sapphire the size of the macadamia nuts he'd been eating glinted on her finger.

"Simone . . ." He didn't know what to say. He didn't even want to be talking to her.

Her eyes locked on his and stayed there, longer than any woman who wasn't one-hundred-percent certain of her drop-dead-gorgeous assets would dare. "Teague, I can tell you have . . . needs that aren't being met. And you know I can meet those needs." Her voice was perfectly sultry and smooth, rolling off her tongue from the depths of her throat, like a siren luring a sailor to shipwreck. "You really look like you could use a good romp. Whaddaya say?" She lifted an eyebrow.

He swallowed hard and looked at her manicured hand lightly massaging his thigh, moving higher and higher. He tipped his head to get the bartender's attention. "Check, please."

Chapter 9

KATE FELT LIKE A kid at a carnival gazing at the bright lights of the rides, only she was staring at the pastel dawn sky. Pinks and purples like she'd never seen streaked the dusty-blue canvas. The fact that she was up at five a.m. checking out a Hawaiian sunrise had nothing to do with Teague not coming back to the bungalow, the dog. She burrowed her toes in the sand and leaned back, enjoying the view, pushing the niggling thoughts out of her head. Would've been easier to make the sun go back down.

It might be the crack of dawn in Hawaii, but it was eleven a.m. back home, so she decided to catch up on a few calls. She went back inside, grabbed her phone and found twenty missed messages—two from Dina. *What a jerk! Does this mean UR coming home now?* Kate's belly did a flop as she advanced the next message. *If it makes U feel better Simone looks trampy in the pics on the net.*

The phone slipped from Kate's hand. He must have been out with Simone last night and the press got a picture. She'd been so foolish, letting a tiny little hunk of her heart think maybe, just maybe, Teague felt something in those kisses. She'd caught him looking at her. He'd whispered her name last night when he carried her to bed while she pretended to sleep. She'd thought maybe . . .

She sank onto the bed. Could she just go home now? Teague probably wouldn't give her any more money if she left, and then she'd lose Mama's house. A summer at Scalia's would've been a killer on her feet, but it would've been much easier on her heart. No amount of money was worth this torment.

She started repacking her suitcase with all the wildly

expensive sundresses, gorgeous tops, and shorts. She tossed in the makeup, the lipsticks, and eye shadows that cost more than she made in a week at school. She put in her gold bikini and picked up her sandals. She snorted and shook her head. They really weren't hers, were they? Neither was the suitcase. None of this was. It was definitely time to pack away this silly, silly dream.

The bungalow door opened. Teague stood in the doorway, wearing the same clothes from the day before.

Kate ground her teeth and threw a sandal at him.

He shielded his face and ducked. "Wow, wrong side of the bed, huh?" He picked up her sandal. "Lose a shoe, Cinderella?"

"And which side of the bed did you wake up on, Prince Not-So-Charming? Or did you two not even sleep?" She rubbed her temples and cursed the sunlight streaming through the door. Then she tossed the other shoe at him.

He caught it and set it down. "What are you talking about?"

Rolling her eyes, she growled the words. "I got a text from back home telling me that pictures of you and Simone last night are all over the Internet." She spread her arms wide in case he didn't understand exactly *how all over the Internet* she meant.

He moved over to her, standing much too close. "What if I did hook up with her? As I recall, you're done with men, you'd never go out with someone like me, and you couldn't get me out of here fast enough last night." He crossed his arms, waiting for her response.

Kate's stomach dropped. She took a step back but he gently took her arm. She jerked it away. "You're right. I don't care," she stammered. "It's just humiliating to have the entire world know you two hooked up last night. I'm going to be labeled as the poor, pathetic farm girl Teague used to get back at Simone." Her hands curled into fists. "It's called discretion—ever heard of it?"

He let out the sigh of a man losing his patience. "Listen, I did see Simone last night at the bar, but we didn't hook up. She suggested it. Put her hand on my thigh, talked about what great publicity it would be for our movie. But I left her at the bar."

"Right. You left Simone Peters at a bar. Simone Peters and her grabby hands." She pointed an accusing finger at him.

"Someone got a picture of you guys together." Kate's throat was tight and she hated feeling so jealous. She had no right to be.

"Alright. Let's see the evidence." He walked over to his bags, grabbed his laptop and settled on the bed. Kate sat next to him. He flipped it open and launched an Internet search. He clicked on a link, and Kate's stomach clenched. Simone and all that wild, kinky blond hair appeared to be nuzzling his cheek, with her hand on his leg. They looked quite cozy, like she was getting ready to eat him with a knife and fork and a dollop of cream.

Kate strapped her chest with both arms. "Looks like together to me. In fact, you could put that picture in Webster's next to 'together.'"

He rolled his eyes. "Damn photographers. They're everywhere. Like I said, she proposed it. And I said no, approximately three seconds after this picture was taken." He crossed his arms, too, and looked at her.

Kate popped up from the bed and planted her hands on her hips. "If you weren't with Simone, then where have you been?"

The words hit her like the eight a.m. Greyhound bus that rolled through Willowdale every Thursday morning. How many times had her mother said that to George? And here she was, repeating history. With a guy she wasn't even dating, wasn't even kissing for real. Crossing the room, she sank onto the couch and studied her feet. The red nail polish was chipping off her toes.

Rubbing his jaw, Teague followed her to the couch and sat down. He dropped his head back and stared at the ceiling. "I can't tell you what I was doing. But I wasn't with Simone, or anyone else for that matter. I couldn't sleep . . . I've got a lot on my mind, and I didn't want to wake you." His leg was touching hers, thigh to thigh.

She looked at him. He appeared sincerely miserable. If he'd been doing the horizontal boogie, he hadn't enjoyed it. But how could she trust him? He was an actor. It'd be awful tough to fake the stubble on his cheeks and the dark circles under his eyes, though. "Does this have to do with the reason you were in Willowdale?"

He chuckled in a way that didn't sound funny at all. "Oh, it's got everything to do with Willowdale."

Kate steeled herself. "Does it involve a woman?" She smoothed her hands down her thighs. "Do you want to talk about it?"

He shook his head. "It's not about a woman, and I don't want to talk about it. But I do want my pretend girlfriend to forgive me. I'll be more careful. The last thing I want to do is embarrass or hurt you." He leaned his head back on the couch and smiled at her. "Please don't leave. I like you here with me. Stay."

Stay. That one word packed one heck of a punch. It sent a warm tingle through Kate. Actually, it was more like a hot flood of screaming, writhing, desperate, panting need than a tingle. Which wasn't surprising since she'd gone through several calendars since she'd last had sex. Did wanting to have sex with him mean she was falling for him? No. No, ma'am, it did not. Falling for him meant her heart was involved and it certainly was not.

So, sex yes, heart no. But still, she didn't want to be used. She looked down at the ring he'd given her and ran the tip of her finger across the big pearl. It was like Teague was two different men. Sweet and kind, but then brash and closed off. "I'll stay here . . . with Eugene."

He closed his eyes. "He's a geek."

"I like Eugene." She leaned against him and all those muscles and set her head on his shoulder. It was a nice shoulder. "I like him a lot." Her eyelids drooped closed like drowsy shades and she tipped up her chin, longing for a kiss, waiting for his mouth to meet hers. The way he'd licked her lips the night before made her belly quiver just thinking of it. Nasty man. She hung there for a moment, waiting for him to do it again. Waiting . . . waiting . . .

"Eugene?" She opened her eyes. "Teague?"

His mouth was open, his breathing deep and rhythmic with a slight, rattling snore.

Kate slapped her hands on her thighs. *Classic! I make my move, and he falls asleep.* She closed her eyes and shook her head, cursing her luck, worse than Marge Graham on Bingo night. That poor woman never won, no matter how many rabbit's feet she spread out in front of her.

Kate watched him doze. The hard edges of his face had softened. There was a vulnerability to him she hadn't seen when he was awake. He looked younger and somehow breakable. This big, hard man seemed like someone she should pet, like an antsy dog that just needed someone to love him, but was frightened of being kicked. But how could that be? Teague could have anyone or anything he wanted. Why did he look so lonely when he didn't have his T-Rex mask on?

She watched him for a while, commanding herself not to touch him. So she grabbed a book, crossed the room, and flopped on the bed to keep as much distance as possible between her and the man she'd bored to sleep.

DINA SLUMPED BACK on the couch and closed her laptop after reading all the gossip swirling around Teague and Simone. Kate wouldn't be able to help her. Not now. George had left that morning, and who knew when he'd be back? Kate would be so mad when she found out what he was up to.

She picked up her cell, took a deep breath and dialed the number she'd been dodging for months. "Mitch? It's Dina. We need to talk."

He said nothing, and she was sure he was going to hang up. "Um, Shelley is over right now, do you think you can call back later?"

Ugh. He was still with his new girlfriend. "It's really, really important."

He was quiet for a moment. "Okay. I'll be there soon."

SHE FROZE WHEN the doorbell rang, but she had to get this over with. When she opened the door, Mitch looked straight at her belly and turned white. "Wow, you got really big."

She pushed him. "Shut up!"

He put his hands on her shoulders. "No, I just mean before you just looked chubby, now you look pregnant."

She knocked his arm away. "Shut up!"

He sighed. "Why don't I come in and stop talking."

She stepped aside and trudged back to the couch, plopping down with a sigh.

"So, what did you need to talk about that's so important?" he asked.

She closed her eyes, took a breath and said, "Yes, you were right, the baby is yours, and I'm not sure what to do." She opened one eye to see his reaction.

His mouth fell open and he shook his head. "Why didn't you tell me the truth when I asked you? I could've been there for you. Now I'm with Shelley."

She looked down at the thumbnail she'd already chewed to the quick. "I didn't want us to be together just because of the baby. I didn't want you to have to like me just for that."

"So you pushed me away? You didn't even give me a chance to get to know you." Shaking his head, he leaned against the back of the chair next to the couch. That made his biceps bulge so Dina had to take a deep breath and refocus.

"I don't want this baby growing up without a daddy, but that doesn't mean we have to be together, like a couple. Obviously, since you're with someone else already." She chewed on her bottom lip, and the faint taste of her cherry lip gloss lingered on her tongue.

He scratched his head. "We'd only been dating a few weeks before you just stopped calling me back. Why call me now? Were you hoping to get back together or something?"

She popped up from the couch and started pacing around the room. "No! A baby isn't reason enough to get back together. I just thought . . ."

Mitch shrugged. "What? This is really confusing, Dina."

She slapped her forehead. "We're already fighting and we're not even a couple."

He closed his eyes and took a deep breath. Pressing his lips together in a thin line, he looked at her. "I just want to understand why you told me the baby wasn't mine, and now, out of the blue, you're telling me it is."

"I don't know. I just thought it was fair to tell you the truth." *Because I don't have anybody else.* "You don't have to be part of this if you don't want to. But do you?" She glanced up at him, not sure how she wanted him to answer that question.

He looked back without saying anything.

Dina's stomach tumbled, and it had nothing to do with the baby.

Chapter 10

DESPERATE TO IGNORE the slumbering man on the couch, Kate tried to keep busy. She felt like a peeping tom creeping around the room while he slept—probably because she was thinking the same inappropriate thoughts a peeper would think; if peepers had a thing for hot, snoring, muscular men, that is.

It was well past noon and her tummy was rumbling, so she ordered room service. She decided to stay outside so the waiter wouldn't wake Teague. And maybe that would give her some space from this man tormenting her even when he was unconscious.

She slipped out the door, but then realized she'd forgotten her hat and sunglasses. Ducking back inside, she fumbled in the dim room, sunblind. She bumped into a table by the door and swore under her breath. A pile of papers slid off the table onto the floor. Kate scooped them up and froze when she saw the notes scribbled on the top page.

$10,576 . . . George Riley . . . Willowdale Town Hall, 12 Main Street.

$10,576. The exact amount George owed in back taxes. Kate's stomach swirled. Why did Teague have this information? Thinking back, she remembered that earlier that morning, he'd set down a few papers when he came in. She'd been too busy tossing her shoes at him to give it a second thought.

"Room service."

The knock on the door startled her and she dropped the papers. Teague woke with a start. He rubbed his eyes and shook his head. "What time is it?"

"Hello? Room service."

Kate didn't know what to say as she opened the door. She

took her food and signed for the meal, but she'd lost her appetite. With a shaking hand, she closed the door, set down the tray, and stared at the papers scattered on the floor.

Teague followed her gaze.

Kate fought back a mix of anger and embarrassment. "Why do you have this information about my stepfather?" she managed to say. "Are you investigating me? You weren't so choosy when you needed a ride."

Teague rubbed his face and stretched. "The press has been poking around, asking about your stepfather's tax bill." He shrugged. "I thought I'd put an end to the questions and pay it off. I made a few calls last night. It's taken care of." He walked over to Kate and picked up the papers.

She crossed her arms and squeezed her eyes shut. "You didn't have to do that."

"It was no big deal, Kate. Our week here in the bungalow will cost more."

Instead of feeling thrilled, she was sick to her stomach. Her throat was tight and her head throbbed. She didn't know what to say—*how dare you* or *thank you?*

He set the papers on the table, then put his hand on her shoulder. "It was a problem I could solve, so I did. One less thing to be questioned about. I left a message for your stepfather, to let him know."

She stepped back. "That's the reason I needed to earn extra cash this summer—to pay off the taxes and save my mama's house. You can deduct it from my fee. Hopefully, I won't cause any more problems for you."

Overwhelmed, she turned away and headed for the bathroom for some privacy. For a moment, a little part of her wished he had done it out of concern for her. But it was only to protect his image. Her biggest problem in the world was just a little nuisance he could easily wipe away. They really did live in two different worlds.

He grabbed her arm. "What's wrong?? You don't have to worry about this anymore."

She pulled away from him. "Don't act like you did it for my

benefit."

"Kate . . ." He reached for her hand and caught her fingers. "I didn't know that's why you needed the money. But if I helped you out a little bit, that's a huge plus. I'm happy to do it."

If only he weren't an actor, maybe she could believe him. But why did it even matter? The tax bill was paid off, and her mother's home was saved—for now. It was the thing she wanted most. She snuck a peek at Teague. Maybe the thing she wanted most had changed. He was holding her hand, and it left her as breathless as she'd be after a few rounds on the dance floor at The Hideaway.

"Hopefully, no one will ask about it at the premiere tonight," he said.

And the nausea returned. In a few hours, Kate would be walking the red carpet on Teague's arm. Had anyone ever thrown up on the red carpet before? Too bad she hadn't tucked a barf bag from the plane into her purse.

"I don't think anyone will notice if I'm not there."

He took a deep breath and slid his hands up her arms. "I'll notice. I want you there." He squeezed her shoulders and the prickling sensation skittered down to her toes.

She ignored the feeling. "Right. Because the cameras will be there."

Teague shook his head. "Kate, I want you with me."

"Still trying to win that bet." The agonizing quiver in her tummy was getting harder to fight.

He shook his head and whispered, "No. That's not why."

Facing each other, the air crackled between them, neither willing to make a move and spook the magic. Kate looked up into his eyes, his lids and lashes at half-mast, moving into a kiss-me-now-you-fool position.

But she was the fool. Kate looked down and stepped back, too scared to make the next move. Too scared it would make her even crazier to have this man. A man guaranteed to break her heart more thoroughly than a rock whizzing through a window. There was no way this could have a happy ending. *Spell broken.* "I better start getting ready," she said to the floor.

His hands slid off her shoulders. "Right. You probably should."

Kate bee-lined it to the bathroom, telling herself to walk it off, like the time she'd been hit with a softball pitch when she filled in for the gym teacher. She stopped and ogled the elegant marble room, which was bigger than her bedroom back home. She washed up in the huge, tiled shower that featured seven different nozzles—most of which she didn't know how to operate, several of which sprayed so hard it hurt. She hopped out and climbed in the Jacuzzi tub to relax and tried not to imagine Teague in the bubbles with her when he rapped on the door.

She squeaked in surprise.

"Sorry to bother you, but your phone's been ringing nonstop," he said from the other side of the door.

"Hang on." She wrapped her soapy self in a plush robe, padded across the cold marble floor and grabbed her phone. She looked at the missed calls. Dina had called seven times in half an hour. *That can't be good.*

Her fingers shook as she dialed. Dina answered on the first ring. "George is gone. Packed his bags and took off this morning."

Perfect. How could she help Dina when she was clear across the world? "Any idea where he went?" She stood there, warm water puddling at her feet.

"He's coming to see you."

KATE WAS STILL in the bathroom with the stylists who'd just arrived. Teague readjusted his cufflinks for the eighth time. Why was he so nervous? It was Kate. He was desperate to be alone with her, to discover every inch of her. To taste every inch. He wasn't even thinking about how his movie would be received by the critics and the judges—which was incredible, because a year ago this film had consumed his life. Now, it was a curvy, silky-haired blonde invading his every thought, even though he had told himself, *No way.*

Pacing the room while she got dressed, he stopped to snap open the cap of her body lotion, taking a deep whiff of the sweet, creamy scent always drifting off her. He dropped the bottle back on the vanity and sat on the bed, his head in his hands. Pulling this off had been trickier than he'd imagined. The mini fridge beckoned, and he tossed back the entire contents of a tiny Captain Morgan bottle.

He wanted to take care of her. Paying off the tax bill had sparked something inside him, something strangely intimate. Her reaction had crumbled his will power. He wanted her to need him.

He froze. *That's it, isn't it?* He smacked his hands together. "That's the key to this whole damn thing," he mumbled to himself. He just wanted her to need him—and want him back. *Exactly!*

He snapped his fingers and stood outside the bathroom door like a horny teenager, imagining Kate's state of undress. This was getting ridiculous. He didn't have feelings for a woman he'd just met. How could he? No. He wasn't falling in love with her. That was his stupid hormones working in overdrive trying to get this party started. That was his problem. He wasn't getting what he wanted. That's why he'd been so desperate to get back to her when he was at the bar with Simone. He'd already had Simone. He hadn't had Kate. That's all it was.

He popped open her lotion again and took in another lungful. Once they finally hooked up, this insane desire would go away. Life would be back to normal. T-Rex would rule the land again. Stomp, stomp, stomp. Shred, shred. Shred. Right? Damn right.

He needed to get her in bed tonight so he could concentrate on more important things. Like his career. Like Stan Remington's next movie. Like the baby. Kate was a nice, curvy distraction from all his worries. He poured himself another drink from the mini bar to help him swallow this new theory.

WHERE WAS THE DAMN mini bar in this place? Kate

definitely needed one of those cute little bottles of booze. Or four or five. George was coming to see her? *Let's panic about one thing at a time*, Kate told herself, while her hair was blown out straight and then reset in big rollers. What was the old man thinking, leaving Dina all alone?

The stylists had interrupted her panic attack, and once her hair was fuller and shinier than nature intended, her two borrowed assistants helped Kate into her dress—one of those size-eight sample dresses, rarer than an albino leprechaun. They draped her in beautiful, sparkly jewelry. "You'll be one of the most gorgeous ladies there tonight," one said, folding her hands against her chest.

She didn't dare to look in the mirror yet. "Thank you."

She leaned toward Kate and lowered her voice. "That lipstick is a stain. Totally kiss-proof, so don't worry about locking lips with that hunk of love you got out there."

Kate's cheeks blazed, and a soft tap on the door startled her. "Ready?"

"I s'pose so," she answered.

Teague pushed open the door and Kate's knees wobbled. His dark tux and silver tie set off the glints of copper in his dark hair and his eyes seemed even brighter blue. She'd never seen anyone so handsome. Never. How could she show up on his arm? She'd look like a backwoods fool; probably get a special award for it. She could strut her stuff back home, but this guy and this crazy world he lived in shook her confidence. At least that's why she figured her hands were shaking.

Teague took a step back and widened his eyes. "Wow."

The stylists smiled and grabbed their things. "We'll be going now." One of the women bopped Teague with a big blush brush. "Don't be messing up all my work on this girl." She winked at him and bustled for the door like a fairy godmother clocking off duty.

TEAGUE WINKED BACK as the stylist scurried away. "I'll be very careful." He had a mind to stay in their bungalow and skip the premiere. Kate looked like a goddess, with her hair parted to the side, and long, flowing waves curling down her back. He could imagine her on top of him, and that hair closing in around him like a beautiful silk curtain. What would that feel like against his chest? He shook his head to clear out all that nonsense. Could they just get this over with already?

Kate smoothed her hands down her torso and along her hips and all that nonsense flooded right back in his brain. "What do you think? Do I look alright?"

He shook his head. "No."

She balled up a fist and planted it on her hip. "Excuse me?"

He grazed his knuckles along her jawline. "You look gorgeous. Amazing. Breathtaking. You pick the adjective." He wanted to hold her tight, keep her away from the camera's glare. He didn't want to share her. Yet, he also wanted to show her off. "I can't imagine anyone more beautiful."

She fingered her necklace. "Now you're laying it on thicker than chicken steak gravy."

What did he have to do to make her believe he wanted her? Every other woman read wild meaning in his most casual comments, but Kate couldn't see him standing there, oozing desire out of every pore? He took her by the hand and pulled her to him. He kissed the tips of her fingers, nibbled a knuckle or two, and wrapped his hand around hers. She let out a breath of surprise. His other hand slipped behind her head and he dipped her, holding her above the ground where she hovered as precariously as this whole thing between them.

She gripped his arms. He liked the feel of her holding onto him. Lowering his mouth, he scrubbed his lips along hers. Her tongue beckoned, searching for his, but he pulled back cause if they got started, there'd be no stopping. His forehead pressed against hers. "That was just a preview." He stood her back up and grazed a finger along her collarbone. "Let's get this premiere out of the way, and we'll pick up from here. And I'll show you I'm not pretending." Because he wasn't—he wanted her.

And he wanted this longing for her to go away.

Kate's mesmerizing eyes were wide and bright. "Sounds like

a plan. Do we have to stay for the whole thing?"

Teague laughed. "We do. Let's get it over with."

Chapter 11

THEY STEPPED OUT of the limo onto a red carpet that almost matched the hues in the darkening sky. "Don't let me fall," she whispered, just imagining the headlines the next day if she fell on her face. *Backwoods Bumbler Bombs on Big Night. Kate Riley Does The Hillbilly Flop.*

"I'm not letting go of you all night. Trust me."

Those words made her chest seize up. She didn't know if she'd ever really trust him. She didn't know if she'd ever really trust any man. But she tightened her hold on his arm and started walking up the carpet as people in the crowd shouted to them and cameras flashed. She just smiled and stayed close to Teague.

"Kate, over here!"

"How about a smile for the camera?"

"How about a kiss?"

The whole thing made her want to run away like a dog that finally broke off its leash. But Teague squeezed her hand, pulled it to his lips and kissed it. A collective sigh rose up from the crowd. Heck, she might have even sighed. A blur of flashes broke her gaze and luckily another star was coming up behind them, catching the camera's attention. Kate and Teague moved on to the open-air seating in front of an enormous projection screen. It was almost like a drive-in movie, but without the popcorn and steamy back windows—which honestly, she'd much prefer.

She spotted dozens of actors and actresses she'd seen on the screen, but here they were just feet away from her, some saying hello to Teague, others shaking her hand—yes, her, Kate Riley from Willowdale, North Carolina, who had only recently plucked a *People* from the beauty shop to take home and read about all of these mythical Hollywood creatures. And here they were in the flesh, talking to her.

"You're Kate Riley, right?" asked last year's Best Supporting Actress Oscar winner outside the bathroom.

"Yes," she managed to say.

The woman squeezed Kate's hand. "Hope the press lets up on you soon."

"Me too," was her clever response. The actress seemed so normal, like a real flesh and blood person—talking to her—that she was a little too stunned to say anything else.

Kate wandered back to her seat, dazed, but not until after saying hello to two other A-list actors. Well, hot damn, this was something else. Kate smiled and nodded as the night unfolded, holding onto Teague like she might float away if she let go. Which she did not, not for one moment. Let go, that is, because she was definitely floating.

Teague wasn't just incredible eye candy in the movie; he was great. He played a wounded American soldier home from Iraq, tormented by what the war had turned him into. Kate wiped away a tear more than once and squeezed his hand. He could be a serious actor, one of the blockbuster stars, she was sure of it. He looked so proud watching the movie, and her heart swelled for him. What the heck was that all about?

The night was warm, but a cool breeze rolling in off the ocean had her clutching her wrap and leaning toward him for warmth. He wrapped his arm around her, and for a moment all was right with the world.

The crowd roared with a standing ovation when the movie was over, and dozens of people shook Teague's hand in congratulations when they tried to leave.

Kate recognized the short, dark-haired woman approaching him. The prison-warden-publicist-goon. The one who hated Kate. Ugh. "This is a wonderful set up for your meeting with Remington in two days," she said. "He's casting his next movie, and it's perfect for you. Devote your full attention to Remington and come to the party by yourself." June looked at Kate like she was a horsefly bobbing in her soup.

Teague smiled at June and Kate recognized it as one of his

fake grins. She was getting good at reading his real moods.

"Thanks for your insight, June. And goodnight." He pulled Kate close and whisked her away. True to his word he had stayed by her side all night, either holding her hand or draping his arm around her waist. They tried their darndest to leave the festival grounds, but someone was always waiting to talk to Teague, often throwing in a question for Kate.

"Teague! Aren't you going to any of the after parties?" A tiny redhead in a white gown skipped up and planted a kiss on his cheek. She didn't even look at Kate.

He stepped back from her. "How are you feeling these days, Kimmie?"

She waved her hand nonchalantly. "Great. Perfect."

Kate noticed his strained smile. "Good. Kate and I are calling it a night." He tucked Kate's hair behind her ear and smudged his thumb across her cheekbone.

She trembled. They needed to get out of there, and fast.

But not before they were besieged by at least a dozen other drop-dead-gorgeous actresses stopping him, asking about his plans, practically rubbing themselves against him like barn cats in heat.

Those women really need to eat. She knew exactly the meal they had in mind, too—the one she was holding onto for dear life. Teague wrestled himself away from the last woman and they finally made their way out of the festival grounds.

She paced back and forth as they waited for their driver. "Don't they read the papers? Don't they know about your country-bumpkin girlfriend? They were totally hitting on you in front of me. Even when you did that thumb thing on my cheek."

His dimples appeared. "You liked that, huh?" The man was way too pleased with himself.

She wasn't going to let him waltz away from her anger. "Anyone would. Any of those women would."

Despite her sour mood, it was a beautiful night. Palm trees rustled overhead, the smell of exotic flowers hung thick in the air, and the moon was a bright beacon in the sky. She took a deep breath, trying to calm herself. She was having a hissy fit right in the middle of a real-life fairy tale. No happy ending ever came out of that.

He tightened his grip on her hand. "Kate, they don't care. I've had girls slip me their number while I was kissing another woman on the dance floor."

She yanked her hand out of his, jealousy dancing through her like a nasty demon child.

He grabbed her hand back, rubbing her knuckles. "You're the one coming home with me, aren't you?"

She stopped mid-tantrum and let her arms fall to her sides. She stared at him. *Mercy, he had a point.* Her heart threatened to pop open like a jack-in-the-box.

He pulled her close and kissed her—and no one was even taking a picture. How 'bout that. His lips melted against hers, his tongue urgent, as she parted her lips for him. Oh, she suspected she would part much more for him before the night was over.

Their kiss continued as Teague's driver opened their door. They tumbled onto the leather seats, their bodies pressed together. Her hands groped his remarkable behind, his wandered over her breasts, then up her shoulders, down her back. He reached for the zipper on her dress.

"Wait until we get to the room," she breathed into his ear, adding in a bite for good measure.

He ran his fingers down her delicate throat, leaving a trail of kisses behind. "I can't. I've waited too long for you."

Kate groaned and gripped the cool leather seat. "You only met me four days ago."

He hitched his leg behind hers and pulled her closer. "That's four days too long. We should have been doing this at Makeout Point."

"Lookout Point." Kate tried to leave space between them, but that was like trying to keep a magnet from sticking to the fridge. "We're almost there. I just can't do this with you in a limo."

"Too tacky?"

She shook her head. "Not enough room."

He laughed and pulled her back for another killer kiss that

left her mouth and her mind numb.

The driver dropped them off at their hotel. Kate wouldn't look at him as they tumbled out, certain he knew what they'd been doing in the back seat. They hurried down the path to the bungalow, sprinting past glowing fountains and trees sparkling with white lights. *Dang, this is a big place. How far away is the beach, anyway?* Kate held up her dress as they ran, Teague pulling her along by the hand. Her giggles echoed across the empty pool area.

By the time they reached the bungalow, they were breathless. Teague fumbled for his key card in his pocket with one hand, while the other wound through Kate's hair as he tugged at her lower lip with his teeth. *Talented man*, she thought.

She squeezed his shoulders and pressed her chest against him. Could he feel her heart thumping?

A man in the darkness cleared his throat. "I see you're enjoying my stepdaughter."

Teague froze and Kate's stomach headed south. Like, direct-flight-from-Charlotte-to-Cancun south. "George? How did you find us?"

"It wasn't hard. Everyone knows where Teague Reynolds is staying."

She rubbed her temples and cursed the horrific karma that worked like a wet blanket whenever happiness snuck into her life. "Why are you here?" But she knew why. Paying off George's tax bill was like dumping a bucket of slop in a pigpen. Once those piggies were fed, they'd be rooting around for more—just like George.

George stood up from the lounge where Teague had massaged the sunscreen on her not so long ago. "I thought I should meet the man who's swept my stepdaughter off her feet, taken her a world away from her family." He crossed his arms and knit his brows together. "I promised your mother I'd take care of you once she was gone. I need to make sure this man is doing right by you."

Her mouth fell open. "You—take care of me?" Her jaw dropped. "You can't even take care of yourself or your daughter.

She's pregnant, if you haven't noticed, and she needs you."

"You need me, too. This seems to be a little more urgent. I want to know what this man's intentions are."

Kate marched over to George and pulled him aside. He'd probably hopped on a flight the minute he found out Teague paid his taxes. "I know why you're here. There's no more money for you. Now go back home."

"Kate, I'm not here about the money. I'm here to make sure you're all right. And I'm not going back. I just got here. I want to see the island." He spread his arms wide and grinned up at the moon like a wolf.

She clenched her teeth. "Then go to your hotel."

"I want to have a word with your boyfriend."

She pressed her eyes closed. "He's not—"

"Are you okay, Kate?" Teague walked up and tucked his arm around her waist.

"No, I'm not."

George waved her off. "Don't listen to her, Teague. It's all good. You know women." He chuckled. "Of course you know women. I think you know women even better than I do. Can you give us a minute, Kate?"

She pointed toward the hotel complex. "Get out of here. This is none of your concern."

Teague grabbed her hand and squeezed it. "It's okay. Go inside, and I'll have a chat with your stepfather and I'll be right back. I promise." He handed her the key card and disappeared into the dark with George.

And before she could squawk, "Hell, no," they were gone.

Chapter 12

TOO ANGRY TO do anything else, Kate opened the door and flopped onto the bed. Beautiful purple orchid blossoms rested on each pillow. She flicked them onto the floor and ate both of the chocolate mints. She balled up the wrappers and tossed them across the room, too. Didn't make her feel any better.

Only George could ruin such a perfect evening. She'd been clear across the globe, but he was still a bigger bother than a recurring bout of the stomach flu. What had her mother ever seen in him? Of course he was handsome. Kate couldn't deny that. Tall and lean, and at age sixty-two he still had a thick head of hair. He'd blend right in with the rest of the Hollywood crowd, fake as plastic. How long would it be before he tricked another woman into loving him, now that her mother was gone?

She stared at the ceiling fan slowly whirling above her, remembering when her mother had met George so long ago. He'd been the perfect guy for a lonely woman, attentive and loving. Just like Tommy had been when Kate first started dating him junior year of high school. Attentive and loving, just like Teague had been all night. That's how it always started; but it never ended that way.

Sitting up, she realized the truth. The sensible part of Kate had abandoned her. Kate kicked off her shoes and wrapped her arms around a pillow. This was stupid. It was a magical evening where she'd played dress-up, and she looked mighty fine if she did say so herself. Only she really was Cinderella with a one-night fairytale pass, complete with the stepsister who needed a keeper.

No prince would come calling when it was all over. She probably wouldn't even get any stupid shoes out of the deal.

She stood up. It was time to step out of this daydream.

Slowly pulling down the zipper of her dress, she let the gown slide to the floor, then changed into her plain cotton nightgown. This wasn't going to happen between her and Teague. She'd gotten caught up in the moment. She was glad George had shown up and stopped her from doing something stupid. She had to remember who she was and the obligations piled up back home. She wasn't destined for love. Certainly not with someone like T-Rex.

She scrubbed off her makeup and brushed out her hair. Tucked under the covers, she tried her hardest to hold back the tears. But they were right there: for her Mama, for the life she dreamed she'd be living with Tommy, for all the hurts and pains and losses.

And one thing was for certain—she couldn't let herself be hurt again. She couldn't go through this with Teague, no matter how tough she was. She thought about calling Tonya or Jeanne back home, but it was the middle of the night in North Carolina. She had to deal with this on her own.

After a good pity-party sob fest, she was huddled in bed when Teague came back half an hour later. He closed the door softly behind him.

"Is he gone?" she asked, her voice thick from crying.

He rushed to her, knelt next to the bed, and brushed her hair off her face with his big, gentle hands. "Hey, you okay?"

She nodded yes. Then she shook her head no.

He smoothed her hair again, twining a piece around his finger. "He's getting a hotel room. He plans on staying for a while. But I don't think he'll bother us again."

She sat up. "How can you be so sure?"

Letting go of her hair, he stood up and took off his tux jacket, then sat on the bed next to her. "I gave him good incentive to stay away."

He'd paid off the fool! "Teague, you didn't have to do that. He's just going to come nosing around hoping for more." She looked away, embarrassed. "I'm not like that, you know. Even though I agreed to this setup . . ." For all her denials, she appeared very much like George. She couldn't imagine what Teague was thinking of her.

"Don't worry. I didn't give him any money. I've got plans for your stepfather. He'll regret coming out here soon enough." Teague peeled the covers back. "Besides, I had you waiting here for me. I was willing to do anything to get rid of him to get back to you." The grin that unfurled on his face hit her square in the chest.

With that, Kate felt her will weaken, teeter and shatter like a vase toppling off a shelf. Her self-control sank to the bottom of the ocean along with Miss Sensible. How bad would it be if she did make love with him? As long as she knew it was going nowhere, she couldn't get hurt, right?

Filled with a surge of need, she grabbed two handfuls of silky sheets. She knew what she wanted; she knew what was going to happen. And that was the difference. This wouldn't lead to love. She wasn't hoping for that. Tommy had broken her heart when she believed he still loved her. The guys she had diddled around with after Tommy were idiots, but she hadn't known that at the time. This was the first time she knew what she was getting into. She could do this. Suddenly, she felt much, much better.

She let go of the sheets, and perched next to him, her legs tucked underneath her. She raised an eyebrow. "Let's remember this counts as fun, not falling for anyone."

Teague pressed a finger against her lips. "No worries there." He ran his finger across her lower lip; she brushed it with her tongue.

Then he pulled her up from the bed. Her feet hit the plush area rug and he dipped her in his arms. She grabbed for his biceps and took hold.

"Isn't this where we left off a few hours ago? Although your dress was a little flashier if I recall. But this one is easier to remove." He grinned and bent down for a kiss.

The strap of her nightgown slipped off her shoulder. She didn't have a chance to catch her breath before his lips found her mouth, his tongue sweeping across hers. Her insides twirled like they were doing the two-step at The Hideaway on a Saturday night, and she knew she would've dropped to the ground if he hadn't been holding her. What hope did she have of resisting this man? What do they say, don't swim against the riptide or you'll drown? She was definitely going to ride this out.

She slid a hand behind his neck and matched his urgent kisses. She reached for the buttons on his shirt with her other hand, loosening them with jittery fingers as he undid his pants and kicked off his shoes. His skin was warm against her palm as she spread her hand across his chest. He stood before her in his boxers as she lowered herself onto the bed. She looked up at him, waiting—waiting for what she had been fighting tooth and nail for what seemed like forever.

Four days really can be a long time with a guy like Teague.

MAN, WHAT WAS he doing, and why hadn't he done this sooner? Would've saved himself a whole lot of grief. He fingered her nightgown and pulled it off her as if he was unwrapping an exquisite gift. "Beautiful," he whispered. He straddled her, running his hands up her hips, over her smooth belly and up to her gorgeous, creamy breasts. He teased her nipples with his tongue, and she shivered beneath him.

"You're nervous."

She nodded, which made him want her even more, if that was possible. Her cheeks were pink and her eyes gleamed dark with anticipation. Her eagerness was as beautiful as her soft, curvy body. It was a delicious combination he planned to enjoy like a decadent dessert.

She ran her hands across his back as he nuzzled her breasts. "Teague . . ." Her voice was huskier and deeper than her usual sweet southern drawl. The sound drove through him.

He wanted her with a fierceness he'd never experienced before. He pressed his face to her chest, feeling her heart throbbing against his cheek, hoping to calm his own. He didn't want to rush this.

Her fingers snaked through his hair while his hands worked under her silky white panties, probing and stroking. He found just the right spot and squeezed gently.

Kate shuddered and arched against him. "You're wicked," she moaned into his chest.

"Yeah, well, you were warned." He ran his hands along her smooth thighs, willing himself to slow down, to enjoy each excruciating moment of sweet intensity. He wanted this woman more than he'd wanted any model or actress who'd found their way to his bed. But he couldn't take chances. The image of another baby on the way flashed in his mind. He imagined the frenzy the press would have with news of two scandalous pregnancies linked to him. Talk about applying the brakes.

He reached over to the bedside table and plucked a condom from the drawer. "I stashed a few here just in case things worked out this way." One corner of his mouth curled up into his trademark devious grin. He couldn't help himself; this smile was the real thing.

Propped up on her elbows, she narrowed her eyes at him. "You're pretty confident."

"Nope, just hopeful. I've imagined doing this since I first saw you leaning against your Jeep, back in Willowdale."

She was so beautiful, with her lips full and wet, her hair in a wild tangle, and those beautiful eyes that threatened to see through his Hollywood veneer. He rolled on the condom and wished there was similar protection for his heart; Kate might whack open a huge crack and slide on in.

KATE WAS SITTING on his lap, but she sensed she was falling. She wrapped her legs around his waist, desperate to have him inside her. How could this desire be real? The times she'd been with Tommy had felt like obligations. Their lovemaking had never brought her much pleasure. But now, she wanted everything she could have from this gorgeous man in her bed. She shimmied her hips, searching for him, ready for him.

"You sure you want to do this?" Teague grabbed a handful of hair and pulled her head back gently, grazing her neck with his teeth.

"Yes," she moaned.

He traced his tongue along her jaw. "How much do you need me?" His voice was a primitive growl.

She shuddered. Maybe this is why they called him T-Rex. He was a perfect monster. The room was whirling, and she thought she might go mad if he didn't bring her relief. "I need you . . . now." She squirmed beneath him.

He laughed low in this throat, then lowered her onto the bed, gripping her hands in his, moving over her, drawing himself along her, until her mouth quivered and the words she meant to say got lost somewhere inside her. They probably weren't fully formed words, anyway.

He nudged her legs open wider with his knee and plunged into her. A scream built deep in her throat, unable to find a way out. She snaked her legs around his and matched his movements, each collision of their bodies sending sparks through her. She was his and he was hers, at least for the moment.

She squeezed her eyes shut, memorizing the feel of his weight on her, the smell of sweat mingled with cologne and the flowery body cream she wore. She moved with him until they rolled together as if she was a wave he was riding. They continued like this, together sensing, needing, pleasing. For how long? Kate couldn't have guessed. Minutes? Hours? He moved faster, harder, until he collapsed onto her, panting. From her moaning and writhing below him, he'd probably figure out that she'd reached the same destination.

After, she arched against him, desperate to keep their flesh together for just a while longer. Teague dropped next to her, still holding her in his arms. "Kate, that was . . ."

She could only nod. Still spinning from the aftereffect, Teague pulled her to him, her back pressed against his stomach. He kissed her neck and she shivered. "So much for strictly business," she said.

"I should have never made that promise."

Kate forced a laugh. She knew who she was dealing with. Teague must've known no woman was a match for his charms.

She was nothing to him. Just the right girl on the right night. But she'd known that going in.

Every detail of the moment hit her: his damp, warm skin sticking to hers, the way his nose pressed into the nook between her ear and cheek, his strong arms wrapped around her ribs. Kate bit her lip, realizing she'd never have this again. *You can't handle this.*

Damn that Miss Sensible always being right.

Chapter 13

THIS WAS BAD—very, very bad. An hour later, they lay in bed, the ceiling fan whirling above them, gulls crying in the breeze. He took a deep breath and sighed, nudging his knees behind hers.

Making love to Kate hadn't fixed things at all. It wasn't enough. She rested in his arms, and he wanted her even more now. He'd never held a woman like this. Sure, women had spent the night, and they'd ended up tangled in each other's arms. But he'd never cradled a woman, squeezing her tight, trying to fuse into one. *Shit.*

It's not that he just wanted another round. He wanted everything from her—to make her laugh, to make her sigh. His mind raced with a thousand ideas of what they could do together the rest of the week. He wanted to see her eyes widen, he wanted to make her giggle and squeal.

Just thinking of it made him squeeze her tighter. She wiggled her rump in response, trying to get closer to him. That just started things all over again. He buried his nose in her hair, clung to her, and wondered how long she would stay his. This wasn't real, what they were doing. Kate was his for a month, if he was lucky. That was their deal. She had obligations back in Willowdale.

And so did he.

He'd better enjoy her while he could. "Ready to do that again?"

She turned to him, flushed and relaxed, looking even more delicious than the first time. "One thing first." She rolled him over on his stomach and sat between his thighs, slightly behind him. She slipped the sheet down past his hips, exposing his rear.

He looked back at her, puzzled. "I'm not familiar with this

one," he said, joking. "But I'm willing to try anything."

She swatted his butt playfully and pulled the sheet back up. He tilted his head. "What?"

She crawled next to him. "Simone's name isn't tattooed on your butt." She sounded surprised.

"Just one of the many lies out there about me."

"The God-in-the-sack one wasn't a lie." She set her hand on his chest and his heart thumped against it. "Although, I could decide for sure if we did that again."

He smoothed his hand over her bottom. "Let's see if I can convince you." The flirty grin that split her face reached in and squeezed his heart. Somehow, Kate had found her way in. But he certainly wouldn't let her know that. He pulled her on top of him. "I'll do my best."

DINA HATED TO admit it, but she was lonely and a little scared, too. Which is probably why she called Mitch again. "Listen, my Dad and Kate are both gone. Would you mind coming over?"

"I've got to work at the hardware store until two, but I can come over after that."

She felt her chest loosen up a bit. "That would be great."

She rushed to her room and rummaged through her closet for something that wouldn't make her look like a bus. She tried on different shirts and dresses until she slumped to the floor. "Oh, it's useless. I'm bigger than a bus."

She wiped her tears away and sat in front of her vanity mirror, staring at all the nail polishes and body sprays lined up. When was the last time she had done her nails? She looked at them and shrugged. Settling her chin on her hand, she gazed in the mirror and looked at herself. Really looked at herself. *You're eighteen, knocked up, and all alone*, a little voice responded. *So what are you going to do about it?*

At least she had her high school diploma. She wouldn't be working at Scalia's forever. But what was she going to do?

No idea, said that little voice.

Mitch came over right after two, like he promised. He brought a bag of goodies for her: Twinkies, Yoo-hoo and chocolate ice cream. "I thought you might be hungry."

Snatching the bag from him, she led him out the back door. They wandered over to the big oak tree and sat down in the spotty shade, where she slid off her black flats and dug her toes into the grass. Even her feet were looking big these days. Being pregnant sucked in so many ways. "Thanks for coming over. I hope you don't think I'm stupid. It's just with Kate gone and my dad gone . . ." She didn't want to say she was scared, like she was some little girl.

He kissed her, probably to keep her quiet. It worked. She was still attracted to him. He was hot and sweet. What more could she want? She grinned and enjoyed the moment, pretending they were a couple again.

He pulled away. "It's no problem, Dina. I like being with you, if you remember."

It felt so good to have him close like this. She rested her head against his shoulder. "I know. Me, too. I just panicked when I found out I was pregnant."

He nudged her with his elbow. "Did you think I wouldn't be there for you?"

She plucked a piece of grass and twirled it between her fingers. "I didn't want you to be with me just because of the baby." *But isn't that why he's here now?* She shook the thought from her head. She needed him. She looked up and smiled.

He broke a Twinkie in half and brought it to her lips. "I probably should have brought you something healthier, but I remembered how much you liked these."

Dina closed her eyes and bit into the moist cake. "Mmm." She finished it off and reached for another.

"I can stay here with you if you want."

That sent her heart thumping. "For how long?" She popped the rest of her second Twinkie in her mouth.

"As long as you need me. Until someone comes home for you."

She chewed on her lip. "But what about Shelley?" she asked

quietly.

Mitch wrapped his arm around her. "You need me more than Shelley does right now. You and the baby." He kissed her cheek.

She leaned into him and her heart settled in place. "Thanks, Mitch."

Chapter 14

TEAGUE HELD KATE'S hand as they drove along the coast, the view more beautiful than any tropical postcard she'd ever seen. She glanced over at him, wondering what was more breathtaking: him or the scenery. No contest.

She sighed. Despite her better sense, here she was having a fling with Hollywood's biggest heartbreaker. She was up for seconds. And thirds. Get it while it's hot, and boy had it been hot. Kate didn't feel like she was being used at all. In fact, she should be paying Teague for the vacation of a lifetime. They were two people enjoying a beautiful tropical island with a side of sex.

She looked at their linked hands and squeezed his. This wasn't going to last forever, but she'd make damn sure he remembered her when it was over. She closed her eyes and smiled.

He squeezed her hand back. "What are you thinking about?"

"Global warming." The windows in the Jeep were down, and the breeze swirled her hair.

He laughed. "I told you it wasn't a bad thing."

"Are you always right?"

"Not even half the time."

They bounced along the winding road to Hana, and Kate gripped the door handle. At times, all she could see was the dense canopy of trees as they drove along the curving road. Vines dangled from rock walls and tiny waterfalls splashed along the stony cliffs. It was as if they were driving into uncharted territory.

The view was spectacular, although the ride was somewhat terrifying along the narrow winding hill. Kind of like this thing with Teague. They pulled off the road from time to time and crept into the jungle to explore hidden pools and waterfalls. Sometimes they ran into other tourists at the different stop-offs. Other times, they were lucky enough to be alone and would squeeze in a kiss while pressed up against a palm tree.

They found a clear, blue-green pool with a ribbon of water cascading from a cliff. It was deserted, except for the two of them.

Teague ran toward the water and crooked his finger. "Come on, let's jump in"

She hesitated and Teague walked back to her, sliding a finger under the waistband of her shorts. "I see. You don't want to get your clothes wet. Whatcha got under there?"

"A bikini."

"Let's see it."

She worked her hands over his shirt. "Get rid of this and then we'll talk."

With a smile, he pulled his shirt over his head and tossed it aside. Then he went to work on the buttons of her shirt, and slid it over her shoulders and down her arms. His hands closed over her breasts, just barely covered by a bikini top. "We're all alone. Should we take this off too?" He toyed with one of the straps.

Holding back a moan, she looped her arms around his neck. "I'm starting to think you're not even interested in swimming."

He kissed her neck, while tracing his fingers down her tummy to unbutton her shorts. "Smart and beautiful. A killer combination." He pushed the material over her hips, letting them fall to the ground. Then he tucked a finger under her bikini bottoms.

She paused mid-kiss. "Oh, no. Your trunks are coming off first."

His hands cupped her rear. "Tempting, but you never know where the paparazzi could be hiding, and no one is seeing you naked but me." He kissed her forehead. "Come on, let's go for that swim." He took her hand and led her to the cove.

Together, they ran into the water. She gasped. "It's cold."

"So much for your global warming concerns."

The blush creeping across her cheeks was certainly warming her up.

He pulled her closer. "Come here. I'll keep you cozy." Taking her in his arms, he kissed her as the water from the falls splashed behind them. Oh, how she'd like a picture of this.

Kate still felt the soreness from their romp the night before as her body responded to his touch. It had been the most intense pleasure she'd ever experienced.

The first time with Tommy had felt forced and hard. It was after one of his basketball games. He'd sunk the winning basket, and she'd been so proud to be the girl walking out of that gym with him. He'd taken her back to his house, saying he was going to get changed and take her out for a late dinner. But his father and brothers weren't home and he'd had all the right words to get her into bed. Four minutes later, she'd wondered what all the fuss was about.

Now she knew.

Teague was working his way under her bikini again, when a snapping twig stopped him mid-grope. "Later," he whispered. "Come on." He took her by the hand and led her out of the pool. "Let's jump off the waterfall."

Kate backed away from him. "I'm not that kind of girl."

He laughed that unforgettable, deep laugh of his. "I've done it dozens of times. It's exhilarating. Come on. Trust me." He held out his hand.

She stared at his hand for a moment, before wrapping her fingers around his. Hand in hand they climbed up the hill to the top of the waterfall and knew she was in deeper than she was telling herself.

"Ready? On three. One, two, three!" he shouted.

They held hands and jumped. They plunged into the deep, cold, water and Teague never let go of her. Their lips found each other's before they even surfaced. His hands patted up and down along her back. "You lost your bikini top."

She shrieked and he pointed to a pair of gold triangles on a string, floating nearby. He swam off and snatched it while she cupped her hands over her chest.

One corner of his mouth curled up. "You just can't keep your clothes on around me, can you?"

Ain't that the truth.

His hands slid over her breasts as he teased her with the bikini he refused to give back. Once she'd been adequately kissed and groped, she slipped her top back on and hightailed it for the Jeep.

They drove along again and stopped for lunch at a fish market. They settled in plastic chairs at a little table outside, the lush forest behind them. Teague stole one of her fried shrimp, but made up for it by feeding her a slice of fresh, juicy pineapple. He let his finger linger on her tongue, and she playfully nipped him.

"I'll get you back for that."

"I hope you do." All day long, her emotions had swayed from wanting to ravage the man again to wanting nothing more than to snuggle into his arms and drink in the beautiful scenery.

After several hours of traveling, they finally made it down to the little town of Hana, where the bright blue sea appeared after a sharp curve, surrounded by lush green cliffs. It was untouched, like they were the first ones to find it.

She covered her mouth, gazing at it. He smiled and squeezed her hand. They parked the Jeep and walked out to the cove where a hot, black-sand beach waited for them. He spread out a blanket and they sat on the sand, comfortable enough with each other to not say much of anything.

Teague collected little white shells and laid them down in the shape of a heart on the sand, surrounded by names and dates and declarations of love other visitors had left behind. He was good, this T-Rex.

"Is there anything we have to do tonight?" she asked, trying to distract her exploding heart.

He smiled. "Just a lot more of this." He leaned in to kiss her, and they were soon tangled together in the sand.

She pulled back from their passionate kiss. "Think of the children," she whispered to him, gesturing to some kids playing in the surf.

He pulled her up from the ground, and they ran laughing to the Jeep, driving back up the road, leaving Hana behind like a lava flow that was hot on their tail.

That's what it felt like to Kate—a hot trail of desire coursing through her. The ride back to their cabana was just as beautiful, but seemed to take forever. This time, there was no stopping at the waterfalls to play. He drove as quickly as possible along the dangerous curves. She had no doubt his thoughts were the same as hers. They needed to be alone, and soon.

When they finally burst through the cabana doors, they made it as far as the couch. The man knew his love scenes, that's for sure. Kate had to hold tight onto the tail end of her emotions or they would spin out of control like the big colorful kites she'd seen kids flying at the beach. Sad thing was, she'd never been much of a kite flyer. She was just waiting for this all to crash.

SO THE AFTERGLOW can last until the next day, Teague thought to himself in bed. *Huh.* He pulled Kate closer, her back pressed against his chest. He buried his nose under her ear. She probably had wondered why he'd been so quiet during much of the ride back from Hana, but she'd looked perfectly happy, her eyes closed, the breeze playing with her hair. And what would he tell her? *I'm trying to figure out why I'm so into you?*

He twined a strand of her light hair around his finger, enjoying the silky feel on his skin. He'd never taken another woman to explore the island, and he'd been here at least a dozen times. He'd always loved the water, always loved swimming, and this was the first time he really shared that passion with a woman. Kate had been enthralled. Teague swallowed hard, pushing back the surprising emotions that fizzed inside him. He'd made her squeal in delight, after all. Had he ever done that for a woman outside the bedroom?

Okay, there was that one time in a tent. But how did this happen? He'd never wanted to share his secret passions with any other woman. Teague ran a finger down her back, tracing a slight tan line she'd developed from wearing that tempting bikini.

Kate was definitely different from any woman he'd known. With the other women he dated, he was mostly concerned about what they could give him—and how well they would stay away from his heart. Premieres and parties didn't offer opportunities to get close, which is why he usually took his dates there. That's why his trips to Hawaii had always been solo vacations. Sure, with a hookup here and there, but he'd never hung out in Hawaii with someone like he was doing with Kate.

Something clenched deep inside his gut. Something he'd never felt before. Scared the hell out of him. But he held her tighter and didn't let go.

DINA SENT KATE another text telling her she was fine and to have fun. She hadn't heard anything from her father, but at least Mitch was staying with her, even sleeping over. It's not like he was sleeping in her bed or anything, but they'd kissed a few times, and she tried to figure out if she was still attracted to him or just grateful he was there for her when no one else was.

She stepped into her uniform, which was getting tighter by the day. She struggled to pull the zipper up in back. Without warning, her tummy tightened. She gasped at the pain of it, stumbled to the bed, and sat down.

"Ready to go?" Mitch asked, walking in. Then his eyes went wide when he saw her white face, and her hand strapped across her belly.

She shook her head, unable to get any words out.

"Are you okay?" he asked.

"I don't know," she managed to whisper. "It's probably nothing." Another pain tore through her and she cried out.

Mitch ran to her, knelt down, and smoothed his hands over her stomach. "Maybe we should take you to the doctor or something." His eyebrows scrunched together and his face paled.

She tried to stand up but collapsed back on the bed.

"Call your doctor," he said. "Where's your phone?"

"In my purse in the living room."

Mitch dashed downstairs and came back with her bag.

Dina dialed the number with shaky hands, described her pains to the doctor and nodded silently. She hung up and looked at Mitch with tears in her eyes. "The baby might be in trouble. They want me to come in."

KATE AND TEAGUE lay on the sand watching the stars, holding hands. Tropical music drifted down from the hotel bar and the warm night air felt moist on her skin. The moon poured pools of silver on the ocean, glimmering in the waves. With Teague next to her, it was the perfect evening.

She sighed. "A star watching the stars." Then she chuckled at the lame joke. "Your parents must be so proud. I know you said you aren't close, but they must be proud, at least."

She felt Teague stiffen next to her. "I wouldn't know."

"What do you mean?"

"I heard they both died."

Kate propped herself up on her elbow. "You heard?"

He was quiet for so long, she thought he wasn't going to answer. But then he finally said, "I haven't talked to my parents since the day I graduated from high school and drove away from home. We were living in Chicago at the time. We moved around a lot. I didn't even go to their funerals."

She set her hand on his arm. "Oh, Teague. Why not?"

He picked a shell out of the sand and palmed it in his hand. "They adopted me when I was two. I was actually born in Raleigh. Not all that far from you. I have no idea why my mother gave me up, but I was a burden to my adoptive parents, too, and they let me know." He flung the shell in the water.

Kate let his words sink in. "They weren't nice to you?"

He closed his eyes. "They didn't abuse me. But I know they regretted adopting me. They always told me their marriage hit the rocks once they got me. Once I left home, we didn't stay in touch."

Kate reached over to rub his arm. "I'm so sorry. Any brothers or sisters?"

He opened his mouth, then closed it and shook his head. "Just me, and that was one person too many in that house. I joined every club and group I could just to stay after school and keep out of their way. That's how I got into acting. The drama club."

A soft breeze rushed past them. "What about your biological parents? Did you ever look for them?"

Shaking his head, he leaned back, leaving a big space between them. "My mother gave me away when I was two. Like she had a trial period on parenthood and decided it wasn't for her. Or that I wasn't for her. Why would I want to meet her? Even now if she showed up, I wouldn't give her the time of day."

Kate sat up and wrapped her hands around her knees. She hadn't expected to hear this, and the pain in his voice weighed on her. "You wouldn't give her a second chance? You don't know what happened."

He shook his head. "There are no second chances on love."

She sucked in a breath. "I'm so sorry." Kate's voice caught on the words, but she understood. She felt the very same way after what had happened with Tommy.

He sat up and folded his arms over his knees, too. "Don't be sorry. I learned early on how to protect myself. Don't let anybody in. Don't let anybody close. So now maybe you understand why T-Rex stomps around like he does. Why T-Rex doesn't ever fall in love and never could. You don't get hurt if you keep everybody out."

The truth hit Kate's heart. He wouldn't ever love anyone. Couldn't. It wasn't just their agreement, it was his reality. No fantasy scenario of hers could ever come true. He'd just told her as much. That's why every relationship of his ended. That's what made him T-Rex.

She let him go when he got up and walked off into the darkness. Because sooner or later, he'd leave anyway.

HE KICKED A STONE along the shore. Why had he done

that? Why had he opened his heart and let her see all that crap inside? Once she knew he had nothing to give, she'd be on her way. This is what he'd been avoiding all this time, airing his garbage.

But Kate hadn't run when he'd told her. She'd listened to him. And she hadn't look at him any differently.

The waves splashed over his feet, soaking the bottom of his jeans. He walked and walked until the lights of the hotel almost disappeared behind him. He thought maybe some distance between them would help. Maybe it would dampen his desire. But with each step, he realized it wasn't working. It was making it worse. He wanted to be with her. That was a frightening admission.

He stopped and looked out across the dark sea. One step at a time, he told himself. That was the first step, sharing his horrible past. And she hadn't run. Could he do this? Really try for something more than a fling? This was the first time he'd even entertained the idea.

He stared up at the moon for a long time. Then he turned and jogged back to the bungalow. Going back was another step . . . a step he'd never taken before.

He burst through the door. She sat up in bed and held out a hand for him. He quickly crossed the room to her and buried his face in her hair.

Neither of them said a word the rest of the night as they fell asleep in each other's arms. When he woke in the morning, it was with a feeling of contentment he'd never known.

TEAGUE CLEARED HIS schedule for the day so they could do all the touristy stuff on the island he always thought he was too good for. It had been fun rediscovering it all with Kate. A pod of dolphins had sailed through the air near them when they'd gone snorkeling. Then they'd taken surfing lessons together, and she'd absolutely kicked his butt and teased him about it for hours. And now they were riding horses along the beach. She'd even convinced him to go to a luau the next day—something he swore he'd never do. He'd blown off numerous parties and premieres the past two days. He felt like a regular guy, not a superstar. She brought out something in him he didn't even know was there.

Perched on top of the horse, she leaned forward to stroke its mane. The horse tossed its head in response. "Do I have to come to this thing tonight?"

He couldn't skip them all. "June's gonna skin me alive if I keep missing all the premieres, no matter how much you pout." Teague smiled at her.

She looked over and stuck out her bottom lip, laughing as the horses trotted along. He stared at her beautiful smile and realized she hadn't worn any makeup. He'd never dated a woman who didn't put on full makeup before they went anywhere, considering himself lucky if they didn't wear false eyelashes. Finding one of those in bed the next day is a frightening thing.

"I doubt she could do that much damage," Kate said.

He lowered his sunglasses and looked at her. "If you don't come willingly, I'll toss you over my shoulder and carry you there myself."

"Hmm. Sounds interesting, but I don't think so." She nudged her horse with her heels and galloped ahead of him, her hair whipping in the wind.

Teague leaned into his horse and caught up to her. "Beat me to that ledge up ahead and you can stay in the room tonight, all by your lonesome. Let's see how good your stunts really are."

"You are so on." Kate's eyes at first widened, then narrowed with determination as she leaned forward and urged her horse on. The animals were reluctant to do more than trot, but she was relentless. Kicking her heels against the horse, she pushed her mare for more speed.

Her horse tore ahead of his and he laughed to himself, knowing how thrilled Kate would be to win and skip the premiere. Then he watched in horror as the big gray beast stumbled in a hole, then landed on its side. Kate went flying and hit her head on a huge rock sticking up from the sand. Heart thundering, Teague jumped off his horse and ran to her. "Kate?"

Her eyes were closed, her body limp. "Kate!" Kneeling beside her, he felt for a pulse. It was light and slow, but she didn't respond to his touch. He squeezed her hand. "Kate!" His stomach dropped and his mouth went dry. The air was sucked out of his lungs. She looked like a doll someone had dropped from the sky. Terror shot through him.

Scanning the beach, he realized they were alone, far from the hotels in the distance. Her horse stood up, shook itself off, and trotted back toward the stable while his horse followed. He fumbled for his phone in his pocket and called 911. "My girlfriend fell off a horse. We're on the beach. Somewhere near Napili."

"Sir, we're sending an ambulance in that direction."

"I'll meet you at the road."

Hanging up, he looked down at Kate. He couldn't leave her here. What if she came to and was disoriented? Hoping that he was doing the right thing, he scooped Kate up, and headed for the road to meet the ambulance.

His feet sank into the sand as he tried to run and he swore under his breath at the fact that he couldn't move faster. He kept glancing down at her. "Kate?" No response.

He almost stumbled, but holding her tighter, he finally made it to the road, his chest heaving and his heart pounding. He willed his wobbly legs not to buckle.

He stood at the edge of the pavement, clutching her against him. Her head lolled over his arm. Cars slowed, drivers craning their necks to watch them. He struggled to catch his breath.

He looked down at her pale face. "Kate, you're going to be alright." It was more like he was trying to convince himself. He kissed her forehead and felt her soft breath on his neck. *Hurry up, already!*

In the distance, he heard the blare of an ambulance. He ran towards it, past the slowed cars and gawking bystanders. Kate felt like nothing in his arms. If he had to, he'd run for hours until he got her help. The ambulance pulled off to the side of the road before Teague stopped.

"She fell off a horse," he gasped. "She's unconscious."

The medic hopped out and frowned. "You should've left her there. You don't want to move someone with possible spinal injuries."

Panic surged in his chest. "I wasn't sure what to do. I had to get her help as fast as I could."

The EMT opened the back doors and rolled out the gurney. Teague laid her on the stretcher.

"We've got her from here."

"No, I'm coming with her." He climbed into the ambulance and prayed the entire way to the hospital. *Please don't take this woman from me.*

Chapter 15

"IS SHE GOING TO be okay?" Mitch asked the doctor while squeezing Dina's hand.

"Just Braxton-Hicks contractions. Nothing serious, but we don't want it to progress to anything worse. She shouldn't be on her feet too much." The doctor looked directly at Dina. "You're going to have to give up that waitressing job of yours."

She felt her eyes pop open. "But I'm not due for six weeks. I need the money."

"It's for the sake of your baby." The doctor scribbled on the chart. "I'm going to recommend bed rest until the baby comes. Do you have anyone who can take care of you?"

Dina's mouth opened and closed as she considered the question, realizing that no, she didn't have anyone who could give her that kind of care.

"She's got me." Mitch smiled down at her while Dina wiped a tear off her cheek.

"Good. We don't want this baby coming early."

HOW MANY PINA coladas did I have last night? Kate woke with a fuzzy feeling in her head and an even fuzzier feeling in her mouth. Her eyes opened to a bright, white room. *This isn't the bungalow.* Damn! It'd been a dream. Only, there was Teague, eyes wide, his cheeks stubbled with whiskers, his eyes bloodshot. Then she remembered. The horse. She fell off. An equestrian, she was not.

He rushed over to the bed. "You're okay. Nothing's broken. Doctors say you have one hell of a concussion." He stroked her hair and held her hand, and Kate wondered if maybe he hadn't been hit on the noggin, too.

She sat up and winced; sitting up wasn't such a good thing. "June's going to kill you. We missed the premiere."

He laughed. "Baby, we don't have to go to the next one, I promise."

Baby? She needed to lie back down. She set her head on the pillow and looked around the depressing room, at all the sterile medical bedding, the bland walls, and thought, *I'm not wasting a minute of my time in here.* "When do I get out of here? Nurses do not make good patients."

"Doctors want to watch you for another twenty-four hours." He squeezed her hand. "And so do I. I'm not leaving you."

She sighed. "I'm so sorry. What a way to spend our time here."

"You're sorry?" He pressed his hand against his chest. "I'm the one who challenged you to a race. It's my fault. Let me go get you something to drink."

He kissed her head, then slipped out of the room. Kate drew up her knees under the hideous green hospital gown. She couldn't believe Teague was here, waiting on her. He seemed genuinely concerned.

He rushed back in with a can of soda, a glass of ice chips, a pitcher of water, and the nurse on his tail. "You're awake now. Good," she said. "We need to have the doctor check you out."

By the end of the day, Kate figured she'd seen nearly every staff member from the hospital. Some brought copies of USA Today and gossip magazines, asking for Teague's autograph and sometimes, even Kate's.

One of the nurses from the maternity ward wandered over, clutching the local paper to her chest. She sighed. "It is so romantic the way you carried her to safety like that. I saw a clip of it someone took on their cell phone. It's on You Tube and all over the 'Net. Oh. My. God. It was like a romantic movie or something." She fanned herself and handed Kate her paper. "Can you sign this?"

Kate stared at the picture of Teague walking down the side of the road with her in his arms. Her insides did a trembling flip-flop.

The next morning, the doctor finally cleared out the room and examined Kate from head to toe. "I think you're clear to go. Take it easy, we don't want another head injury. Don't do anything foolish."

A little late for that, buddy. She was nothing *but* foolish.

TEAGUE HELD HER by the elbow as he walked her down the path to the bungalow. His heart had been caught in his throat until the doctor gave Kate the all clear. He wanted to whisk her back to L.A., back to the safety of his home, but the doctor thought it was best to give her a few more days' rest.

Kate gently dislodged her arm from his grip. "I'm not an invalid."

"I just don't want you to trip or anything. I'm not leaving your sight. We're hunkering down in the bungalow for the rest of the festival." He unlocked the door and held it open for her.

She stepped inside. "What about your meeting with Stan Remington?"

He groaned. "I can put it off."

She turned to give him a look. "I'm not a Hollywood insider, but I know it's an important meeting. You can't miss it. Not on my account."

"Shhh." He picked her up and laid her on the bed, and she slipped off her shoes and stretched out like a cat.

She looked up at him. "I could use your assistance here," she practically purred.

He rubbed his hands together, ready to serve. "What? Can I get you anything?"

"You can get in bed with me." She patted the huge mattress.

He shook his head and took a step back, bumping into one of the tables. He straightened the bowl of fruit on top. "No way. I'm not going to do anything that could hurt you."

Sighing, she lowered her head back onto the pillow. "Trust me, you might blow my mind, but you're not going to actually hurt my head."

"No." He felt several different body parts strongly objecting to that decision.

"Please?" She parted her lips and widened her eyes. There must be some secret female manipulation class he didn't know about. Kate had mastered it.

He lowered himself on shaky legs. "I am going to sit on the couch where we'll be nice and safe." But Teague wasn't. No, he might as well be swimming with sharks out in Kapalua Bay with a *"Come bite me"* sign hanging around his neck—written in blood. He'd only known her for a week, but Teague was falling in love with Kate Riley.

There, he'd admitted it. Coming so close to losing her cemented the deal. To put a cap on the whole thing, June had called earlier and read him the riot act for looking so darn romantic in all the pictures. Damn the entire free world and their cell phone cameras.

"You look positively in love. What were you thinking?" June had asked him. "Do you know they're calling you T-Wrecked now?"

"Calm down, June. This won't change a thing." He'd actually hung up on her. And turned off his cell.

Kate's sweet, clear voice pulled him back to the present. "Are you really going to stay over there all night?" She twirled her hair around her finger and pouted, then hopped off the bed and sauntered over to him.

Teague closed his eyes. "Stay in bed, Kate."

"I will if you come join me."

He sighed. "Fine. But we're just going to talk. That's all."

"Good. We can talk while we do it." Kate bounced back on the bed, and Teague sighed.

Who knew head injuries could make a woman horny? "Be careful."

"Too late for that."

Wasn't that the truth? He laced his fingers in hers and wondered if he could actually keep his hands off the rest of her. He was a knot of emotions: relieved that she was all right, angry that it happened in the first place, desperate to sear his flesh with hers.

"Please humor me. If anything else happened to you . . ."

She groaned and plopped back on the bed. "Fine. Rock paper scissors? Truth or dare? I seem to remember you being pretty good at twenty questions."

Oh, he had so many things he wanted to ask her. He snuggled up next to her and put his arm around her. He kissed her head and got the rundown of her life: from the prize-winning Halloween costume in fifth grade, to the little collie dog that ran away when she was seven, to the sadness of watching her mother's marriage dissolve.

They spent the night without removing a stitch of clothing. And that's when Teague knew. He really *was* in love.

Damn.

"I DIDN'T KNOW if you wanted grilled cheese or peanut butter and jelly, so I made both." Mitch stood in Dina's doorway, holding a plate in each hand.

Dina sat up. "I'll eat both. I'm starving."

Mitch set the plates on the table next to her and wiped his hands on his pants. "Is there anything else you need before I go to work?"

"You're leaving?" Dina's eyes widened. "What if something happens? What if I have those pains again?"

He sat on the bed next to her. "Then you call me or you call the doctor."

She grabbed Mitch's hand. "I'm scared." And she was—about having the baby, about losing the baby. About losing him.

He patted her hand. "Me, too. But we'll get through this. Together."

"Together?" She nibbled on her bottom lip. "Really?"

He nodded. "I told Shelley everything and broke up with her."

Dina gasped, then covered her mouth with her hand.

"What?" Mitch asked. "Is it the baby?"

"Yes," she lied. She wasn't exactly certain why her stomach had turned upside down at his news. Was it a good upside down or a bad upside down?

Chapter 16

STARING AT THE CLOSET of designer clothes that still seemed far too flashy for a gal most comfortable in old jeans, Kate sighed. She did not want to go to this party. She wanted to stay in with Teague, clothing optional. An A-list party held the same appeal as a trip to the dentist; and old Doc Miller wasn't so handy with the drill anymore.

"What do I wear to a meeting with Hollywood's hottest director so I don't ruin your action-hero career—if I haven't already?"

Teague laughed. "That's not going to happen. But wear a nice dress. Anything will be perfect on you." He was dressed in linen pants and a jacket, looking like perfection—as usual.

Kate piled her hair in an easy twist on her head and put on a long, slinky sundress. Hopefully, he'd be the only one looking at her.

His fingers slipped under the straps. "Just figuring out the terrain so I can take it off easier later."

She wrapped her arms around his waist. "You're finally confident that I won't break?"

She meant her body, not her heart, because that was sure to break when this whole thing ended. On top of the head injury, her emotions were suffering from a major case of denial. Kate was falling for him. There, she said it. Maybe it was some reverse Florence-Nightingale-nurse thing, but the way he'd been taking care of her cleaved her heart in two.

He pulled her closer for a kiss. "I don't know if you'll break or not, but I'm going to be very slow . . . very careful . . ." He growled those last few words and she laughed. They held hands as they walked through the resort, under the canopy of palm trees to the waiting limo.

STAN REMINGTON'S PARTY was at his home on a hill overlooking Kapalua Bay. The place was packed with people, most of whom took special notice of Kate, some even gesturing or jerking their chins in her direction as they pointed her out to friends.

"I'm going outside," she said, rubbing her arms, wishing she was a chameleon that could press itself against a stucco wall and disappear.

"I'll get us drinks and be right out."

"No, take your time. Do what you need to do with Remington."

He gazed into her eyes and set his hand on her lower back, then looked over at Stan with a sigh. His shoulders slumped, having to make a decision between the two of them.

"Go," she whispered, slipping her hand from his and ducking outside to make it easier on him.

She snagged a couple of coconut shrimps from a passing waiter and found a seat, mesmerized by the waterfall pouring out of a hot tub into the pool. Spotting an empty tennis court off to the side of the house, she considered hiding out there. Instead, she took off her sandals and dipped her toes in the warm water.

What was she doing in this bizarre, make-believe world? She was desperate to get away from these fake people. That's what she had thought about Teague at first. But he'd surprised her. He was wonderful, and some woman would be very lucky to have him on day, if he ever brought his heart out from its shell. She'd been so wrong when she first met him, believing he was anything like Tommy or George.

She frowned. Where had George gone? She hadn't heard from him since he'd shown up at the bungalow. Teague had promised he'd be leaving them alone, but who knew what kind of trouble he was getting into? Thank goodness Dina was texting her so Kate knew she and the baby were alright.

She sensed someone approaching her and turned around, hoping it was Teague. Wrong answer. It was his publicist, June, probably coming to drown her.

She smiled at Kate and took a seat next to her. "I'm

surprised to see you here. I thought Teague was coming solo."

Kate shrugged. "I said I didn't mind staying behind, but he insisted I come. He's been fretting like an old lady ever since the accident."

June leaned toward Kate and wrapped her fingers around her forearm. "I don't know what's going on with you two, but if you really care about him, you need to leave. Stan Remington is now considering a few other actors for this upcoming role. Because of you."

Kate opened her mouth to say something—she wasn't sure what—but didn't get the chance.

June released her arm and pointed a finger at her. "This was going to be a career maker for Teague, and he's very close to losing it because of you and this stupid romance. Remington is very aware of what goes on the press. He likes bad boys and wild partiers to take on his roles. People who will get him press, someone who lives up to the role in real life. Everyone's saying Teague's whipped. And that's not good for his reputation. We've worked too hard to get him where he is. You're ruining him. End this."

Kate's throat was hot with rage. "Shouldn't Teague get a say in this?" She could barely get the words out.

June twisted her thin lips. "He never knows what's best for him. That's why he hires people like me to make those decisions for him. The best thing you can do for him right now is to get on a plane tomorrow morning and go home. He needs to do something to reclaim his T-Rex reputation."

Kate wanted to argue—push her in the pool even—but there was a tiny voice inside whispering, *She might be right.*

June seemed encouraged by her silence. "You can take my limo back to the resort, pack up your stuff. I'll tell him you're leaving. He'll only try to stop you. If you care about him, trust me—this is what you need to do for him." She paused and her voice softened, if that was possible. "And you certainly must know that this relationship doesn't have much of a future. You know his track record. Save yourself some hurt and get out now."

Kate wished she felt more upset by her suggestion. Instead, she felt resigned.

June reached into her purse and pulled out an envelope. She flipped opened the top, revealing a stash of cash. "I've got an incentive for you to take me up on my offer."

Fortunately, the people mingling and chatting outside didn't seem to notice the humiliating conversation. Kate pushed her hand away. "I'm not taking your money to leave Teague." She stood up and shoved her feet back in her sandals. Crossing her arms, she stared across the pool at a neglected palmetto tree tucked in the corner. Everything dies, just like this foolish game they'd been playing. She knew it'd been coming, and here it was.

That's when she realized the truth of it all. Teague wasn't like George. *She* was. Pulling Teague down, ruining his life, just like George had messed things up for her mother. Things would have been so much better for everyone if George had just left them years ago.

Like I'm going to do now.

She wasn't going to be the reason Teague didn't get where he wanted to be in his career. She loved him and wouldn't hurt him like that. Beyond the money he'd offered her, she had no reason to stay. She'd promised him a month; certainly he wouldn't pay her if she left now. But twenty thousand dollars wasn't worth ruining things for a man she loved. How could she ever enjoy living in Mama's house, knowing the deal had cost him his career?

She hoped the few days they spent together had been enough of a distraction to keep his secret safe back in Willowdale, whatever it was. But now she needed another diversion to draw attention away from her so she could slink back into her quiet little life. And once again, she was going to do what she had to do to make things right.

She sighed and looked over at June, who was still clutching the cash. "Put the money away. I'll go on my own. Tell him I had an emergency at home, and I can't take the Hollywood fast lane. Tell him it's over. Tell him he's better off without me."

For the first time, Kate saw a smile from June, who patted

her knee. "Good girl."

KATE STUMBLED OUT of the limo and lingered in the lobby. She knew what she had to do, but she had to rustle up the courage first. Hard to do when your knees are knocking. She straightened her shoulders and told herself this was for Teague's good—and her own.

She got on the elevator and pressed the button for the 27th floor. She rang the doorbell for the suite and stood there long enough that she assumed Simone was out. But the door opened as she was walking away.

"Hello?"

Kate spun around, stunned again by how beautiful Simone was with her halo of curly, golden hair and perfect petite body. *Life sure ain't fair.* "Hey, Simone. It's Kate Riley. Teague's . . . girlfriend. Well, not anymore." She fiddled with the strap of her dress. "Listen, we had a falling out, and I thought maybe it wasn't too late for the two of you. He's at Stan Remington's party. I'm sure you're welcome to go."

Simone tilted her head. "Are you shitting me?"

Kate shook her head and clutched her purse in front of her. "This is all too much for me. Teague's a great guy, but I'm not cut out to be his girlfriend."

Simone shrugged. "Thanks for the heads-up. I'm going to freshen up and head over to that party."

KATE GRABBED HER suitcase, giving the room a second glance to make sure she didn't leave anything there except for a piece of her heart. She snapped her gaze away from the big, beautiful bed where she and Teague had shared . . . what *had* they shared, really? A good time, and that was it. It would have to be enough. She was opening the door to leave when her ring clinked against the doorknob. She took it off and left it on the bedside table, along with a note that said, "Thanks, Eugene. Best job I ever had."

TEAGUE SCANNED THE crowded room for Kate. He'd been so busy with Stan he hadn't had a moment for her. He spotted June and waved her over. "Where's Kate?"

"She went back to the room, wasn't feeling well. But she told me to make sure you stayed here," she said.

Teague nodded and went back to the little group Remington was entertaining. The two of them shot some pool and downed martinis as the party thinned out. He was smart enough to let the old man win a few rounds. Once the room cleared, they settled on a big, white leather couch and started talking shop.

"You're here alone?" Remington asked, stretching his arm along the back of the couch.

Teague shrugged. "It appears that way, yes."

Creases etched the tanned skin around his eyes. "Good, good. So you've heard about my next project?" His voice was slow and deliberate, just like someone would use to command a room. The doorbell rang and Remington scrunched his bushy white eyebrows together. "Hold that thought."

Teague crossed one leg over his knee and bounced his foot, waiting for Remington to return. He hadn't realized how much he really did want this role. Even though Hollywood had been an escape from his personal hell, he did enjoy the work. Loved it, in fact. This movie could land his name among the big time action stars: Diesel, Willis, Schwarzenegger. He couldn't wait to tell Kate about it.

Remington sported a big smile as he walked back from the door, someone trailing behind him. "Teague, I think you know Simone Peters, right?"

Chapter 17

"TABLE SIX IS READY to kill me. How long till that chicken parmesan is finished?" Kate tucked her hair behind her ears and glared at the cook behind the steam table.

He swiped his sweaty forehead with the back of his hand. "Cool it, Hollywood. It's ready." The cook slid two plates toward her, his chubby cheeks red from the heat. "How's Dina?"

She set the plates on her tray. "Scared. Being alone on bed rest isn't what most girls do the summer before they're supposed to start college." Kate still hadn't been able to forgive herself for being away while Dina was going through complications with her pregnancy. *I never should have left.*

He nodded. "Guess that worked out good for you, taking over for her here. Sorry to hear you lost your job at the school. But Sam's thrilled to have you back. Says business has doubled since you started waiting tables."

Kate shrugged. "Glad someone's happy."

She set the tray on her shoulder and pushed her way through the swinging doors, ducking out of the path of another waitress. The owner might be happy with her, but the rest of the staff resented all the attention she was getting. *Bunch of surly toddlers.* She sighed. No matter. Just one more problem to deal with. She'd come home and found a registered letter from the school district informing her she'd been let go from her position as middle school nurse because of "inappropriate behavior detrimental to the students." Someone had snapped a few shots of them frolicking under the waterfall that day.

Well, she had said she wanted a picture of it. At least it hadn't been a topless photo. She blushed as she remembered the view of her bikini top floating in the current.

Everything had gone wrong since she'd left Teague in Hawaii two weeks earlier. George had called to say he wasn't going to be back home for a few months, that he was trying to break into Hollywood as an actor, the fool. Turns out, Teague had introduced him to his publicist, June. Then, she found Dina on bed rest. Worst of all, she missed Teague. It seemed like they had tucked in months of a relationship during that time, even though it had only been a week.

She had to remind herself the whole thing hadn't been a dream. And she had to remember it meant a whole lot more to her than it did to Teague. She'd seen a few clips on TV that he'd already moved on to Simone. She'd cried herself to sleep that night and then reminded herself who she'd been dealing with: Teague Reynolds. The man who admitted to her he could never love anyone.

He'd had his fill and moved on. That's how the tabloids told the story. So much for Kate being the one to break things off like he'd promised. She'd endured more pitying looks than she could stand since she'd been home. She thought about wearing a t-shirt around town that read, "I'm fine. Really."

Kate dropped off the plates at table six. "Is there anything else I can get you folks?" She smoothed her hands down the red, flowered dress with the big, puffy white sleeves, aware of how ridiculous a grown woman looked in this costume.

The woman paused for a moment and then looked up at Kate, wrinkling her nose in curiosity. "What's Teague Reynolds really like?"

Her husband set down his fork and rolled his eyes.

Kate forced a big grin. "He's exactly like the magazines say." She walked behind the hostess station and slumped against the wall. This was some sort of karmic payback. One week in paradise with a guy like Teague certainly came with an awful big price tag.

After allowing herself five minutes to grumble, she stood up, brushed off her apron and poured drinks for the table of four in the corner. Because that's what her mother always did, no matter what had gone wrong. You brush yourself off and move on. And Kate had plenty to move on from.

TEAGUE GLANCED OUT the window at Stan Remington's office. He was about to sign a contract that would change his life. This was what he had been working toward with each calculated move to take the right role, to date the right girl. But it didn't feel as good as he'd imagined. Kate had already changed his life. But then she'd left him, and he certainly couldn't blame her. Her life had been nothing but trouble once he'd shown up in town. Her stepfather had skipped out, the press was on their tail, she'd been injured. Anyone would've run.

When June told him that Kate had said he was no good for her, he silently agreed. She was right to leave him. He laughed softly to himself. He did tell her to go ahead and break his heart. He never imagined it could happen.

"Just sign the last two pages and we've got a deal." Remington tapped his pen on the contract spread out on his big Brazilian cherry wood desk.

Teague scrawled his name on the dotted lines while his agent sat smiling behind them. He had about two months to resolve things with Jennifer and the baby. His nephew. His only real family. What was he going to do with a newborn? If Stan Remington thought Kate was bad for his press, what would a drooling, cooing child do for his image?

Worry about that later.

Remington pumped Teague's hand and clapped his back. "Welcome to the majors, kid. You're gonna be a big star."

THE HOSTESS PEEKED behind the partition. "Kate, got a new table in your section."

"Be right out." She straightened her apron and tried to force a smile. No luck. She just couldn't do it. Grabbing her order pad, she headed back to her section. Her sturdy, white nurse shoes stopped in their tracks. *Shoot.* What did Mama always say? *Don't complain, 'cause things could always be worse?* And something worse had just parked its butt at one of her tables.

She gritted her teeth and took her time walking over. "Afternoon, Chief Larsen." She hadn't seen him since getting back to town. They'd managed to stay friends all these years after the breakup—she'd even urged Tonya to go out with him. But that rat had called the tabloids on her and Teague.

He beamed at her. "Hi, there, Katie. Got all of that Hawaii sand out of your hair yet? I saw some of the pictures and I must say—"

Kate cut him off. "Our specials today are the eggplant parmesan or our four-cheese ravioli. Can I start you off with a drink?"

He patted the seat beside him. "Care to join me?"

She wouldn't look at him. "Absolutely not."

"Oh, now that you've had a taste of the glamorous life, you're too good for the little folk in Willowdale?"

She tapped her pen on the order pad, biting back all the vile things she wanted to say. None of this would have happened if he hadn't tipped off the press. "What can I get you to drink?"

"A cola would be fine, and I'll try those raviolis."

She took his order and sent his drink out with the busboy. What was he doing in here, in her section? Tommy was definitely a Jelly Jar diner kind of guy.

Someone had left that week's *People* behind the hostess station, just to annoy her, no doubt. It was open to a page with Teague and Simone strolling down a beach. A beach very similar to the one she and Teague had walked along. She tossed the magazine in the garbage and totaled up the check for table six. She ignored Tommy as she dropped it off and went back to get his food.

She held the plate of raviolis on her tray, hoping he'd burn his tongue. "Here we are," she said grabbing the plate off her tray.

"Guess who I saw in town today?"

She pressed her eyes shut. "I don't care who you saw in town today."

"Ah, I was wrong, then. I thought you might be interested to know I saw Teague Reynolds over at the park."

Kate's eyes popped open and she froze. "You're a liar," she said through her teeth, holding the plate midair.

Tommy chewed on a toothpick and shrugged. "You could ask the woman he was with. Although she was in a delicate condition. Might not want to upset a pregnant gal."

She stared at him, waiting for him to say he was kidding. But he didn't. He shrugged. "Just reporting the facts."

She shook her head and closed her eyes. So that was his secret. A baby. First Tommy and now Teague had gotten someone pregnant? No. Years of hurt coursed through her veins like rain in a bloated river. Years of saying, "No, no it's alright. Tommy did the right thing. I'm just fine." She opened her eyes and saw Tommy's smirk.

A shot of pain whomped her square in the chest. She lowered the plate and dumped the raviolis on his lap. "Careful, darlin', they're hot."

He jumped up, brushing them off and shrieking more like a little girl than a big, beefy cop.

"Oops. Sorry, maybe this will cool you off." Kate poured the rest of the soda on his lap. "If you're so sure you saw Teague Reynolds, maybe you should call the press again. I know what good friends you are with the media in Asheville. Hope they rewarded you well for the big scoop."

Tommy brushed at his pants. "I didn't call anyone! I told you I wouldn't, and I didn't. Just thought you'd like to know the truth about your big-time boyfriend is all. And look how you thank me."

She tossed her tray on the hostess station and took off her apron.

Sam, the owner, ran out from the kitchen. He hurried over to Tommy, dabbing at his pants with a kitchen towel, while hollering at the bus boys to bring a mop. "What's gotten into you, Kate? Don't bother coming back. I don't care who you dated in Hollywood. We don't treat our customers like that here at Scalia's. You're fired."

"God bless America," Kate said, walking out the door. Didn't matter if she lost her silly waitressing job. She was done in this town and had no idea what to do next. She looked up and down Main Street, chewing her bottom lip. She should really call Tonya or Jeanne for some chocolate therapy, but she was too stunned at the moment.

After walking in circles for a few moments, she leaned up against the building and started hyperventilating. Tommy was lying, right? But Teague did have a secret he was hiding in Willowdale. A pregnant mistress certainly was something for a guy like him to hide. She slid down to the ground and tucked her head between her knees, trying to breathe.

She told herself she was going to drive straight home and forget about Tommy's wild accusations. But of course, once she gathered her composure she drove toward the park. She slowed down and passed the kids' playground, packed with children flying on the swings, mothers worrying after the little tots running around. She was congratulating herself for being right about Tommy lying, when she spotted a couple tucked back in the park on a bench under a tree.

Yep, T-Rex himself with his arm around a young woman. He smiled at her, and she laughed at whatever he was saying. She was beautiful, with wavy, dark hair, and long, elegant fingers laced over her big baby belly.

Kate's own stomach threatened to hurl its contents. She sped off, wondering who she was more ticked at: Teague, for being there; or Tommy, for being right.

TEAGUE WALKED JENNIFER back to her room at the Willowdale Residential Treatment Center and Living Facility and stopped in at the director's office. He sank into a leather chair and dropped his head in his hands. "What do you think we should do about this?"

Jane Johnson took off her glasses and rubbed her eyes. "Mr. Reynolds, Jennifer understands she is having a baby and seems quite happy about it."

He swallowed hard, hating what he was going to say. "With her . . . condition, can she even take care of the baby? She can't even take care of herself."

She shook her head and smoothed her hand across her legal pad. "No, she can't. I have to admit, this is a new one for us. We're figuring this out as we go. What would you like to see happen? You have a role in this, too. You're the child's uncle."

He looked out the window behind her, lost in thought. An uncle. Finally, he had an actual link to his biological family. Too bad he had no idea how to deal with this. "I just don't know what to do." He pulled a wad of cash from his wallet it and slid it across her desk. "Make sure she has everything she needs. Including privacy. I appreciate your discretion so far. The press cannot know about this." Money. That was all he had to offer. He was useless.

She held up her hands. "Trust me, I know. Look what happened to poor Kate Riley for being linked with you. Who knows what it would do to Jennifer?"

His hand froze over the woman's desk. "What are you talking about?"

She closed the file and looked up, surprised. "Kate lost her job at the school because of racy photos of you two in all those magazines." She shrugged. "The school district figured it wasn't appropriate for her to keep working with the middle-school students after . . ." She waved her hand in the air looking for the right word.

He tugged his hand through his hair. Damn. He'd been nothing but trouble for her. Whether he was two or thirty-two, Teague was nothing but a burden and bad luck to the people around him.

He pushed up out of the chair. "Thank you, Miss Johnson."

He had to find her. He had to apologize, to ask for a second chance. He'd been miserable without her. He knew why she'd left, of course. Which is why he shouldn't have gotten close to her in the first place. But he had, damn it, and he wanted more. Maybe he could make it right and take care of her now that she didn't have a job. Maybe Kate really did need him, after all.

He stopped at the reception desk and asked to borrow the phone book. His movie scripts were thicker than the little volume of numbers for Willowdale. The number and address for Kate's stepfather were listed and he jotted them down. He settled behind the seat of the new car he'd bought specifically for driving to Willowdale so he wouldn't raise suspicions taking a cab. He'd never be willing to ask a stranger for a ride again.

Teague called Kate but it went straight to voice mail. He didn't leave a message. What the hell had she been through since their breakup hit the tabloids? Of course, the truth never hit the papers. No, the press didn't know that Kate had been the one to leave. Instead, it showed him back together with Simone, which wasn't right either. What he thought were going to be test shots for the movie were being billed as a romantic reunion, with poor Kate left in the dust.

Teague drove away from the residential center, wishing he had the perfect character he could pull out of his acting bank to smooth things over with Kate. But he was too nervous to be anyone but himself.

KATE JUST KEPT DRIVING, unsure where she'd end up. She laughed in a not-funny-at-all way, thinking how she'd felt the same way when she'd first picked up Teague a few weeks back, having no idea where they were going. Maybe that's why she found herself pulling into the same diner where they'd shared lunch.

The bells on the door at the Kissin' Counsins chimed as she pushed her way in, but the place was just as empty as it had been when she'd brought Teague here. She sat in the same booth they'd shared, wondering why she was torturing herself.

If only she would've told Teague, *No, you can't have a damn ride.* She sighed and looked out the window. Would she really give up the week they had together?

No. It had all ended messier than a frog in a blender, of course, but those moments when she felt like they were really together, like he had really cared? Nothing would ever match that. Not many people ever get to experience something like that; she'd been lucky to have it for a sliver of time. It hadn't been love on his part, she knew that, but it had been something special.

"Can I get you something, darlin'?"

Kate looked up to see Delores.

Her smile fell. She stuck a pencil behind her ear. "Oh, hi there, 'hon. How you doing since all that Hollywood fallout?"

Kate tried to put on a brave face, but her fake smile crumbled and her lip quivered.

Delores pushed in to sit next to her and patted her hand. "There, there. It's gonna be alright."

Kate could only shake her head, no.

"Listen, sugar. I saw the two of you here that day, and I know sparks when I see 'em. You had something, and it'll come back if it's meant to."

Kate thought about Teague and the woman in the park. "I don't think so."

Delores was quiet for a moment. "I feel somewhat responsible for this."

"What do you mean?"

She fiddled with silverware on the table, straightening it just so. "It was me that called the press that day you were here."

"What?" Had she heard her correctly?

Delores let out a big sigh. "My niece is a reporter in Asheville. I knew it was a scoop seeing a big star like Teague Reynolds in town. I asked her who might pay for information like that." She looked down at her shoes. "My diner has been struggling for some time. I couldn't lose it. Not after so many years."

Kind of like how Kate wasn't willing to lose her mama's house. Kate knew desperation. She sat there with her mouth open, not sure if she should laugh or cry. "Seriously? It was you?"

Delores nodded, looking a bit sheepish.

Dang, she owed Tommy a super-sized apology. But what if Delores hadn't called? Kate never would have gotten on that plane with Teague. She never would have been in his arms . . . in his bed . . . "It's okay, Delores. I only hope they paid you well."

Her eyes brightened. "Oh, they did. Five thousand dollars. It'll keep me going for a bit longer. And after that?" She shrugged. "What I wouldn't do to have some of those pieces back your mama bought from me."

"What are you talking about?"

"She bought some valuable Depression glass from me. Well, wasn't so valuable at the time, but it's skyrocketed since. Do you still have it all?"

"I don't know. I think so."

"I'd love to take a look sometime."

"Stop over whenever you'd like." *I've got nothing planned—for the rest of my life.*

Chapter 18

KATE CALLED JEANNE and Tonya and told them to double-time it to her house. She must've sounded hysterical on the phone because they both peeled in her driveway moments after she got home.

After pouring some sweet tea, Kate gave them the scoop. They sat next to her on the couch, each holding one of her hands as she sniffled her way through the latest developments.

Tonya frowned. "I liked this story better when Tommy was the bad guy."

"A lapful of pasta is pretty funny, though," Jeanne said.

Kate started laughing, then crying, then hiccupping.

Once she stopped her blubbering, Tonya got a devious look on her face. "You know, you could make some money yourself and tip off the press that he's got a pregnant girlfriend in town."

"And look like even more of a fool?" Kate shook her head. "Besides, you know I'm not the vindictive type."

"Except for the raviolis," Jeanne pointed out.

"Damn girl, I didn't think you were the type to jet off with someone like T-Rex," Tonya said. "Calling the tabloids would pale in comparison."

Jeanne shrugged. "If Delores got $5,000 for her tip, imagine what you'd get? It sure would help with the bills now that you've been fired from two jobs."

Kate blew out a long breath. "Tempting." But she didn't want to be the latest person to betray Teague's trust. He'd said he couldn't trust anyone. Kate wanted to prove him wrong on that.

After a few more tears, the girls scooted off home, and Kate crawled into bed. But she wasn't there long before she heard Dina grumbling that she was hungry.

"I don't even have time for a dang pity party," Kate mumbled to herself, shuffling downstairs to make dinner.

After asking Dina what she wanted to eat—much like a waitress, Kate noted—she was soon stirring spaghetti on the stove. Just the thought of Italian made her stomach churn after what happened at Scalia's, but you don't say no to a grumpy, pregnant teen. The doorbell rang and she seriously considered running back upstairs to hide under the bed. *What now?*

She wiped her hands on a towel, took a deep breath, and opened the door. Tottering back a step, she tried to swallow. *Breathe, breathe, breathe.* But she couldn't. She pointed a finger at Teague. "I don't know want to know what you're doing in town. I just want you to leave."

He braced himself against the door. "Kate, I'm sorry. About everything." He looked at her, his eyes searching hers for something—what?

She didn't care. Whatever he wanted from her, he wasn't going to get it. "I said leave. I don't want you here."

He nodded. "Okay. I understand." Clearing his throat, he stared at the ground. "I've got something for you." He reached in his pocket and handed her a cashier's check.

She took a step back, like the check might nip at her. "You don't owe me anything. I didn't even help you for a month like I promised."

He ignored her and pulled another check out of his pocket. "And here is your bonus. Your twenty thousand dollars for winning the bet. For not falling for me." His mouth turned down. Had he ever looked so sad?

Kate put the brakes on her sympathy and said nothing. She couldn't fess up how she really felt. Not now, knowing he'd had a pregnant lover all along here in Willowdale. How many times in her life would Kate Riley be played the fool? Never again, that was for sure. "I don't want you or your money."

Teague tucked the check in the mailbox mounted by her door. "You lost your job because of me. I owe you something for that."

She held up her hands. "I broke our agreement. I didn't stay

with you for a month. You don't owe me nothin'. It's over. Go."
She reached for the check and tore it into pieces and let it fall like
snowflakes at her feet. That money would've paid the bills for
quite a while. But she wasn't accepting pity payments, not today.
Not ever.

And certainly not from him.

Teague blew out a deep breath. "Okay. I just want to say
sorry for everything that's happened. I didn't think about the
long-term consequences. I shouldn't have put you in that
position just to save myself."

She raised her chin. "I was stupid. I should have known
better. You're T-Rex. I knew full well how this would end."

Teague stood there for a moment, then he nodded and
walked slowly down the porch steps.

Kate shut the door and slid down to the floor. Her heart
was pounding and tears stung her eyes. She was just one of many
women he'd been stringing along. Everything she thought she'd
felt for him hadn't been real. That pregnant woman in the park
was very real; along with his arm around her and the dreamy
smile on her face.

She knocked her head against the door, trying to knock
some sense into herself. If only she could forget him: the way
he'd kissed her, the gentle way he'd held her, the delirious way
he'd made love to her. She'd been dumber than dirt. She sat on
the floor, wallowing in her misery for a few minutes. She
deserved that much, at least.

A rap at the door jerked her heart out of place. Was he
coming back? She flung open the door and when she saw who
was standing there now, her stomach dropped, much like that
plate of raviolis back at the restaurant.

Tommy was wearing street clothes. His uniform was
probably already at Speedy Dry Clean. She wondered how he'd
explained the sauce stain. "You okay, Kate?"

She stepped back and crossed her arms. "You tell me. Are
you here to arrest me?"

He laughed and then tried to look stern. "I probably should,
but that'd be too embarrassing for me, bringing you in for

assaulting an officer with pasta. Dolly would never let me hear the end of that."

She balled up her fist and chewed on her thumb. "I apologize. I don't know what came over me." But she did, she knew exactly what had hit her.

Rocking back on his heels, his voice softened. "I could've been a little more sensitive, delivering news like that. Did you go and see for yourself?"

She nodded and looked away. She couldn't bear to see him relishing the moment. "Yes, I also found out you didn't tip off the press. A waitress at a diner a few towns over did. So, sorry about that, too." Kate shuffled her feet and kept her gaze on the ground. "Any idea who Teague was with?"

"No, I didn't recognize her. I could do some poking around if you'd like."

Kate shook her head. "It doesn't matter. So you were right. Are you happy? Is that why you came over? To gloat?"

He shook his head. "No, to make sure you're okay."

"I'm fine. Now if you don't mind, it's been one long and lousy day. I'm going to check on Dina and lie down."

He took a step wider and crossed his arms. "Well, that's also what I'm here about. The kids. What do you think we should do?"

"The kids?"

"Dina and Mitch."

Kate gripped the door. "Your little brother Mitch is the father?"

Tommy grabbed her arm, stepping a smidge to close to her. "You didn't know?"

"She wouldn't tell us." She pinched the bridge of her nose and worked it out in her head. Kate and Tommy would be linked forever by this child.

"He was staying here at the house with her while you were out in Hawaii. You didn't know that, either?"

Damn. What *did* she know? Kate knocked her head against the wall again. "You better come in."

KATE AND TOMMY sat across from Mitch and Dina, who were doing their best to not look at each other, like surly toddlers after a fight. "So who's going to explain what happened between the two of you?" Kate asked.

Dina rolled her eyes. "Geez, didn't Teague show you how that worked?"

Kate grumbled something under her breath and jumped when Tommy set his hand on her arm. She cleared her throat. "I mean, why aren't you two talking? You're about to be parents."

Dina tipped up her chin. "Mitch thinks we should get married."

Mitch crossed his arms, which were still a bit gangly. He wasn't a hulk of a man yet, like his brother, although he was getting there. "What a jerk I am, right?"

Dina turned to him, waving a finger. "But you don't really want to. Look what happened to Tommy when he left Kate. I'm not settling for that. I want someone who loves me."

"Leave us out of this," Tommy said sternly.

Dina ignored him. "You probably still like Shelley just like Tommy still loved Kate when he got married."

"Dina . . ." Kate warned.

"I left Shelley for you, Dina. I wouldn't have even gone out with her if I'd known." He ran his hand through his hair. "You and I were only going out for a month when you got pregnant, and we broke up before I even knew. Who could be in love after a month? I'm trying to do the right thing."

Kate had been in love after just a week. But that was all in the past.

"I told you to use a condom!" Dina shouted.

Tommy looked like he'd rather be in the middle of a cavity search—on the receiving end. "Let's keep those details to ourselves. How do you plan on supporting this child by yourself, Dina?"

Dina chewed on a fingernail. "I'll figure it out. Mitch'll owe me some child support, right? That'll help."

Kate reached over to pull Dina's hand away from her mouth, but Dina shooed her away.

Mitch planted his palms on his thighs. "Sure. I'll have tons of money to give you when I'm paying for college and making no money."

"Maybe you should get a job instead," Dina suggested.

He jumped up, knocking his chair over. "Maybe you shouldn't try to run my life."

Kate made a time-out sign with her hands. "Guys! You're already acting like you're married. You're never going to know if you really love each other if you're not even spending time together." She stood up and picked up Mitch's chair. "Don't make a decision yet. Pick up where you left off. See if you really do love each other."

Tommy nodded. "I can help you two out with some money if you want to move out, Mitch, and get an apartment so you two can be together with the baby. I want you two to give this a chance."

"They can stay here, Tommy. They're gonna need some help with the baby, and I'm not exactly busy right now," Kate said.

Dina looked at Kate. "I'm not getting married unless I'm in love." She shook her head and looked at Tommy. "Not like you and Ellen, Tommy, and not like my dad and Mama Margaret. Would you want that, Kate? Would you want to be like Mom and Dad? Aren't you glad you found out about Teague?"

Dina should've had just punched her in the gut. It wouldn't have hurt as much. But it was true, and she didn't want Dina repeating those mistakes. Kate didn't want to either, which is why she'd been smart, sending Teague away. He'd admitted to her once that he couldn't love anyone. And for all she knew, he had a full-fledged love affair going on with the mother of his child. What more convincing did she need? Clearly, she was a fool and a half when it came to matters of the heart.

Mitch rubbed Dina's shoulders and she sighed, leaning into him. "Okay, let's give this a try. But I'm not getting married unless we're in love, Mitch."

He wrapped his arm around her. "Okay."

Tommy clapped his hands. "Great. Why don't you kids plan

a date for this weekend, and pick up where you left off?"

"I'm on bed rest," Dina reminded him.

"That'll make it tough to spend quality time together," Tommy said, thinking.

"I like Kate's idea," Mitch said. "I'll move in—I'll sleep in the basement. I'll be here with you whenever I can."

"Sounds like a plan to me," Tommy shifted in his seat. "I mean, she's already pregnant. What more could happen? And maybe you'll fall in love, get married, and this thing will work itself out."

Kate looked at Mitch. He really was a great kid, good-looking, too. She laughed to herself. Four brothers in that family and each one of them handsome. And single, come to think of it. Just like his brothers, Mitch was tall and well built, with blue eyes that had certainly unnerved many a girl, just like Tommy's had. Though Tommy was the only one with the dirty-blond hair. Mitch's was dark brown like his other brothers with waves Tonya could never copy down at her salon. Any other girl probably would have jumped at his marriage proposal, especially with a baby on the way. Dina's indecision was a shocker.

Dina looked up at Mitch and squeezed his hand. "Okay. You can help get the baby's nursery ready. I was thinking a Noah's Ark theme? I saw the cutest decorations at Walmart." And she was off and planning, Mitch holding her close.

Kate let out a long, slow breath. Soon enough, there'd be three people in her old home to look after: two teens and a baby. It wasn't going to be easy. If only she could run off with Teague again. But she had responsibilities. Big-time responsibilities. It was her destiny. The jet-setting week she'd spent with Teague had been the stuff of make-believe. This was her real life and she needed to forget about her ridiculous happily-ever-after scenarios that kept nipping at the edges of her every thought. She had to help these kids make it all work out.

"And you can start with a romantic dinner right here Saturday night." Tommy offered. "Kate and I will get it all set up for you."

"We will?"

"Only you can do the cooking, and I'll be the waiter. We all know you were one lousy waitress."

TEAGUE IMMEDIATELY flew back to L.A. after leaving Kate. For days, he moped around his house and cancelled all his appointments. He figured a few drinks could help him forget her. He was wrong. June finally picked him up in her own car and dropped him off at the new hip bar of the moment to get him back on the scene. It was no surprise to find Simone there.

She sat on his lap in the VIP room of the bar, like an alley cat that just kept coming back no matter how many times you pushed it away, and it took everything in him not to toss her off and march out the front door. Her arms were looped around his neck, and three martinis had left her giggly and off-balance, so she kept slipping off his lap.

"Don't let me go, Teaguey. Not this time. Don't let me get away again." She hiccupped in his ear.

Teague detached himself from her grip and headed for the restroom. He needed a break from her and her cloying perfume, her forced, high-pitched laugh. Stan Remington had cast her in his next movie, too, and the director liked the idea of the two of them getting back together. Anything to keep buzz about the movie in the press. Teague had signed a ten-million-dollar contract for the role and filming would be starting in Australia in two months. He should be on top of the world, pounding his chest.

But all he could think about was Kate and those heavenly eyes. The way her mouth had felt on his, like it had been made expressly for his pleasure. They way they'd fit so nicely together—in more ways than one. He splashed cool water on his face and looked at himself in the mirror. It was not the image of a happy man.

The door to the restroom opened and Simone tottered up behind him. "Let's get out of here." She set her hand on his thigh, her thumb grazing his crotch. "Unless you want to do it right here." He hadn't made love to her in the two weeks they'd supposedly been back together. Hadn't even kissed her. He knew she was doing her best to make that happen tonight.

He tried to push past her, but she grabbed his hand, leading him out of the door. Resigned, he realized he might as well get her safely to the limo. Any man would be thrilled to have Simone Peters leading him from a bar with that sassy little flip of her hip.

But Teague closed his eyes and tried to imagine it was Kate. Of course, his hands would have been all over Kate. They probably wouldn't have even made it out for a night on the town. He'd be happy at home with her, talking and laughing. Okay, making out and making love, too. Lots of that. But he wouldn't need much more than that with Kate.

He followed Simone into the waiting limo, and she was on him before the door closed. "What are you waiting for?" she breathed into his ear. "I'm here. I'm yours."

Her breath was warm on his skin, and he pulled away from the boozy smell of her. "I'm only doing this for the cameras, Simone. We are not back together." He laughed to himself, thinking how he was posing for the cameras with yet another woman. Nothing much in his life had been real, had it? But that wink of time he'd had with Kate had been the closest thing to real he'd ever known.

Simone leaned closer, apparently immune to the word *No.*

He slid his hand out of her grasp. "I don't want you, Simone. Let's just keep this up in public for Remington. I don't care if you go out with other guys. Might make the whole thing more interesting."

She snorted, shaking her head. "It's that hillbilly chick of yours. Priceless." Her golden eyes flashed a warning. "Oh, you are so going to regret this."

"I already do." He told the driver to stop and got out to hail a cab. What would another trip to Willowdale hurt?

TONYA PULLED THE shade closed on the door of her salon and led Kate to a chair. "We've tried chocolate, we've tried ice cream, this is the last trick up my sleeve. A new 'do. Maybe some highlights, too."

Kate plopped in the seat ready to whine. "Just trim the ends. Teague liked how natural my hair was."

"Liked. Past tense. And who even knows if that is true? He's a liar."

"And a cheater," Jeanne offered.

"He didn't cheat," Kate said

"He's with Simone now." Jeanne held up a magazine with the two of them on the front cover.

Kate snatched it from her and tossed it aside. "Not really. It's just for the movie. But even so, I left him. So, he's not a cheater."

Tonya spritzed Kate's hair with water. "What about the pregnant girlfriend?"

"Clearly he got her pregnant before he was with me. That woman was round," Kate said.

"But he's a liar," Jeanne said, her eyes narrowing.

But he wasn't. He hadn't lied about anything. He just hadn't told her about the girl. That there was someone else. He'd never made any promises to her. So why had she expected any? Kate sighed. "I don't care what you do to my hair."

"Really?"

Kate panicked. "No, not really. Give me some highlights, I don't care. Nothing's going to shake me out of this mood."

"I should shave you bald for cutting us off like you did when you left town with him."

"He had a secret to hide and I couldn't trust myself not to tell you guys it was just a setup. That we weren't really dating."

Jeanne snatched a cookie from the pile of goodies in front of them. "I think you should find that woman and confront her."

"She did nothing wrong. Besides, Teague said she needed protecting." Kate shrugged. "Trust me, I wouldn't wish a go-round with the paparazzi on anyone." Not even the baby mama of the man she loved. "And don't forget, I've got my own pregnant gal to contend with. Two might do me in."

"Are Mitch and Dina going to keep the baby?"

"They're going to give it a shot. So we better hurry it up here, gals. Forget the highlights and just give me a trim. I gotta get home and make sure she's okay."

"CAN I HAVE ANOTHER grilled cheese?" Dina asked, holding out her empty plate right as Kate sat down on the couch with a magazine.

Kate forced a smile. "That didn't occur to you when I was back in the kitchen?"

Dina shrugged and flipped through the Babies'R'Us catalog. "Sorry. Cravings, they just pop up, you know?"

Kate frowned. "No, I don't." And probably never would. "Anything else?"

"I'll let you know," she said without looking up from the page of baby swings.

Kate had been trying to keep the bickering with Dina to a minimum since she was on bed rest and all. *What doesn't kill me makes me stronger, what doesn't kill me makes me stronger*, she chanted, unwrapping two slices of cheese.

Tommy and Mitch walked in—without knocking—so she made a few more sandwiches.

As soon as she slumped onto the couch, Dina said, "Kate, could you get us—"

"Drinks," Kate finished.

"Stay put, Katie. I'll get some sodas." Tommy patted her knee and pushed up from the couch. "Just because we're waiting on you two this Saturday for your special dinner doesn't mean you can take advantage of Katie like this."

Dina tucked her blanket around her. "Did everyone forget I'm on bed rest?" Her lower lip popped out in a familiar pout.

"Did you forget Kate's not your maid?" Tommy asked. "Have some respect for the woman who's keeping this roof over your head, keeping your baby from coming early and trying to keep you together with the daddy." He stomped off to the kitchen and Kate followed so she didn't have to hear Dina's grumbles.

"Wow," Kate said. "Thanks."

"I don't like to see people take advantage of you. Like Teague Reynolds. What he did to you was wrong."

"You weren't much better to me," she said quietly and looked at the ground. She'd tried to play it off for so long like it was no big deal. Like Tommy was doing the right thing marrying Ellen when he got her pregnant. Kate and Tommy had been broken up when it'd happened, after all. Still, it hurt.

He set down the cans of soda and was silent for a moment. "I'm sorry. Sorrier than you'll ever know." He stared at her. "But I hope I can rely on the excuse of my youthful stupidity. Just like Dina can. But Teague? He's a grown man."

Kate knew she couldn't argue, couldn't explain how wonderful Teague had been. "Alright. Truce." She offered him her hand.

He shook her hand, then brought it to his lips, and she thought, *Oh, no. Hell no.*

Chapter 19

"MR. REYNOLDS, Jennifer does not want to give up her baby."

"I don't want her to either," Teague said. "But I'm not sure what the solution is."

Miss Johnson steepled her fingers in front of her. "We're considering a few different options. An open adoption might work, if she had visitation rights. Have you considered asking for custody of the child?"

He shook his head. "Impossible. We could never keep it a secret."

She dropped her hands to her desk and tilted her head. "How bad would it be for people to know the truth?"

He shook his head. "Very bad. For everyone involved."

She shrugged. "Very well, then. We've only got a month before her due date. We need to make some decisions. Would you like to join her for her ob-gyn appointment tomorrow in Whitesville? They're doing another ultrasound. You could see your nephew."

"Absolutely. I'll be there."

He left the Willowdale Residential facility, determined to speak to Kate. He had to try again. Maybe he could make things right between them. Maybe she'd even join him in Australia for a few weeks. They seemed to do the adventure thing well together. They could pick up where they'd left off.

Teague parked down the street from Kate's house. He was working out in his head what he could say to her to get her back in his arms. What he wouldn't do for a scriptwriter's help. He watched her house, trying to work up the guts to go over. He did a double take when a police cruiser pulled up. It was the police chief—her ex-boyfriend—climbing out, carrying a bunch of flowers.

Kate grinned when she opened the door and let him in.

Teague squinted as if he might not be seeing things clearly. But no, that really was the chief and Kate had been happy to see him. A flood of curse words pummeled his brain. He'd driven her back into the arms of the man she once loved. The man she claimed she hated. Somehow, her rejecting him hadn't hurt as much as seeing her with someone else. He started his car and sped away. *This time for good.*

KATE'S STOMACH CLENCHED when Tommy walked in with the flowers. It was a big bunch of red roses like Teague had sent her back in LA. The memory of it sucked the air out of her lungs, like a balloon letting loose.

Tommy saw her expression and pulled one of the flowers from the bunch and handed it to her. *Ugh. He thinks I'm pining for him!*

"I should've taken better care of you when I had you," he said. "Did I ever send you flowers?"

Kate shook her head. She wouldn't take the bouquet. "Leave it in there for Dina. She might count to make sure it's an even dozen. I don't think you should mess with a pregnant gal's emotions."

Tommy frowned and tucked the flower back in.

"Let's get ready for the kids." Kate set the flowers on the counter and scrounged around under the sink for a vase. There hadn't been too many flowers in her house growing up. A few "I'm sorry" bouquets George had sent to her Mom, but that's it. She pulled out a vase, filled it with water, and set the flowers in.

"I went into Whitesville and got the kids surf and turf. I bought extra for us. Figured once they ate and settled down for the movie, we could enjoy dinner, too."

Kate bit her lip. She didn't want to spend any more time with Tommy than necessary, but she wasn't going to ruin the kids' night. She opened the cupboard and reached for a platter on the top shelf. She stood on her toes and grabbed at it with her fingertips.

Tommy came up behind her and plucked the platter from the shelf. He set it in front of her and kept his hands on the counter, circling her. "Katie."

She held her breath; she was not going to do this. "Tommy, we've got a lot to do before Mitch gets here." She wouldn't turn to face him.

"We've got some time," he said, brushing her hair off her shoulders.

She pushed her way out of his arms and set two plates on the kitchen table.

He sighed and walked toward the door. "I've gotta grab something from the cruiser."

Kate set the steak knives next to the plate and considered the shiny weapons. *Too tempting*, she thought, putting them back in the drawer.

Tommy came back in, holding up a bottle of champagne. "Nice, right?"

Kate put her hands on her hips. "Dina can't drink alcohol. She's pregnant."

He stuck the bottle in the fridge. "It's not for the kids. It's for us."

"Why would we need champagne?"

He shrugged. "A new start and all. We're going to be related, we're going to be aunt and uncle to this baby."

And that's all we're ever going to be. She dumped the bagged salad in a bowl. "Speaking of the baby, make sure Mitch shows up to the ultrasound tomorrow. Dina said he's been cagey about whether or not he's coming. Is he getting cold feet? He's the one who was pushing to get married. If we're going to do all this work to get them together, we better make sure he's still got his heart in it."

Tommy shrugged. "People can change, you know. Feelings change. Sometimes it takes a while before you realize what you've lost. Years, even."

She shut her eyes. Was there any way this night could end without a fight? "And sometimes it takes years to realize how wrong someone really was for you."

"I'm not giving up on you."

"You're going to be one disappointed man."

"You're not still pining over T-Rex, are you?" He hitched up his jeans. "If I see him in town again, I swear I'll find a reason to toss him in jail. He did you wrong."

She slammed the basket of cherry tomatoes on the counter. "No, he didn't. I left him."

Tommy's eyes went wide. "Why would you do something like that?"

She shook her head. "It's complicated."

One corner of his mouth quirked into a smile.

"No. It had nothing to do with you. Sometimes two people just aren't meant to be together."

"What did you expect? You knew he was no good getting into it."

She had. She'd fought it tooth and nail, knowing exactly the kind of guy he was, but she'd fallen anyway like a damn fool. She thought she saw something that just wasn't there, like when the moon casts shadows in your room that make you think you're seeing a ghost. That's what her romance with Teague had been: a shadow that had never been there.

The doorbell rang and Kate hurried over, almost as nervous as if she was expecting the date. Mitch stood there with his hands stuffed in his pockets, studying his biker boots.

Kate smiled and held the door for him. "Hello, Mitch. Welcome to Chez Willowdale. Please have a seat while I let your date know you have arrived."

But Mitch hesitated. "Do you really think this is a good idea?" He'd put off moving in, and Dina said he was calling less often. Which probably meant ten times a day instead of twenty.

Kate laughed. "A gourmet dinner date isn't a good idea?"

He frowned. "No, I mean pretending like this. We're supposed to get to know each other better, but this isn't real. Once the baby comes we won't be enjoying fancy candle-lit dinners. Playing make-believe doesn't make you love someone."

Wasn't that the truth. She smiled at him and squeezed his

bicep. "You're a pretty smart kid. Just come in and enjoy the night for what it is."

He stepped in and Kate led him to the couch. "I'll let your date know you're here." She dashed up the stairs and found Dina sobbing in her bed.

"What?" Kate asked, uncertain she could douse another fire today.

"This is stupid."

If one more person calls this stupid . . .

"I didn't want him, but now I do . . . and now . . ." She took a deep, shaky breath. "Now he doesn't want me. Love is so stupid."

You're telling me, sister. Kate smoothed Dina's shiny black hair. "It sure is, honey. But I don't think Mitch doesn't want you. I think he's just realizing how real this all is. I think you're both a little scared. So go downstairs, enjoy your dinner and don't think you have to plan out your whole future tonight. Things'll work out. I promise."

Dina nodded and swiped the back of her hand under her nose.

Kate followed her downstairs. Mitch popped up from the couch and smoothed his hands down his dress pants. "You look pretty," he said quietly.

Dina blushed and lifted her gauzy skirt off the ground. "You don't think I look like a blimp?"

He shrugged. "Maybe a hot air balloon, but not a blimp."

She blushed and gave him a playful shove, and he didn't quite look her in the eyes.

If not for Dina's bitty bump—which wasn't so bitty anymore—Kate would've never believed these two had gotten naked together. *Odd time to get shy with each other.*

Tommy stepped out of the kitchen and Kate caught her breath. He'd changed into a tuxedo. He brought a tray of appetizers over to Mitch and Dina. "Prosciutto-wrapped asparagus spear?" He handed Dina a napkin and she picked one off the tray.

Kate had never seen this elegant, sophisticated side of

Tommy. She shook off the feeling and dashed into the kitchen for the sparkling grape juice.

"Tonight we're serving surf and turf with twice-baked potatoes, soup and salad. For dessert, we have tiramisu. Dinner will be served in half an hour. Feel free to stroll the grounds while you wait." Kate tried not to giggle. This was kind of fun.

Tommy flipped on some romantic music, and they hustled back to the kitchen.

"Nice music," Kate said. "Where'd you get it?"

He shrugged. "Downloaded some stuff from my music library."

"Right. You're the romantic music type."

He stopped and took her gently by the arm. "Kate, a person can change. And sometimes if that person is lucky, they get a second chance. That's what I'm hoping for."

She pursed her lips. "There are no second chances on love, Tommy."

He ignored her and grabbed her other hand and slowly moved her to the music.

She looked up at the ceiling. "Tommy . . ."

He pulled her closer. "Shhh."

Dina walked into the kitchen with her empty glass and her eyes popped open. "Sorry to interrupt, I was . . . uh, looking for another drink."

Kate pulled herself away from Tommy and scurried to the refrigerator. "You didn't interrupt, we were just goofing around." She filled Dina's glass—without looking her in the eyes—and went to work on the salad.

Kate was cheered to hear the two kids chatting in the living room, laughing a few times, even. Luckily, she and Tommy were both too busy for any more impromptu dancing. What bothered her even more than his gumption was her lack of outrage. She tried channeling the hurt she'd felt over the years, but it just wasn't there. She felt . . . numb.

When they sat down to eat, Mitch pulled out Dina's chair for her. Kate set their salads in front of them and slipped out onto the back porch to give them some privacy. She sat on the swing and stared out at the big back yard. She took a kitchen timer with her, set for ten minutes when she'd go inside and serve the main course.

Tommy settled onto the swing next to her. "I think it's going well, don't you?"

The night was warm and moist. She took a deep breath. "Yes. I was surprised how shy they were at first, but they seem to be settling in. You'd think they hadn't . . ." Kate cleared her throat. "Thanks for your help with this. These two need to make a real shot at having a family."

Tommy slid his hand over hers. "But they're still just kids. It might do them well to see us together. With your stepfather gone now, you're gonna need some help supervising this fledgling little family. Might be a smart idea to give them a positive role model. What do you think, Katie? Would you marry me?"

Kate pulled her hand away. "Marry you?" she managed to whisper. This seemed more serious than his feeble offers at The Hideaway.

"I made some stupid, stupid mistakes. But we were kids. And kids make mistakes, look at Dina and Mitch." He dragged his knuckles along her cheek. "I didn't realize how much you meant to me until I saw all those pictures of you with Teague. Damn near ate my heart up. You're the best thing that ever happened to me, and I blew it. I blew it big-time." He pulled his hand away from her face and gestured behind him. "If those two can work to make love happen, why can't we?"

Kate didn't immediately argue back. She was so tired, she couldn't even round up the right words to fight it.

Tommy seemed to take that as a good sign. "And face it, kid. You need me. No job, sullied reputation . . ." He let the words hang there for good effect.

Marry Tommy? She could never marry Tommy for love. But he did raise some good points. Could she marry him for convenience? Her nose wrinkled just thinking of it. She wondered if this was how her mother felt when George proposed. Kate wouldn't be the first person to accept a marriage proposal that wasn't grounded in true, heart-swollen love.

"Think about it," Tommy said, patting her hand. "There are some very good reasons for the two of us to be together. Not the least of which, I love you. Always have. And besides, don't you want your own baby? Even though Ellen and I got divorced, Jane is the best thing that ever happened to me. Love that kid. Don't you want that? That biological clock of yours has got to be ticking."

And her kitchen timer went off. "Time for the main course," she said quietly.

Tommy stood up. "I'll get it. You think about what I said." He left her on the deck, and she wondered how she could even be giving a serious moment's thought to this preposterous proposal.

DINA STABBED A piece of steak with her fork and was grateful to keep her mouth busy with something other than talking. Why was this so hard, sitting here with the guy who got her pregnant? She studied her plate, pushing around a stray pea with her fork.

"The food is good," Mitch said. "This was really nice of them."

Dina nodded. "Do you think something's going on between them?"

Mitch set down his fork. "Do you? Kate just hooked up with a movie star. You think she's going to be happy with someone like my brother?"

Dina shrugged and put her hands in her lap. "She loved him before. And it's not like she has a choice now. Teague's with someone else, and Kate has no job."

"You think she should settle for Tommy?"

Dina felt her throat close up. "You think we should settle for each other because of the baby."

Mitch threw his napkin down. "The baby is a very good reason to settle. We have to be realistic here."

Dina pushed away from the table, crying. "So you *are*

settling. I don't want to make you do something you don't want to do."

"I never said I didn't want to do it! I've been pushing to be part of this even before you admitted it."

Dina walked to the stairs and turned around. "I'm not feeling well, and I'm sure arguing like this isn't good for the baby. We've got an ultrasound tomorrow at ten if you're interested."

Kate and Tommy ran in from the deck. "Everything alright in here?" Kate asked. "Where did Dina go?"

"Upstairs." Mitch turned up his hands. "This didn't exactly work out. Thanks for trying. I'm not sure what's going to happen with us."

Chapter 20

"PLEASE, LET'S JUST wait five more minutes." Dina watched the door of the exam room for Mitch. "I told him about the appointment. I figured he'd come. Maybe." She smoothed the blue paper gown across her thighs and nervously swung her legs off the end of the exam table. A florescent light flickered overhead.

Kate patted her hand. "I'm sure something came up with work, or maybe he's having car problems."

"I have a cell phone. He could call." Dina's big eyes were slick with tears.

The ultrasound tech cleared her throat. "I'm sorry. We're booked solid today. We have to get started."

Dina sniffed and lowered herself onto the table, the sound of paper rustling beneath her. The tech lifted the gown and squirted her belly with jelly. She moved the wand over her tummy while Kate and Dina gazed at the screen.

Dina sucked in a breath. "Oh! That's my baby?"

The tech nodded and grinned. "There's your baby's heart. See it beating?" She pointed to a tiny, fluttering image on the screen.

Dina nodded. "Can you tell if it's a boy or a girl?"

"Yep. You want to know?"

Dina nodded enthusiastically.

"You're going to have a little girl."

Dina cupped her hand over her mouth, and Kate felt her own womb tighten with longing for a child of her own. Tommy had been right, what he'd said the night before. Only, she was pretty certain a baby would never be in her future. She wondered what kind of father Teague would be to his child.

Once the procedure was over and Dina's belly had been

wiped dry, the tech handed Dina a picture of the baby's profile and a DVD recording of the whole procedure. Dina slid down from the table and checked her phone, frowning.

This is not the time to bolt, buddy, Kate thought. Mitch better have one heck of an excuse for missing this appointment.

TEAGUE HELD JENNIFER by the hand as they walked into the doctor's office. "You're having a little boy. Are you excited?" he asked her. He tugged his ball cap brim lower and adjusted his sunglasses.

"Yes. I name him T, like you." She laughed and sat down in a chair while Teague checked them in. He was nervous, too, and dropped the pen a few times as he filled out her information.

He turned around and knocked right into someone, clumsy fool that he was. This was no way to lay low, bowling people over. "I'm sorry," he said quietly.

"Teague?"

He'd know that voice anywhere. He looked up at her. "Kate? What are you doing here?"

She blinked a few times. "This is my stepsister, Dina. She's expecting a baby in three months."

Dina looked as if she'd forgotten that she was carrying a child. She lifted a shoulder and dropped her chin, gazing at him coyly. "Hey, Teague. Nice to meet you."

Kate gently whacked her with a handful of pamphlets. "Go wait in the car."

Dina slunk away, watching him over her shoulder.

Kate turned back to him, shaking her head. "What are you doing here?" She crossed her arms over her chest and tapped her foot.

He couldn't lie to this woman. Not anymore. Not about this. He let out a deep breath. "Come here. I want you to meet someone."

She shook her head and stepped back. "I already met the other woman you're sleeping with, back in Maui. I don't need to meet another."

He shook his head. He was surprised how calm he felt when he was no longer desperate to cover up the truth. It felt good. "I haven't hooked up with Simone again, no matter what you read. And I'm not here with a girlfriend. I'm here with my sister."

Her face didn't change, didn't morph into relief like he hoped it would. "I thought you said you didn't have any brothers or sisters." A cool tone laced her voice.

"You're right. I did tell you that, to protect her." He held up his hands. "I didn't think I had any siblings until I got a call from the director of the facility where she lives. They tracked down her family to figure out what to do about this baby. And that's how, after all these years, I found out I have a sister. Would you like to meet Jennifer?"

Kate looked over at his sister. "Sure." She followed him over to the plastic row of chairs in the waiting room.

Jennifer looked up, and Teague watched Kate take it all in with one quick glance at Jennifer's features: her mouth agape ever so slightly as it always was, her eyes just a little too wide, the too-big grin that broke out. "Hi," Jennifer said in her deep, slow voice.

Kate stuck out her hand. "Nice to meet you, Jennifer. When are you having your baby?"

Teague's heart swelled as he watched her treat Jennifer like any other person—like a lucky woman waiting for her baby to be born.

Jennifer shook her hand vigorously. "Three weeks, then four days."

"That's so exciting. Congratulations!" Kate said. Her voice sent ripples of longing through him.

Teague squeezed Jennifer's shoulder. "Can you stay here while I walk Kate to her car?"

Jennifer nodded.

Kate followed Teague outside and it took his every ounce of power not to wrap her in his arms, so he took a step back. "Now you know my secret. The one you helped me keep."

Kate looked off and nodded. "I can see why you needed to keep it quiet." The breeze ruffled her hair and he moved to brush it off her cheek, but stuffed his hands in his pockets instead.

"Yes. And I owe you more than I could ever give for helping me do that. I really hope that despite everything that's happened between us, you can keep this a secret. I don't want Jennifer hurt by the press. It's not good for her or the baby."

"And it's not good for you," Kate added with a frown.

He shrugged. The truth of it hurt him. She thought he only cared about his image, his reputation. "You know the drill."

"And you don't think June'll find out?" She pursed her lips.

Did she have to be so cute when she was being difficult? "I fired her after the film fest. Couldn't stand another moment with that woman, no matter how good of a publicist she was." He grinned. "But don't worry. I introduced her to your stepfather. He's hell-bent on carving out a career in Hollywood. June is smitten enough to think she can help him do it. They're going to drive each other crazy. But that should help the family finances, no?"

Kate pinched the bridge of her nose. "I thought he was talking nonsense about becoming an actor. But she's trying to help him? That pretty much guarantees he'll never come home."

"And that's a bad thing?" Man, Teague was so bad at this stuff.

"His daughter is expecting a baby. She's only eighteen, she's all confused and we're the only family she's got. And it's not like he'll be sending the money home."

"Oh," he said quietly. Maybe that's why she'd turned to the police chief for help. She certainly couldn't shoulder this all on her own. She needed someone after all, but it wasn't him.

She grabbed his hand and squeezed. "I won't tell anyone about Jennifer. But I think people are going to find out. It's a small town."

He swallowed and found his voice. "I've been paying her residential facility pretty well to keep a tight lid on it. So far, so good." Teague wanted to pull Kate close and carry her off to his motel room and start all over again. But he dropped her hand and backed away from her to make sure he wasn't tempted. She had a new life, she had no room or need for him. She was working things out with her ex, trying to get her life together. He'd only make things worse. *Ride off into the sunset, dude . . . this party's over.*

Kate stood there quietly for a moment, then sighed. "It was good seeing you. Good luck with everything—the movie, the baby. Congratulations."

Crickets chirped in the fields behind the office and the sun beat down on the back of his neck. Teague nodded. "Thanks. Jennifer and the baby will be the only people I know who are really related to me. I'm very excited, actually."

"Did you find about anything about your parents? Your biological parents?"

He shook his head. "I only found a record of us being given up for adoption at the same time. There's no information about my mother or father." He shrugged. Water under the bridge. "I've gotta get back in there for Jennifer's appointment."

"Sure, of course. I've got lots to do, too."

Right, like the police chief. The thought made him wild.

"Take care, Teague." Her smile was cheery as ever, although her eyes didn't match the mood.

But he smiled and did the hardest thing he'd ever done. He walked away from the woman he loved. Guess she was right, after all—some people aren't meant for love.

COULD SOMEONE BE *more disinterested?* Kate plopped her painting gear in the spare bedroom with a huff. Teague couldn't get away from her fast enough. But he certainly had his own issues to deal with, just like she did. Their week in Hawaii had been pure fantasy for both of them, as it turned out.

Kate snapped open the newspaper, scanning the want ads before she laid it on the floor to and started painting the room a lovely, pale pink for the baby. But there wasn't much work available that interested her. Not that she had the luxury of being interested in her work. She doubted she'd ever work in a school again. But she needed something to bring in money. She laughed to herself. It seemed like yesterday that summer had rolled around and she was looking for a temporary job. How her world had changed. Delores was coming over later to check out Mama's Depression glass, but that certainly wouldn't bring in much.

She rolled another stripe of paint on the wall and wished she were doing this for her own child. Dina was in bed, crying because Mitch hadn't shown up for the ultrasound. He'd been the one wanting to marry Dina. Now the roles were reversed. She didn't know much about astrology, but she figured the planets must have been all out of kilter. Nobody was getting what they wanted these days.

After covering the first wall with paint, she called Dina in to take a look. "Come see, it's so pretty."

Dina didn't answer, so Kate wandered into her room. Dina was tucked into a little ball, sobbing quietly.

Kate squeezed her shoulder. "Honey, it's going to be okay. This is a scary time for both of you."

Dina reached for Kate's hand. "I just don't understand."

"The two of you are going through a whirlwind of emotions. And let's not forget you're pregnant. I've heard those hormones and all those changes can turn you upside down." *Not to mention you had the diva thing going on before this anyway . . .* "You've got so much to deal with. But you've got to be willing to fight for what you want."

Dina sat up and blew her nose. "So, why aren't you fighting for Teague?"

Well, that was one way to slow down a conversation. She turned up her hands in a helpless gesture. "There's not really anything to fight for. There wasn't much there to begin with."

"Does this mean you're getting back together with Tommy?"

"Uhhh . . ."

The doorbell rang and Kate patted Dina's hand, wondering how much more drama she could stand in a day. It better not be Tommy looking for an answer to his crazy proposal. Did Dina know about that?

She opened the door. *Hello, drama.* She braced herself against the doorframe. "Mitch. I'm not sure if I'm glad to see you or not. Dina's really angry you didn't show up for the appointment."

He shuffled his feet. "I know. I was scared to come. Scared to see a real live picture of the baby. Makes it kind of real, you know?"

She closed her eyes and nodded. "I can understand that. It all looked pretty real in the doctor's office, but if you're coming in to break that girl's heart you're going to have to do it another day. Dina's really upset, and I'm worried about her."

"Do you think she'd be upset if I gave her this?" He snapped open a white velvet box. A tiny solitaire diamond sat on top of a gold band.

Kate blew out a breath. "I don't know. Let me see if she wants to talk to you." What was it with the Larsen boys and this rash of proposals?

Kate knocked on Dina's door. "Mitch is here to see you. Should I send him in?"

Dina sat up in her bed. "No!" She patted her hair and stripped off her ratty shorts. "Not yet. He can't see me like this. Give me a few minutes. I'll come down when I'm ready."

Kate trotted back downstairs and let Mitch in. "Give Dina a minute. It might help if she catches you doing this." She handed him the paint roller and directed him into the nursery. "I'll give you two some privacy. I'll have my phone on if you need me."

Kate hopped in her Jeep and headed for the park. She'd take a walk around the jogging loop and blow off some steam. Seemed like a good plan. When she got there, she settled on a bench instead, too tired to do a few laps. She crossed her fingers that things were going well back home. She frowned. Her home for now. The taxes were paid off, but now she didn't have a job. Was it just fantasy to think she could keep Mama's house with no steady income?

A smart woman would accept Tommy's proposal. It really was best for everyone. But Kate wasn't a smart woman. She'd had the misfortune of feeling the intense burn of desire with

Teague. He'd ruined her. Hell, she was imagining him walking across the park to her right then. She'd never be able to shake him.

Only, he really was walking toward her.

She looked up at him, shielding her eyes from the sun with one hand. "Why are you still here?"

He sat on the other end of the bench. "I'm staying in Willowdale until Jennifer has her baby. Rented a room at the Be Wright Inn. I like this park. I wanted to come out here, think some things out." He set his arm along the back of the bench, his hand just inches away from her. "I'm glad I did."

Kate crossed her leg and bounced her foot. "So, you're going to be here for a while."

"Yep." He looked over to the playground, mostly empty in the hot afternoon sun. "What are you doing out here?"

"Giving Dina and her boyfriend some space. They're trying to work things out before the baby comes. What about Jennifer's baby . . . and the father?"

He shook his head. "She won't tell us who it is. But she said no one hurt her. I figure it was one of the other residents."

"Is she going to give the baby up for adoption?"

"No. I won't allow it. I'm still trying to figure it all out. Maybe I can hire someone to care for the baby full time at the facility. I'm just not sure."

"Could you adopt the baby?"

He shook his head.

"What about an open adoption, where you and Jennifer could have contact with the child?" She placed her hand on his arm and it felt so good to touch him again. Such a strange mix of emotions mingled in her heart, being here with him like this.

Hesitating for a moment, he set his hand on hers. "How are you doing, Kate? Looks like things are working out with the police chief. I'm happy for you."

She shook her head. Surely she hadn't heard him right. "What are you talking about?" How could he have known about Tommy's proposal?

Teague propped his elbows on his thighs and gazed out at

the park. "I was coming over to talk with you the other night and I saw him at your door with a bunch of flowers."

Kate froze, then she laughed.

"It really wasn't amusing at all."

She scooted closer to him and set her hand on his leg. "No. We were throwing a romantic dinner for Dina and Mitch, the baby's father. That's his little brother. We're trying to get them together. Like I said, it's been rocky. Tommy brought flowers for their dinner."

She could feel him taking a deep breath. "So, you're not back together?" His voice was so hopeful her chest tightened at the sound of it.

"No." She wanted to rest her head against his shoulder, but held back. "Not that he's given up trying yet, but I don't love him."

Silence settled between them.

"What were you coming over to talk to me about that night anyway?" Kate asked, her silly, silly heart doing a little dance.

He closed his eyes and let out a breath. "I wanted to know if you really meant what you told June, that I was no good for you. I was hoping I could change your mind. But then I saw the two of you . . . so I left."

Kate held up a finger. "Wait one minute." She hopped off the bench and clenched her fists. "I told June *I* was no good for *you*. She tried to pay me to leave, said I was ruining your chances for the big time. But she didn't have to give me a dime, I left on my own. I didn't want to ruin your career—I love you too much." Kate gasped at what she'd said and turned away from him, cupping her elbows, wishing she could disappear. How had that slipped out?

Teague sat there, saying nothing. He reached for her hand and pulled her back onto the bench. "How could you think that? It was only a few days, but you were exactly what I needed. Kate, you're . . ."

"You were in danger of losing a huge movie role because of me. How could it ever work between us?"

"I'm the one who ruined your life. You lost your job, you

got hurt."

Kate watched a squirrel scamper up a tree. "Aren't we a sorry pair?"

"Perfect for each other, when you think about it." He pulled her to him. Their kiss was cautious, as their lips remembered how this thing worked.

"Should we be . . ." Kate tried to protest, tried to fight what they were doing.

His lips spread into a grin as they pressed against hers. "Yes. Hell, yes."

He led her to his car, never losing contact as they raced back to his room at the Be Wright Inn. He swung open the door of the dank, dark room and carried her in.

She slid out of her paint-stained jeans while Teague pulled off his shirt, backing them up to the bed. They were on top of each other without a word, their fast, heavy breaths the only thing between them. He ran his thumbs over her eyebrows and kissed her forehead.

Then his mouth found hers, and that same spark ignited between them. It was familiar, comfortable—and thrilling. Kate curled her legs around his, desperate to be one. But Teague was taking his time, enjoying every inch of her, exploring and touching, kissing and caressing.

"Teague . . ."

He mumbled something from behind her knee and rolled her over onto her stomach.

She groaned and grabbed the headboard. "You're killing me here."

"Hmph," came a sound from the small of her back.

"Could you please make love to me now!" she finally wailed.

He grinned, his teeth slick on the skin of her neck. "I am, to every inch of you."

He rolled her over and she collapsed in defeat, realizing she was his in every way.

And that's when he plunged into her. Wicked, wicked man. She gasped and moved with him, shuddering. Her body reveled in the pleasure while her heart slipped away like a feather floating down a river. She wondered where it would end up.

HE COULD NOT LOSE her again. He held her long after they had tumbled into that wild place of ecstasy that came so easily for both of them. But there was something different going on here each and every time he was with this woman. It wasn't a fluke; it wasn't the novelty of being with this what-you-see-is-what-you-get southern beauty after so many Hollywood phonies. No, it was the thing he'd been afraid of the first time he thought, *Hmm, what about a go-round with this gal?* Something in his brain had been smart enough to say, *Back off, buddy, she could be the one.* But of course, he hadn't listened.

Thank goodness.

Never had he made love to a woman and felt his heart respond as strongly as parts farther south. Damn the press, damn his handlers, damn it all, he wanted her for keeps. This is what he'd spent his entire life avoiding. Closeness, someone who cared about him. Someone he cared about. Someone who could share the love budding in his chest for this child who wasn't even born, who wasn't even his, who was the best chance to right all the wrongs in his life. And he wanted Kate to be part of that, too.

It was like he'd been searching for all of these puzzle pieces his entire life and they finally landed in his lap. It was love, honest-to-god-love, that's what it was . . . as well as he could guess, because he certainly didn't have much experience in that department.

He stared at her: cheeks glowing, skin damp, smile twitching as she rested. His. All his. That's what he needed. He squeezed her tight. He could only hope to god she needed him, too.

"I forgot to tell you something back at the park," he said.

She opened her eyes. "What?"

"I love you, too."

She smiled. "Good." And she drifted back to sleep and he

watched over her with a heart that felt full and whole.

"MARRY ME, KATE."

She sat up, pulling the sheet around her. Her words came out in a whisper. "You're crazy." *Plus, I've already got an offer on the table.* But one moment with Teague had erased any question of whether or not she could spend her life with Tommy. It would never work. Not after remembering what it felt like to be with someone she truly loved.

He got up and rummaged in his suitcase. He grabbed her left hand and slid on the antique pearl ring he'd bought that first day together. "This is just for now. I hadn't exactly been planning to do this." He laughed and dropped to his knee, totally naked. "Marry me, really." He looked up at her with wide, hopeful eyes.

Kate's hand fluttered over her throat, imagining how wonderful it would be to say yes, but she was too stunned to say anything.

He sat on the bed beside her and laced his fingers through hers. "This is perfect. We can adopt Jennifer's baby. No one would have to know about my sister's situation. We'd be a family."

The bubble of happiness in her heart popped. Kate was too tired, too exasperated to cry. She sighed, letting out the regret that came with her next words. "I can't. You just want us to pretend again. It's no different than when I was posing as your girlfriend. It's no different than when I pretended my stepfather wasn't running around on my mother, pretending we were a happy, normal family. It's not real."

The noisy air conditioner blew stale, cold air across the room as she clutched her pillow to her chest. "I've lived lies my whole life and I won't do that again. Not even for you, Teague. I'm sorry." She handed the ring back and slid off the bed, searching for her clothes.

She watched him sitting there, saying nothing, not even fighting for her. He didn't really want her. He just wanted a way to keep that baby and keep it all a secret.

"Good luck, Teague." She meant it, too. She wanted the best for him, even though she wasn't the one who could give it to him. She dressed, then slipped out of the room and started walking back to her Jeep at the park.

It was a long stretch of road for a broken-hearted woman to be walking alone with her thoughts.

DINA AND MITCH were painting the nursery when she got back to the house. Mitch reached up to dab the spots Dina missed and Kate thought, *This might work out, at least.* "Looks good, guys."

Dina turned to her and beamed. "Thanks. Mitch is going to move his things in later today, if that's okay."

"Absolutely." That was one problem smoothed over for now. Maybe someone would get their happily-ever-after in the end.

Later that night, Mitch and Tommy lugged in a dresser and bed for the basement rec room, while Kate cleared out boxes and bags of junk to make some space. The four of them collapsed on the deck afterward with a pizza and a chorus of cicadas providing the dinner music.

"So, I said yes to Mitch," Dina said.

"Yes to what?" Kate asked.

"His proposal." She clapped her hands together. "We're going to get married."

Tommy whopped Mitch on the back. "That's great. I'm happy for you kids."

"When exactly are you hoping to do this?" Kate asked.

"Soon. Before the baby comes." Dina rubbed her tummy and looked happier than she had in a long time.

Kate nodded, imagining the work and the money it would take to pull this off. "We've got some planning to do."

"We were thinking something small, of course. We thought maybe right here in the back yard?" The more Dina talked, the more excited she became. "We could have the reception here, too. Get a big tent and tables and all that."

"We'll have to take a look at our finances," Kate said quietly, swatting away the tiny bugs gathering near the porch light. Dina didn't know how dire the financial situation really was. She had promised her she'd be able to fix things, but she hadn't.

"Did I tell you my brother Brad's starting up a catering company with his friend, Jeanne?" Tommy asked.

Kate sat up. "My friend Jeanne?" Man, she'd fallen right out of the loop after her adventure with Teague. She winced just thinking of him.

"Your friend, his friend, whatever. I bet they'd be able to throw one hell of party. I think I could cover the cost for the kids," Tommy offered. "This can work. And it might be the right opportunity for a double ceremony. Have you thought any more about my proposal?"

Well, isn't this a hoot.

Dina's head snapped in Kate's direction. Mitch's eyes went wide and Kate looked for a place to hide as she hissed at Tommy. "I thought this was a private matter."

He shrugged. "We're all family here, dealing with some big issues." He settled his arm on her lawn chair.

She pushed his arm away. "I think we should talk about this later, alone."

Dina clapped her hands and squealed. "Oh, Kate! It would be so perfect. Say yes. We could be brides together."

Kate dropped her head back and looked up at the moon. It was full, no surprise. "Tommy, I don't want to get married for all the wrong reasons. Maybe it's never going to happen for me. But neither of us deserves less than true, wild crazy love."

He rolled his eyes. "That's just fairytale stuff. Nobody gets that."

Some people do, she thought. Just not me. "I'm sorry."

"I'm not taking no for an answer, Kate. You need me, and you're going to realize it sooner or later." He pushed back his chair and stomped off into the night.

Mitch popped up from his chair, scratching his head. "I

better talk to him or something." He chased after him.

Dina crossed her arms and glared at Kate.

She just wasn't making anyone happy today. Not even herself—because it would have been so nice and easy to say yes to Teague.

Chapter 21

"COME AND SEE the baby."

Kate almost dropped her cell when she heard Teague's voice. She hadn't expected to hear from him again. It had been a long week since she'd last seen him.

When she didn't respond, he quickly added, "I'm sorry to bother you, but I just had to share this with someone."

"Jennifer had her baby already? Is everything okay?"

"Yes, he's almost three weeks early, but he's beautiful and perfect, and Jenny's thrilled. She's even told us who the father is, and he's here, too. One of the fellow residents—she was trying to protect him. I guess he's her boyfriend. The staff is still trying to figure out how they were able to . . ." He cleared his throat. "We've got ourselves one interesting situation here. But I really want you to meet my nephew. That's all, as a friend."

Could she do that? Just as a friend? She'd take what she could get. "I'd love to."

Kate picked up a tiny teddy bear and a big bunch of flowers before she drove to the hospital. She tapped on the door, and Teague rushed to greet her. "Wait till you see him." He grabbed her hand and pulled her into the room.

Kate hugged Jennifer and handed her the gifts while Teague plucked the baby from its bassinette. "Have you ever seen anything so amazing?" He gazed at the little bundle in his arms. The man looked like he'd never seen a baby before. Kate thought back over his history and realized he probably hadn't.

Kate offered a finger to the grunting, squirming little guy with swirls of auburn hair pasted to his wrinkly scalp. He grabbed it and he might as well have reached in and squeezed her heart. This was not the thing a twenty-six-year-old woman in love with the man next to her needed to see. She wanted a baby—a baby of her own. Teague's baby.

She might as well wish for the moon.

"Want to hold him?"

She nodded. "What's his name?"

He blushed a little. "Jennifer named him Teague."

Kate looked over at Jennifer and the baby's father, whispering and holding hands. "Will they be able to raise him on their own?"

He shook his head. "They're both almost like children themselves. I guess an open adoption is the best scenario. The facility won't allow me to hire a nanny for the baby . . . I just don't see another option."

It would have been very easy to say yes, let's do this. Let's raise this child, let's get married. But a relationship based in lies would collapse down the road. Mama and George had shown her that. It was impossible, really.

He cleared his throat. "I've got to get things settled before I start filming next month. Maybe I'll move them to be near me in L.A. I'm going home tomorrow and I'll look into some facilities. After that, I'll look for parents for the baby."

Teague would never have reason to come back here, she realized. Which was just as well. "I hope it all works out for you." She had to leave before the tears took over. "I've got to get going." She forced a smile. "We're planning a wedding for Dina and Mitch. Lots to do." Her voice sounded thick and forced.

They faced each other, neither of them wanting to admit this might be the last time they ever saw each other. "Send me a postcard from Australia."

"I will. If there's ever anything you need . . ." He reached out his hand for her, but she wouldn't take it, so he dropped it to his side.

There would always be something she needed from Teague. Something she could never have.

KATE DIRECTED THE catering crew setting up tables and tents in the back yard. She swiped her hand along her forehead.

Tommy looked surprisingly handsome, cool and collected, and totally opposite of the frenzy Kate was feeling. She wanted to bop him over the head with one of her shoes. He came up behind her and squeezed her shoulders.

She squealed. "Don't do that."

"What are you so nervous about? This isn't your wedding. And I'm still waiting on you, Katie. It's the right thing for us. " He grinned and nodded, like that might convince her.

She ignored him. "Did you get the keg yet?"

"Yep. And the cake and the flowers and the fifteen other things you put on my list. I'm reliable. I take care of this community. I can take care of you."

"I can take care of myself, Tommy." She pushed past him and decided to check on the pastries in the kitchen for the third time. If only she could see beyond their past, it might work. He still had the good looks that had buckled her knees back in school. And he certainly had seemed like a different guy these past few weeks. But he had one big thing going against him. He wasn't Teague Reynolds.

She reached into the closet for one of the sundresses she'd worn in Hawaii. She clutched it to her chest, inhaling the scents still mingled in the gauzy fabric. She could smell Teague and suntan lotion and a dozen memories. She shoved it back in the closet and picked out her simple standby black dress. It reminded her of her life—practical and predictable.

Kate expected a nervous, quivering Dina. But she was calm and smiling. Kate helped her into the sleeveless white dress that she'd picked out and assured her she didn't look like a Macy's parade float, then gave her a last-minute hug.

Dina froze for a moment, then hugged her back. They hadn't shared too many hugs growing up. Life was just changing all around her.

"Thanks," Dina whispered. "I know we haven't always been the best of friends, but I'm glad that's changing." She tucked a stray hair behind her ear.

"Me, too."

Kate scurried out to the back yard, herded the guests to

their seats and cued the school's music teacher they'd hired to play the violin. Tommy walked Dina across the deck and down the stairs, and Kate sent a thousand curses out into the universe, hoping George would be punished for missing this. She'd called him at least a dozen times, begging him to come home.

"I've got auditions, Katie. Being a Hollywood actor is not an easy gig."

Which made her even more impressed with how Teague had been right there for his sister, and he actually had a real career in Hollywood.

Dina had tried to pretend she wasn't bothered by it, that she was happy and proud of George for chasing this dream. But Kate knew better. The girl was putting up a good front. A year earlier she would have had a foot-stomping hissy fit if she didn't get her way.

Dina walked toward her groom, clutching her gardenias and rubbing her belly. Kate frowned, hoping the Braxton-Hicks wasn't kicking in again.

Mitch held out his hand for her and kissed her once she reached him. Not a sweet peck on the cheek, but a kiss probably similar to the one that started this whole thing, what, nearly eight months ago?

The preacher cleared his throat and started the ceremony.

Tears pricked her eyes right from the get go. Oh, shoot. She'd never been weepy at weddings before, but this one hit her. Maybe because it was her stepsister, but more likely because she was certain she'd never be the one up there in front of a minister, in love, looking forward to a life together with someone.

A hankie appeared in front of her and she saw Tommy offering it to her. "Thanks," she whispered.

He set his hand on her shoulder and surprisingly, she let him keep it there for the rest of the ceremony.

DINA AND MITCH danced under the twinkly lights in the reception tent. Kate frowned while watching them, thinking Dina had spent way too much time on her feet for a mama-to-be on bed rest. When the song ended, she pulled Dina off the dance floor and plopped her in a chair. "Rest," she commanded.

"I'm fine. It's my wedding, what could go wrong?"

"Maybe you should," Mitch said, squatting beside her, rubbing her tummy.

"Oh, lord. We're married two hours and you're already telling me what to do?"

And they're off, Kate thought, rubbing her temples.

Dina was mid-sentence, still arguing, when she caught her breath. Her mouth turned into a tiny "o" and she looked down at the puddle between her legs. "I don't think that's pee."

Mitch hopped up from his seat and started pacing. "Oh, crap. Oh, crap. Oh, crap."

"It ain't that either, honey," Dina said, surprisingly calm, reaching for another piece of cake on a nearby table.

Crap is right, thought Kate. The baby wasn't due for another six weeks. Kate scanned the crowd for Tommy. He was clear across the tent at the bar. She cupped her hands to her mouth. "Tommy! Get over here. We need you."

He dropped his drink and sprinted over. The music stopped and the crowd stared at the commotion.

"What is it?" He surveyed the scene and kneeled next to Dina.

"Her water broke. Are you having contractions?" Kate asked.

Dina nodded, finishing her cake.

"We gotta get her to the hospital."

"We'll take my cruiser. Help me get her up, Mitch."

"I'm coming, too," Kate said, following. She caught her friend Jeanne's eye. "You're in charge of the party."

"Sure thing. Now get that girl to the hospital!"

Dina was the only one not panicking.

Kate grabbed some towels from the house and lined them along the back seat. Mitch laid Dina's head on his lap and stroked her hair. She caught her breath each time a contraction kicked in, and they were coming more quickly than Kate would've liked.

Kate hopped in the front and Tommy flicked on the lights and sirens and sped toward the hospital in Whitesville.

"How quickly can you get there?" she asked.

"It's a forty-five minute drive if you're doing the speed limit, which I won't be. I'd say twenty-five minutes at best."

Of all the units they'd covered in nursing school, obstetrics was her least favorite. "Can you make it twenty?"

"I'll sure try, darlin'." The car lurched forward and Kate gripped the seat and said a few silent prayers.

Dina was moaning every three minutes, so Kate guessed that's how quickly the contractions were coming. She'd called the hospital and they had a crew ready to meet them at the ER. "Hang in there, sweetie, we're almost there."

Mitch was green and speechless in the backseat and she wondered who'd toss their cookies first.

"It's coming!" Dina shouted. She'd lost her cool the minute Tommy flicked on the sirens.

"Hold it in," Tommy said, hitting the gas. "We're five, six minutes away."

Kate slugged his arm. "She can't hold it in. Pull over."

Tommy pulled the cruiser into an empty parking lot. This is a bad way for a preemie to be coming into the world, Kate thought, pushing Mitch out of the way. "Get in front," she told him.

They swapped seats and Kate shouted to Tommy to keep driving. The car pulled back on the road, and she took a deep breath before checking out the situation. She didn't see a head crowning. "I think we can get you there in time, but I'm right here if we don't. So relax, squeeze my hand, and breathe." OB might not have been Kate's favorite rotation in nursing school, but she did remember one thing: if the patient is talking, she can't push. "Keep talking Dina, sing if you want, but do not push. Tell me again what you got at your baby shower?"

Dina started rattling off a laundry list of bibs and booties and toys and, somehow, they arrived at the hospital. The medical team was waiting and Dina made it up to the delivery room before giving birth to little five-pound-eight-ounce Ashley ten minutes later.

Kate slumped against Tommy outside Dina's room and laughed. Then cried. "Why is everything so crazy lately?"

He kissed her head—yes, kissed her—and said, "That's life for you. And I reckon it's a lot easier when you're navigating the rough spots with someone else. So whadda ya say, Kate? Don't you think its time we end this nonsense and get hitched?"

Kate was too tired to argue. She was not going to deal with this, not tonight.

"That wasn't a no." Tommy seemed just as surprised.

Kate shrugged. She just didn't have the strength to consider his question. She'd talk to him tomorrow, really explain why it just wouldn't work. But right then, she just wanted a moment of peace.

They went back in the room to take another look at their niece. They peeked at little Ashley snoozing and sucking her thumb, and Tommy slung his arm around Kate's shoulder as they walked out of the hospital.

"Better get back and start cleaning up the mess from the reception," she said

"Nah, we need a drink. Let's go celebrate." He pulled her in for a kiss, but she leaned back from him and he dropped his hand.

"You go on ahead. I'm too pooped." She'd raise a toast to her new niece another day.

Chapter 22

TEAGUE SET DOWN his beer and counted the hours before he could leave this town. At least he'd never have to come back and see Kate again once he moved Jennifer near L.A. He didn't think he could handle seeing the only woman he'd ever loved; the one woman he couldn't have.

The door to the bar burst open and Teague looked up. It was the police chief. Teague looked for Kate, but it appeared the chief was alone.

"Hey, hey, everyone! I've got an announcement to make," he bellowed, and the bar quieted down. "Kate Riley has finally agreed to marry me. Drinks are on me."

The bar erupted in cheers, everyone jostling to shake the chief's hand. Teague resisted the urge to smash his glass against the bar and slunk out before the chief spotted him.

He slammed his hands on the steering wheel. Damn, he'd screwed up. What had he done to send her rushing back to that hound? The chief was a cheater and he'd lied to her. And Kate had said she wanted the truth. How could she go back to a guy who'd given her nothing but lies?

And suddenly it was like the clouds had blown out of the sky and he got it. Kate wanted the truth. That was it. He wasn't going to get her unless he could be truthful about everything. Could he do that? How long had it taken him to admit the truth to himself?

He stared out the window at the trees swaying in the warm midnight breeze and shook his head as the realization sank in. But could he be truthful about everything? Jennifer? The baby? All those damn newspapers and TV shows. If not for them, they'd have no problem making this thing work.

He ran his hand down his face wondering how he could fix

everything. Then he realized those damn newspapers and TV shows might be able to help. He didn't believe for one minute she wanted to be with the police chief. He had to take a chance. But if it didn't pan out . . . he'd blow everything for nothing.

KATE TROLLED THE produce aisle, looking for the strawberries Dina had requested. She was enjoying being waited on, and Kate was happy to do it. Her mama would have been doing it if she were still here.

"Hi, there, Kate." Delores looked up from the cantaloupe she was poking. "That was some big news about the baby."

The last two days had been a whirlwind—cleaning up from the party, visiting Dina in the hospital, dealing with questions like this one. "Yes, but Dina's fine and everything's good." Was there anyone in this town who didn't know about the dramatic race to the hospital? That's Willowdale for you.

Delores put her hand on her hip. "I was talking about Teague Reynolds' baby."

Kate said nothing. The words just wouldn't come out. But Delores must have understood her confusion from the terror in Kate's bulging eyes.

"You didn't hear? He's adopting a baby. His sister's baby. I just saw it on *Entertainment Tonight* . . . and he talked about you, too." She pointed a finger at her. "I would have gotten a bundle for that scoop."

Kate left her half-filled cart parked next to the melons, raced back home and flipped on her computer. *Come on, come on!* She logged onto the *ET* website and clicked on the video links. Teague was holding the baby as the reporter interviewed him. "This is not the T-Rex we've come to know. Tell us about this baby, Teague," said the beautiful blonde.

And Teague explained how he'd gotten a call that he had a twin sister, also given up for adoption years ago, and that she was having a baby she wouldn't be able to raise, for reasons he didn't want to discuss. He didn't talk about her mental challenges.

"All these years and you didn't know you had a sister?"

"No. It was a thrill to meet her." He smiled his gorgeous Teague smile—the sincere one.

"And so you're going to raise this baby on your own?" the reporter asked.

Teague looked at the camera. "I certainly hope not. I've proposed to a woman I hope says yes. So, I'll ask her again—Kate, will you marry me?"

"Kate?" the reporter asked.

"Kate?" Tommy asked behind her.

She slapped the lid of her laptop shut, but it was too late.

"Teague Reynolds just proposed to you?" Tommy asked, palming his gun.

She nodded.

"But you said yes to me last night."

"I didn't say yes."

"You didn't say no. I took it as a yes."

"Tommy, I just didn't feel like fighting after everything with the baby."

He blinked for a moment and deflated. "Guess that means you won't be wanting this." He held a small white box in his hand. He popped it open to show her the engagement ring, which appeared to be a honking two-carat solitaire. "I thought I'd get you a new one, start with a clean slate and everything." He rubbed his hand over his eyes and sighed. "I told everyone at the bar you said yes. When I said we should go out and celebrate, and you didn't argue, I just thought . . . well, I thought you were on board. "

She hugged her arms around herself. "I thought you meant we were going to celebrate the baby. I was too tired to argue about all that marriage talk with you again. It's just not right for us. Never was."

He snapped the box shut. "I see."

"It wouldn't be fair to you. I'm sorry . . ."

He laughed softly. "Guess I deserve it. Payback's a bitch, even six years later."

"So you're not mad?"

He puffed up his red cheeks and blew out his breath. "Oh, I'm pissed as hell at Teague. But not at you. You didn't stand a chance against him." He turned to leave and then stopped. "So his sister lives in Willowdale, too? That's who I saw him in the park with?"

She nodded.

"What a coincidence."

She shrugged. "I guess."

He was putting it all together. "You two didn't meet on the Internet, did you?"

She hesitated long enough to give him his answer.

He hooked his thumbs in his pockets. "What was it then?"

Hell, Teague had probably explained the whole thing on TV; no use keeping secrets anymore. "He was trying to protect his sister. Some photographer was following him. He bumped into me and asked for a ride. When all the photographers were at the airport, he offered to pay me to be his girlfriend so the press wouldn't know why he was really here." Ugh, that sounded bad saying it out loud. Really bad.

"He hired you to be his girlfriend and you said yes?" He clucked his tongue. "That surprises me even more than if you had been getting it on at Lookout Point."

Kate struggled for the words to defend herself, but he was right. She opened her mouth to say something, *anything*, but Tommy waved a disgusted hand at her and quietly left.

She slumped on the couch, feeling anything but happy. Eventually, she lumbered back to the computer to make sure she'd really seen a marriage proposal on *ET*, for crying out loud. And she had. But Teague handled the "so they both lived in Willowdale question" a bit differently.

"Yep, that's why I responded to her email on the Internet dating site. I was intrigued that they were from the same town. It was like, fate, or something."

Kate winced. Teague hadn't told the whole truth. But soon enough the gossip express would get the real story out, thanks to her.

The thrill of his proposal was gone. Things just couldn't

ever work out between them.

Each time the phone rang—and boy, did it ring—she waited to hear Teague's voice. But he didn't call. He didn't show up. And when the news hit the press later that day about the way they really met, she knew why he wasn't calling. She'd blown the lid off yet another secret he was keeping—their ridiculous arrangement. If he was too embarrassed to tell the truth about that, then what was the point?

The only bright spot in the days that followed was Delores's visit. She arranged an auction to sell off the most valuable of Mama's antique pieces, giving Kate twelve thousand dollars in the bank. Kate was stunned to see what some of the pieces went for and decided she'd be scouring garage and estate sales the very next weekend. After sitting down at the diner to celebrate, Delores made Kate a deal. "Why don't you come into business with me? You do the hunting and I'll do the selling."

Kate had found herself a new career after all. *I don't need a man to take care of me.* She tipped her nose up in the air just thinking about it.

A week had passed since Teague's TV proposal, but she hadn't heard from him. She wondered how angry he was with her. The doorbell rang one morning—earlier than the UPS man would be showing up and earlier than any of her friends would be rolling around. She thought maybe, maybe, it was Teague, but it wasn't. It was a tiny, withered woman clutching her purse.

"Can I help you?"

"Are you Kate Riley?" she asked in a whisper of a voice.

She sighed. "Yes, how can I help you?"

"I'm hoping you can help me find Teague Reynolds. He's my son."

SHE THOUGHT SHE'D lost the connection on the phone because Teague hadn't said anything in like, a minute.

"I know you probably don't want to see me, and that's totally fine, but you've got a woman here sitting with a world of hurt. What do you want me to tell her?" Kate asked.

"I'm here in Willowdale with Jennifer. I'll be right over to tell her myself."

WHO TO DEAL with first, Teague wondered. Kate was pissed, he knew that. She hadn't called him, hadn't given an answer to his televised proposal. She was probably livid that he'd lied about how they met. Here he was trying to start over with her telling the world the truth about the baby, and he'd blown it with another lie.

But his mother. Where to start there? *You ruined my life? How could you just give me away like a book you didn't want to finish? Why didn't you love me enough to keep me?*

But all of his tough talk washed away when Kate opened the door and he said, "Where is she?" He'd deal with Kate later.

"In the living room. I'll be on the back deck to give you some privacy."

"No, stay. I want you to know everything about me, Kate. No more secrets."

Her eyes bulged at that, but she just nodded and led him into the living room.

His mother was smaller and sadder than he'd imagined. He'd been ready to demand proof of her wild accusation that she was his mother, but he knew when he looked at her: the hair, the eyes, the guilt.

She smiled and he wondered if she'd always looked so ragged, or if the years had just worn her down. "Your hair was that beautiful color the day you were born. You and Jennifer, both with those dark waves. People would stop me on the street to get a better look at you two."

It was like a punch in the gut, hearing how they'd been a family. "What about our father?" he heard himself ask. He paced the room, fighting all the conflicting feelings roiling inside him.

She waved a weak little hand in the air. "Oh, he took off before you were born, and I had no means to track him down. Truth was, I didn't want to share you with a horrible man like that." She smoothed her cotton skirt, the one she probably wore on special occasions like this, although it looked old and faded. He wondered how many special occasions she'd had in her life.

He swallowed hard and tried to channel all the anger and hate he'd felt the last thirty years. He wanted to storm out. He wanted to scream at her. He wanted to demand proof she was who she said she was. But the familiar rage just wasn't there. Something had changed inside of him. So he sighed and said, "Why did you give us away after two years?"

"I didn't." Somehow, the woman slumped in her chair even more. "You were taken from me."

Kate froze and Teague's heart seemed to stop. "Taken? Why?"

She dropped her face in her hands and sobbed.

He sat next to her and surprised himself by gently rubbing her back.

She looked up and wiped her eyes. "Because of Jennifer. Her—injuries."

Teague backed away. "What did you do to her?"

She reached in her purse for a hankie and blew her nose. "Negligence, that's what the police said. Child endangerment. All sorts of charges to confirm what I already knew—I was a horrible parent. But I was so tired that night. I had you two in the tub—gosh, how you loved your baths. Always loved the water. You were splashing and laughing and you got your pajamas on the floor all wet. I went in your room to get new ones." She took a deep quivering breath, and Teague rubbed her back again until she found the words to continue.

"And suddenly, it was too quiet. Jennifer was face-down in the tub and you were trying to pick her up . . ." Her hand hovered over her mouth and she worked to regain her composure. "It was a miracle, really, that she lived. But she had serious brain injuries. And since I was going to be serving time in jail and had no next of kin or anything, they placed you both in foster care, although Jennifer needed a special living situation with her needs."

Her hands were on her knees, shaking, and Teague wrapped his fingers around hers and squeezed. It felt to him like grabbing a lifeline when you're kicking and flailing underwater. It was terrifying, yet a relief at the same time.

She squeezed back.

He heard Kate sniffing, or maybe that was him, because he felt tears streaming down his face. Tears. T-Rex was crying. Damn. "Why didn't you ever get us back?"

"I was in jail for two years. That was a long time to convince myself that I was a bad mother who didn't deserve children. I gave up rights to you, thinking it was for the best. I'm so sorry. I've been sorry for years. I never had the courage to look for you, because I figured you wouldn't want anything to do with me. I've lived in Whitesville ever since my release. Had no idea where you two ended up." She took a deep breath. "But once I heard your story of finding your long lost sister, and adopting the baby because she couldn't take care of it, I just knew you were mine. I'd seen you before, recognized your first name and thought, could he be my little boy? But when I heard that story the other night on the TV, I knew."

He sat there for a while, letting all that sink in. "You named me Teague?"

She nodded. "Teague and Jennifer McHenry."

He stared off, a million puzzle pieces falling into place now that he'd found the one missing link.

She set her hand on his knee and he looked at her. She drew in a deep breath. "Is there any way you could give me a second chance? Let me into your life after all these years?"

Teague stood up and looked out over Kate's backyard. He'd imagined a moment like this for so long. Only, he'd imagined confronting his mother, showing her what she'd missed out on and telling her to get lost. He never dreamed he'd consider forgiving her for what she'd done or even considering to let her back in.

That wall he'd constructed in his heart to keep people out had stood guard for a long time. But he could feel the bricks tottering out of place. And he had Kate to thank for loosening them up.

He turned to his mother and held her hands in his. "Yes. I

can give you a second chance . . . Mom. Someone recently showed me that real, true love is worth a second chance." He looked at Kate, and she smiled at him.

They hugged and cried and his mother finally raised her pale face to him. "Do you think I could see Jennifer?"

"Yes, but I need to talk to Kate first about some important things."

"No, Teague, go with your Mama. We can talk later."

Teague grabbed her by the hand. "You're coming with us. I'm not letting you go again, Kate."

Chapter 23

ONCE HIS MOTHER was settled in her hotel room after the teary reunion with Jennifer and a damn hard time prying her away from that baby, he and Kate headed back to her place. Not one word had been mentioned about their relationship or the proposal on the ride over. But she brought him up to date on a new antique business and let him know she was doing okay on her own. Turns out she didn't need him or Tommy.

And that made him love her even more.

She led him into her house, got them both a drink—scotch on the rocks, after a day like this—and she sat and looked at him and said, "So."

"So," Teague repeated with a weak laugh. "So . . . it turns out there's something worse than Internet dating when you're a movie star."

"What?"

"Hiring a woman to pretend she's your girlfriend. Remington dumped me from the movie. Looks like I'm going to be here in Willowdale for a while."

Kate caught her breath. "I'm so sorry. How can he do that?"

He lifted his eyebrows. "Oh, there's all sorts of clauses in those contracts. Adopting a baby, that would have been tough to fire me for. But hiring a girlfriend? My lawyer said that broached fraud and moral indecency blah, blah, blah."

Kate shook her head. "I'm sorry. It's my fault. I told Tommy and he told . . . everybody." This time, she knew it was him. Couldn't pin this one on Delores.

Teague shrugged. "It doesn't really matter. I'm not that upset, not really. At least we're keeping the rags in business, the two of us."

Kate shook her head, still not able to understand. "Why did you do it, though? Why did you tell everyone about the baby when you tried so hard to cover it up?"

He jumped up and walked over to her, kneeling beside her. "Because you were right. Even if you didn't want to spend your life with me, I was tired of hiding secrets, too. I didn't want to do that to little Teague. I can't change my past, but I can change his future." He looked down. "Of course, then I blew it by not being honest about how we met."

She nodded and then he took a deep breath, ready for the most important line of his life. "What about our future? Have I blown it? Or do we have a second chance?"

DID HE REALLY WANT to try this? She couldn't believe it. Kate shrugged. "You tell me, have I blown it? I lost you a movie deal, probably ruined your career."

"And you made my life one hundred percent better than it was. It was one more secret we shouldn't be keeping. I'm not embarrassed by how we met. I'm just thrilled that we did." He took a deep breath. "I know you don't need me, Kate. You're doing a fine job taking care of yourself. But I hope you want me. Because I want you—more than anything. Marry me, Kate."

She squeezed his hands, wanting to say yes. But something was holding her back. "Where do we go from here? I can't move to L.A. with you. I've still got Dina to look after. And what are you going to do, move Jennifer and her boyfriend there with you? And what about your mom?" She closed her eyes and shook her head. "It might just be too much for us."

"Isn't there room for all of us in Willowdale?"

She looked up at him. "You know that you can't keep any secrets in a town like this."

"We're not keeping secrets anymore."

She smiled. "No, we're not." She looked in Teague's kind, happy eyes. Those eyes that had looked at his mother and forgiven her instantly. If he could give love a second chance, so could she. "I guess we should call Delores and tell her to get the word out. Yes, Teague Reynolds, I will marry you."

He swept her up in his arms and kissed her, and she felt that spark again. It probably would be there forever. That spark had always been the one true thing between them.

Epilogue

"ARE WE THERE YET?" Kate asked, as Teague drove her Jeep down a long dirt road.

"Almost. Close your eyes and don't open them until I tell you."

She sighed. "This is awful close to Lookout Point. I hope you're not thinking about taking advantage of me . . ."

He laughed. "You're already pregnant, what could happen? Plus we're married. It doesn't have the same allure anymore."

She playfully tried to whack him with her eyes closed but missed. "Can't we play twenty questions?"

"Truth or dare. And I dare you to be quiet and wait for your surprise."

She crossed her arms and sighed.

He drove along a bit more and then stopped the car. "Wait, let me get the door for you." He hopped out, opened her door, and helped her slide out of the seat. Then he took her by the hand. "Follow me . . . just a few more steps. Now open your eyes."

Kate opened her eyes and saw a big, beautiful home overlooking the valley. Four giant white pillars lined the front of the brick home surrounded by big old trees and beautiful gardens. She couldn't even count how many windows she saw. She turned to him. "What is this?"

A huge grin split his face. "This is our new home. I had it built big enough to fit any of our family that could possibly want to live here."

Kate's hands cupped her mouth in shock. "It's gorgeous . . . it's . . . gigantic. What about Mama's home?"

"You did mention it would be a perfect antique store. Time for you and Delores to move out of that old café." He reached for her hand. "Come on. Let's look inside."

She followed him in, stunned. An enormous crystal chandelier sparkled in the front hall. A fireplace stretched to the ceiling in the living room off to the left, much like the one at Teague's home in L.A. This kitchen was even bigger than his. He ran up the stairs in front of her and proceeded to show her all the bedrooms. Then he opened the door to a small pink bedroom next to theirs. It was the same color she'd painted Ashley's nursery for Dina.

"It's for the baby," he said.

She nodded, unable to say anything.

He swallowed hard and his face was pale. "Do you like it? I took a chance keeping this a surprise. We can sell it if you don't want it."

Kate shook her head. "I love it. Absolutely love it. But how did you do all this? You've been off filming." The crazy way they met had ruined his action-star career, but it gave birth to a very successful start in romantic comedies for Teague.

But not before they'd flown back to Hawaii to elope. They had managed to dodge the cameras by booking two different locations for their secret ceremony and then snuck away to exchange vows on that black-sand beach in Hana. And to her delight, Kate had discovered that the seashell heart Teague had made was still there. Not a picture of their wedding existed.

"I've had construction crews working on this round the clock. I know I said no more secrets, but this seemed more like a wonderful surprise than a secret. How do you like the view?"

Kate looked out over the rolling valley. "It's incredible. This whole thing is amazing."

"I thought it would be a great place to move Jennifer and Darryl into their special suite with the baby, and we've got a suite for my mom. Heck, Dina and Mitch can live here too, if they want. And George, too, if he ever finds his way home." He took her in his arms and squeezed.

"It's perfect." It was wonderful, scary and crazy. It was real. Kate winced as the baby kicked, evidently as excited as she was about how this was all working out.

"You're perfect." Teague rubbed her belly.

Kate leaned into him. "I think we'll live here happily ever after. It's the perfect ending."

He kissed her on the lips and worked his way down to her round belly before planting another smooch there. "This isn't the ending. This is our happy beginning."

Coming Next!

MAN OF THE MONTH

Book Two of The Willowdale Romances

Lisa Scott

Excerpt

Chapter 1

Jeanne's champagne sloshed over her glass as she tried to find it with her lips. Lordy, was this her third . . . or fifth? She'd never been much of a drinker, but it was the only way she was going to get through this night. Either that or one of her pecan praline pies. Not just a nibble, either—the whole dang thing. In the end, the champagne would do less damage to her hips, so here she was drowning in the bubbly.

Aiming for her mouth again, the flute disappeared when someone plucked it from her sticky fingertips. "Hey!" she protested, grasping at the air.

Brad towered over her, frowning as he snatched the glass. "Jeanne, what's gotten into you? Tonight of all nights?" A few people turned to stare.

She hiccupped. Covering her mouth, she shot Brad her nastiest glare, but ugh! The man was handsome even when he was mad, with those chiseled cheekbones and that pitch-black hair falling in his eyes. "Shoot, Brad!" She stamped her stiletto and wobbled, grabbing his arm for balance. Her hand locked onto rock-hard muscle and she nearly whimpered.

Instead, she lied. "I need that drink to ring in the New Year. I'm fine!" she shouted over the music and laughter at the party and plastered on a great big smile. Seemed like everyone in Willowdale, North Carolina, had turned out for the bash, even Chester Miller. He hadn't left his house since 1998, and here he was chasing the old Mercer twins around the living room—and they were enjoying it! Was she the only one here faking the fun?

Brad's stern look disappeared and out came a smile that could blind the sun. "You don't need any more, not tonight. Now, get over here, girl. The ball's dropping." He linked his fingers with hers, pulling her through the crowd until they had a good view of Times Square on the giant flat-screen TV. Couples bunched up together in the crowd, preparing for the countdown. Brad snaked his arm around her waist, his thumb stroking her black satin dress. The warm feeling coursing through her body had nothing to do with all those glasses of pink bubbly.

They counted down together. "Three . . . two . . . one!" Horns blared, confetti flew, and it felt like a slow-motion movie scene. She turned to him, locking her eyes on his, bright blue and smoldering under a lock of hair. His eyebrow hitched while his mouth formed a perfect pucker. A shiver shimmied down her spine then back up again. With a swipe of her tongue across her lips, she sucked in a breath, closed her eyes—

And Brad planted a big kiss on her cheek. "Happy New Year, kiddo," he whispered in her ear.

Her heart sank faster than the ball they'd just watched, just like it did every time she realized her perfect guy could never be more than a friend. Dang. She swallowed back the sob crawling up her throat. Didn't go down as easy without the champagne.

She forced a smile. "Happy New Year, Bradley." Then she grabbed her glass, slurped the last of her drink, and pushed away from him. Stumbling through the crowd, she made her way toward the back deck of her friend Kate's enormous house. The damn place was probably bigger than the Smart Mart over in Whitesville.

After indulging a few of the regulars from the Jelly Jar diner with celebratory hugs and kisses, she finally slipped outside, relieved to drop the fake smile. Pulling her wrap tight around her bare shoulders, she leaned against the railing and let out the tears she'd been holding back. The champagne glass slipped from her grasp and crashed onto the patio below. That only made her cry harder—like she needed more proof she really didn't have a grip on things and hadn't for a long time.

Jeanne sniffed and her bottom lip wobbled like a bumper threatening to fall off an old truck. She wasn't one to fall apart all pretty. When she crumbled, she was a downright mess.

Soft, downy flakes fell from the sky, tickling her nose. She brushed them away like gnats. That damn kiss on the cheek shouldn't have been a surprise. She'd known for a few years now that Brad would always be just a friend, for several very good reasons. And now that they were business partners, becoming a couple would be as stupid as topping their famous rum pound cake with hot bacon drippings. Normally, she could deal with it. Just tuck away that painful longing like a brochure for a month-long cruise you could never afford to take but still liked to dream about.

Guess something about the promise of new starts and a new year and maybe all that champagne brought hope rising up inside her. Only to be popped like a silly soap bubble. Of course, the bad memories from that New Year's Eve so long ago chased away the good feelings, too. She sucked in a shock of cold night air and shivered.

Folding her arms on the railing, she rested her chin on top. She shouldn't have come to this party. She should have volunteered to babysit so her sister, Becca, could've gone out. Little Emma was just three months old and the most beautiful thing Jeanne had ever seen. That was weighing heavy on her heart, too, reminding her how badly she wanted to be a mama. To have the perfect family she'd never had, and how unlikely that was going to happen anytime soon.

The deck door slid open and the sounds of music and laughter spilled out. She stood up and pressed her fingers under her eyes to catch any dribbles of mascara. Was she the only person in the world sobbing in the New Year? Taking a deep breath, she turned to see who was coming outside. Please don't be Kate or Tonya. Didn't know if she had the strength to lie to her friends about what was wrong. They could sniff out a fib faster than Doc Louie's bloodhounds.

"Why'd you rush out here?" Brad asked.

Dang, worse than Kate or Tonya, Jeanne thought as she turned away. "Guess I don't feel like celebrating tonight."

"Sure looked like you were having fun." He rubbed his hands together. "It's freezing out here." He took off his jacket and draped it over her shoulders. His fingers grazed her arms and she felt goose bumps answering his touch.

His big, warm body pressed up next to hers and he planted his elbows on the railing as he looked out over the yard and the pool tucked away for the winter. "This night's hard for me too, Jeanne. Eighteen years is a long time, but still . . . It hurts, I know."

She shook her head and shrugged off the idea. She didn't break down like this every year. Why this one? "No. That's not it. Your mother died that night too, and you're not out here crying."

Brad winced and closed his mouth. He was quiet for a spell. "You still upset we didn't land the catering gig for the Willowdale New Year's Bash? You know Kate threw this party just to hand us a catering gig, right? Not a bad consolation prize."

She nodded. "I know. Kate's a great friend and the New Year's Bash was a long shot. We're not ready for that yet."

He leaned into her, his breath hot on her cheek. "Cheer up, kiddo. It's a new year. I'll make you a batch of those rum balls you love so much to start it off right." He frowned. "Nothing with alcohol for you. How about chocolate silk pie? You love my chocolate silk pie."

She loved his everything. "No, thanks."

"Damn. You turned down pie. You are upset." He nudged her with his elbow. "You pouting 'cause I took away your drink?

You're a lightweight and you know it. I've gotta look out for you."

Shaking her head, she sucked in a deep breath. "I'm pouting because . . . I'm lonely." She sniffed, her emotions ready to tumble out like a bunch of peaches in those flimsy paper bags the Save More uses. "I'm sick of being single. I want a family."

He looked up at the sky and let out a long sigh. "How can you even think about romance when we just launched Elegant Eats I sure don't have time for dating. What makes you think you would?"

She lifted a shoulder, a strand of hair tickling her skin. "I'd make time. The alarm on my biological clock is blaring." Cue the dramatic eye roll. "Never mind. I forgot—you don't have one of those timers." The champagne had loosened her tongue more than she realized. Things always got ugly when their talk turned to babies.

Brad's hands went up and he stepped back, his best cowboy boots thunking against the wooden deck. "Jeanne, you can't be mad at me for being honest. It would be a mistake for me to have children. But I know that's what you want, and I respect that. Just don't look down on me. I'm being responsible, not getting into a situation I don't want to be in—can't be in."

She nodded, not looking at him. It was the one thing about Brad that was a deal breaker and they both knew it. Jeanne wanted kids more than a stray dog wanted a warm home, and Brad was a wolf who'd always be on the run.

The music thumped inside as they stood there, frozen, while a whole world of silent hurts tumbled between them. His hand cupped her elbow. "It's a new year, a new start. Why not resolve to get out there and meet someone?"

Her soft laugh left a puff in the air between them. "Brad, I know practically everyone in Willowdale. There's no one here for me to date unless one of the biddies down at Tonya's salon has a handsome grandson locked up in her attic. Besides, matchmaking and me just don't mix. Things got real ugly when Faye Jenkins tried setting up her son Leroy with me and Tonya and Kate—all at the same time."

"Leroy Jenkins is a fool. Course it didn't work out." Brad tipped her chin up with one finger and she swallowed a cry. "I've got lots of great friends from here to Asheville. Good men."

Sadness tightened her chest, and she brushed off the suggestion with a big wave, stumbling as she made the gesture. Brad steadied her, his hands on her waist like he might lift her up and kiss her long, hard, and good.

Which, of course, he wouldn't. Been there done that, decided it wouldn't work.

He pulled his hands away. "No, really. Make it your New Year's resolution to go out with a new guy every month until you meet Mr. Right."

She laughed in a not-funny-at-all way. "Listen." Her finger poked his hard chest. "I don't drink mocha double lattes just to seem trendy, I don't wear push-up bras just 'cause I don't got the goods, and I don't do blind dates just 'cause I'm lonely as sin."

Brad pushed away her finger and groaned. "But these guys will all be pre-screened by me. Who knows you better?"

The truth of it slapped her heart. The man she loved knew her even better than her sisters or her girlfriends did. "You want to set me up with a guy?"

He nodded. "One guy every month. The Man of the Month."

She hiccupped and pressed her hand to her mouth. "The Man of the Month," she said through her fingers. "You're kidding, right?"

"Nope. There's your resolution, J."

She loved when he called her that.

He grinned, looking way too smug. "It's a brilliant plan."

"Good lord." It was so silly she couldn't even find the words to argue against it. No way, no how, was she agreeing to such foolishness. But when she looked up at those take-me-now eyes, his perfect lips, and those big biceps flexing as he leaned against the railing—imagining herself all tucked up in them—she knew she needed to do something to get Brad Larsen out of her system. And that's how she found herself saying, "Okay, Brad. Man of the month. Sign me up."

"YOU DID WHAT?" Tonya choked on her sweet tea at the Jelly Jar diner the next afternoon. Two old-timers at the counter turned around from their coffee and pie and squinted in their direction.

"Shh! And shut those blinds, would you?" Jeanne winced and rubbed her temples. "You heard me. I agreed to let Brad set me up with a different guy every month. It's my New Year's resolution. Wasn't my idea." There had to be some grace period for a do-over on a resolution, right? She could not go through with this. Her mama was probably rolling over in heaven at the thought of it. At least she thought that's what her mama would do. Jeanne didn't remember much about her.

More heads turned as Tonya, in her tight jeans, popped up to lower the blinds. She planted a hand on her hip. "You mean, Brad-I-love-him-but-won't-ever-admit-it Brad." She plopped back in her seat, her dark curls bouncing on her shoulders. A week ago, her hair had been straight and red. Tonya thought the best advertising for her salon happened right on her head.

Jeanne glared at her. "You know which Brad I'm talking about. Business-partner-best-friend-Brad." She pushed away her burger and fries, realizing her stomach wouldn't appreciate that.

Kate wagged a manicured finger at her. "I saw you tossin' back the drinks. A bottle of champagne can make a girl agree to all kinds of crazy things."

"Especially when that girl is actually in love with the man trying to set her up with his buddies," Tonya added, dragging her French fry through a puddle of ketchup.

Kate nodded. "That's even more powerful than a bottle of bubbly."

Jeanne squeezed her eyes shut. "Will you two let up on that? Just because we dated for like a month a while back does not mean I'm in love with Brad Larsen. That's when we figured out we were meant to be just friends. We want different things. So give up that goose chase, girls. Brad and I were never an item and never will be. We're friends. And business partners. That's it." She sighed. *Right. And after my New Year's resolution, I'll give up lying for Lent.*

Tonya pretended to zip her lip while Kate nibbled on her own. "Yep, that's what you've been telling yourself for a long time, Jeanne."

"Because that's the truth." Jeanne sat up straight, trying to channel a bit of confidence. "And the more I think about it, the better Brad's idea sounds. He probably does know some very hot men, and I get to go out with one a month." She crossed her arms and nodded. She had to prove to them she wasn't in love with Brad—which would be as easy as convincing them she didn't like chocolate. "It'll be fun."

"You're right. It does sound like a good plan. Kind of makes me wish I wasn't married," Kate said, tucking her silky blond hair behind her ears.

Jeanne gave her a look. "Right. You'd give up the hottest guy in Hollywood for a shot at some of Brad's redneck friends." Kate had married actor Teague Reynolds in the biggest slice of gossip ever served up around these parts. But news of this resolution would get tongues wagging, too. Jeanne rolled her eyes just thinking of it. Maybe she should buy a honkin' pair of sunglasses and a great big hat to disguise herself on these dates.

Tonya looked down and tapped a shiny blue nail on the table. After a deep breath, she lowered her voice and took on a serious tone. "Alright, I'm just gonna come out and say it. You don't think it's a little strange to be in love with him after what happened with your parents? Why him, of all people?" Her eyes slowly met Jeanne's. "You might want to sit down and make a list of all the reasons you love him and ask yourself what's really going on here." She shrugged. "Lists always help me. It's just—I know Dr. Phil would have something to say about this."

Jeanne's mouth opened and closed a few times and she looked away. "No! I'm not in love with him. We worked that all out. He's out of my system. And that would be weird, right?"

Neither of them answered and she noticed Rita's daughters taking their time cleaning up two booths over. The diner and the beauty shop were the two biggest transmission points for gossip in this town. News of these monthly blind dates would spread like a pandemic.

Kate snagged an onion ring from Jeanne's plate. "And you two are so different. He's a total control freak and you like the unexpected."

"I wouldn't call him a freak," Jeanne said. "He just likes things to be planned and orderly. I really admire that."

"He washes his truck every Saturday morning, rain, shine, snow, or hail," Tonya said. "While your apartment hasn't been clean since you moved in."

Jeanne glared at her.

Tonya held up her hands. "Hey, I'm not saying we're going to call Hoarders or anything, you just like to be surrounded by stuff. And he is not a stuff kind of guy."

"And don't forget he alphabetized your spice rack," Kate added.

Jeanne threw up her hands. "And it's so much easier to find things now. Except for turmeric. I always spell that wrong."

Kate sighed. "We just want you to be happy, Jeanne. Whatever it takes. You deserve it."

"Why don't we set you up with Tommy, instead?" Tonya asked. "If you like one brother, the other might do."

"Now why would we do that?" Kate asked.

Tonya shrugged. "We've both dated him and can vouch he's a good kisser." Tonya pointed at her. "Plus, he's got a kid, so we know he can make 'em and take care of 'em."

Jeanne balled up her napkin and tossed it at Tonya. "Is today January first or April first—because you have got to be kidding me. Getting Ellen Lewis pregnant by mistake while he was on break with Kate doesn't count as wanting children." She tipped her chin in the air. "Plus, he's nothing like Brad."

"You're mighty quick to defend Brad." Tonya's eyes narrowed to devious slits. "Admitting it is the first step to solving the problem."

Jeanne's voice strained with a thread of hysteria as she rose to her feet. "There's no problem. Why would I agree to a year's worth of blind dates if I wanted to be with Brad instead?"

Plenty of heads turned at that, and Kate pulled her back into the booth. "You're absolutely right. You and Brad are just friends."

They poked at their food, but ate nothing. The three of them without empty plates was like two-stepping to rap—it just wasn't right.

Tonya finally piped up, her good-natured mood returning. "Keep us updated, girl. We want to dish after every date. Who knows, maybe Mr. January will be the one?"

"When's your first date?" Kate asked, finishing her milkshake but stopping when it got to the noisy slurping part. Gotta ramp up the class once you marry into Hollywood. "Jeanne, you should wear that silk V-neck cream dress. It makes you look like a B cup."

Tonya raised an eyebrow. "Or maybe even a C cup if you get him drunk."

"Hey, you're a real C cup, Tonya. Maybe you should go on the date," Jeanne said. Tonya was sorry and single, too.

Tonya ignored her. "Whenever it is, stop by the salon first. I'll hook you up with some highlights and make this brown hair sing," she said, fingering Jeanne's hair.

Jeanne slapped Tonya's hand away and shrugged. "I'm not doing a makeover for this. And I'm not sure when the first date is. Suppose I'll find out in a bit. We're catering a party in Whitesville tonight. Gotta get to the kitchen, hangover and all." She slid out of the red leather booth and waved goodbye to the girls and wondered if she could ever shut off her feelings for Brad, because lying about it was certainly taking its toll. Slumping behind the wheel of her car, she asked herself if Man of the Month might be the way to finally do it.

"Yeah, when the devil starts serving sweet tea, heavy on the ice."

Chapter 2

Jeanne dropped the stack of linen napkins she was folding. "My first date is Friday? This Friday?" She grasped the table to catch her balance.

Brad folded his arms and gave her a smile she wanted to smack right off his face. "It came to me first thing when I woke up this morning. The guy who rents from my brother, Jake, in Whitesville would be perfect for you. Sam's Mr. Environment; he rides his bike everywhere. That's important, now that you're going green these days."

She rubbed her temples, but nothing was making this headache go away. "I put in energy-saving light bulbs because they were handing out free samples at the hardware store." She planted a fist on her hip, her silver bracelets clinking. "I'm not exactly green, Brad. But I guess concern about the environment is good. He's not out saving whales or anything is he? Not that I don't like whales . . . What does he do for a living?"

Brad shrugged. "Not sure."

"Is he good-looking?" *Say, someone well past six feet, broad shoulders, thick, black hair, such as yourself?*

Brad stroked his chin. *A strong jaw like that would be nice as well,* she thought. With a dimple smack dab in the middle, too. Made her melt whenever she looked at it too long. He'd been so intriguing back in school when Principal Willis made sure not to put any of the Larsen boys in class with any of the Clark girls after the crash. Too awkward, she'd heard the teachers say. But she could always spot Brad a mile away in the hallway, thanks to the dimple. The one that was currently winking at her.

"Is he good looking?" Brad repeated. "I guess. It's hard for me to say. I'm a guy." He dropped another stack of laundered napkins on the table to be folded.

"So, you don't really know him, you don't know what he does, and you can't say if he's good-looking or not." She counted off the disturbing facts one by one on her fingers. "Basically, you're setting me up with this guy just because he has a bike?"

Brad set his hands on her arms and pulled her close. "He was the first guy I thought of."

A laugh escaped from her pursed lips. "Perfect qualification right there."

"I didn't want you to chicken out. I figured we'd better strike while the iron was hot, while you were still keen on the idea."

"Still *keen*? I wasn't keen about it last night, and I'm still not." But she did like the way Brad was holding her in his arms like that. Possibly to shake some sense into her, but still, it felt nice. And he smelled good, too. Always did. "This is stupid, looking at it now that I'm not drunk and crying in the dark. You had me at a disadvantage last night." She raised an eyebrow. "One might even argue you tricked me."

A hurt look crossed his face, like a kid who learned he wasn't going out for an ice cream after all. "But you promised, J."

She pushed past him and picked up the linens she'd dropped. "This is the thanks I get for giving you an antique butter churn for Christmas? Do you know how many shops I scoured to find that?"

"Hey, it was my favorite gift this year. I'm going to put it front and center in the entryway and tell everyone it's yours."

"No room for it at home, huh?" She thought about his everything-in-its-place lifestyle the girls had been mocking. They weren't off base on that one.

He scratched his head. "Someone might see it there. It's better suited here."

Brad admired old kitchen gadgets, but didn't like admitting it to anyone else. She lowered her voice. "And what if I tell everyone that's your collection out in the lobby?"

His jaw dropped. "You wouldn't. Don't use my love of

vintage kitchen tools to get out of this. You know I love it. And I . . ." He fumbled for his words. "And I just want you to find someone."

"Why do you care? You said it yourself—I should be concentrating on the business, not my love life." Hard to believe they had once put pleasure before business when they were a couple working together at The Hideaway. *That was a long time ago.*

He grabbed a few napkins from her and helped fold them. "I just hate seeing you so sad. You deserve to be happy."

She nodded, wishing she felt the same way, wishing she could be happy without him. He reached for another napkin and their fingers brushed. Just that little swipe of flesh sent an embarrassing surge of lust straight down to her toes. She jerked her hand back.

She thought she'd had her feelings for him under control for a while, that she'd shut them off completely after they decided they'd never work as a couple. But the feelings were back full force. "You're right. How bad could one blind date be?"

Brad rubbed the back of his neck. "That's the spirit. I'll call and tell him you're in, then I'll give him your number."

Jeanne hoped her heart would flutter just a whisper at the idea. But it dropped like a brick in her chest. "Great. Thanks, Brad. I'm so lucky to have you . . . as a friend."

He nodded and finished folding the last napkins. "So, back to business. The desserts are prepped for the banquet tonight. We've got three cases of champagne coming in. I'll be handling those." He winked at her and she winced.

"Don't worry." She held up a hand. "I won't be drinking champagne again until we ring in the next decade."

"Or maybe at your wedding?" He waggled his eyebrows. "I've got a good feeling about this."

SHE GROANED WHEN he said it, but Brad kept his smile wide and tried his best to sound encouraging. He wasn't sure if he was pulling it off. Despite everything he felt for her, he knew damn well he wasn't the guy to deliver Jeanne's happily-ever-after dreams. And she deserved nothing less. Bottom line, she wanted a kid, the dogs, the big back yard—and he didn't. After his mom had died in the crash, his dad started drinking more. While his mother had been a weepy drunk, his father was a mean drunk who seemed to find a reason to smack him and his brothers every day—him, especially. Brad wasn't so sure that mean streak hadn't carried on down the line. He would not screw up a kid like that. He wasn't going to perpetuate those bum genes by having a kid. No, parenthood wasn't for him, no matter how much he loved Jeanne.

He looked at her brunette waves tumbling over her shoulders, imagining her hair spread out on his bed, her bright green eyes looking up at him longingly. Damn, the things he wanted to do to her. Their month together three years ago hadn't been enough.

He finished folding the napkin and went into the kitchen to get away from the one thing he wanted but could never have.

But she followed him in, creamy skin, perky nose, and all. "So, I was thinking. Since you forced me into a New Year's resolution, it's only fair I come up with one for you, too." Her grin left him tingling in all the right places.

He draped a dishcloth over his shoulder. "Stop right there. I am not agreeing to the woman of the month club. I'm all business these days. I told you that."

Jeanne frowned at him and even looked cute doing that. "Fine. Then let's come up with some resolutions for Elegant Eats." She hopped up on the counter.

"That's not a bad idea. What are you thinking?"

She crossed her legs and leaned back. "We should aim for ten new clients."

"Sounds good." *Looks good*, he thought, surveying her long, lean body. *Knock it the hell off.* He studied the tile floor but couldn't get rid of his randy thoughts.

"And booking more parties than Events Extraordinaire."

His eyebrows shot up. "Okay . . . we could try. But they're in Whitesville and they've been in business longer than us, remember."

Ignoring him, she continued. "And finally, landing the next New Year's Eve Bash."

He whistled. "That's an ambitious list. Makes Man of the Month look amateur. We should step that up to Man of the Week." Only because he liked to make an art of torturing himself.

She whacked him with her towel. "No way. You're lucky I was drunk and defenseless when you concocted this fool plan for once a month. I should have whooped your butt last night just for suggesting it."

He uncovered a tray of desserts at the end of the workstation, prepped for the party that night. "Good thing I can always buy you with sweets." He brought a Mexican wedding cake cookie to her lips, the tip of his thumb brushing her lower lip. It was soft and warm and he remembered how nicely it had fit against his that time they'd kissed.

Her eyes fluttered up to meet his. Then she closed them and took a bite of the powdery cookie; crumbs of sugar stuck to her lips. Damn, he loved watching her eat. Sinful. If she were his, he'd feed her like this every night.

He cleared his throat. "That's what I'm going to do every time you complain about this—feed you. That'll keep you on board."

"You're evil."

He winked at her. "I know." But if he was one-hundred-percent honest with himself, this resolution was more for him than her. Because the sooner Jeanne was taken, the sooner he'd be forced to move on from the woman with the lips and the eyes and the laugh that killed him. The woman who could never be his. The woman he'd wanted since he'd snuck a kiss during naptime in kindergarten.

Acknowledgements

Writing is a tough thing to love. This book wouldn't have been written without the help, support, and encouragement of so many fellow writers, including Nancy Edwards Johnson and Aileen Nalen, and the many great folks in my writing group, LCRW. It doesn't hurt to have an incredibly supportive spouse who takes the kiddos to the movies so I can write without stopping to pour juice or referee fights, and has never once questioned why I spend so much time at the keyboard. Thanks to the great group at BelleBooks for taking a chance on me. And thanks to the stranger who inspired this story: a hot guy getting into a hot car with California plates in my tiny New York town that got me thinking, "What's a guy like you doing in a place like this?"

About the Author

Lisa Scott has wanted to be an author since getting her first creative writing assignment in second grade. But first, she worked as a TV news reporter and anchor for nearly two decades in Bangor, Maine, Rochester, New York and Buffalo, New York. She now enjoys making up stories instead of sticking to the facts. She's a voice artist in upstate New York, where she lives with her husband, two kids, two cats, a dog, and a pond full of koi fish. Like on her on Facebook at Read Lisa Scott.

CPSIA information can be obtained at www.ICGtesting.com
Printed in the USA
LVOW051812150513

333884LV00006B/602/P